Wealth and Worth

Sean Cutler

Lasagna **Hill**

Published by Lasagna Hill
Books@LasagnaHill.com

ISBN 978-0-9935354-0-6

For Kelvy.

Wealth and Worth

Chapters

Wealth and Worth

Chapter One

Mrs. Bennet was in a high state of euphoria; an alien pleasure ran through every inch of her sixty-four year old body like nothing she had experienced in her prime. Her young lover was barely of legal age and already outperformed her husband, even in his youth.

She loved her husband; she would often look into her lover's eyes and imagine it was her husband who made her feel this way. Whenever she caught the odd glimpse of his face in the solid gold photo frame on her bedside table, she would recoil and immediately look in another direction.

So, when she heard his booming New York accent from behind her lovers back, she shut down. Her body went into shock and without thinking, shoved the young man off her. When she reopened her eyes, expecting to see a man in a rage, there was no one. In the space where she swore she heard his voice come from, was the television.

He was standing on the steps of their hotel, the hotel she lived in and loved with every breath in her lungs; the hotel that had afforded her the life she lives today.

The way it had transformed over the years since they purchased it, often gave her a pause for thought.

Her husband, Mr. Bennet was giving a press conference, but she had no idea, about what. She had learnt long ago, not to ask too many questions about his business. It was her husband who dealt with the hotel; it was her job to stand by his side and look beautiful at all times. When they married, he had promised her that she would never need a job, and was too attractive to work; a promise he had never broken.

Her lover laughed as he turned around and saw him on the seventy inch TV behind him; he took the remote from the bottom of the bed and muted his voice. He knew that Mrs. Bennet would appreciate not hearing his voice while they fucked on her martial bed.

He laid her back on the bed, gliding his hands up her smooth and firm stomach as he climbed back on top of her. His penis had not taken any notice of the interruption her husband had caused, and was ready to resume where they had left off.

"No," she muttered in a hushed tone. She was not an American like her husband, but English. She feebly tried to push him off her, but he was too close not to continue and breathily told her so.

Without any resistance, he entered her. She was no longer in the mood; she lay there so he would hurry up and leave. She moved her head so she could look over his shoulder and read the bottom of the screen.

What was he up to? She thought. It wasn't a complete surprise to see her husband on TV; he was a well-known man, particularly in New York. He would often feature on local TV and would appear as a talking head, giving his opinion on a wide range of topics on a National news channel.

If she strained her eyes, she could just about make out the writing on the bottom of the screen. As the letters slowly formed into coherent letters that she was able to make out, she felt her lovers body clench as he exploded inside her.

Her lover let out a roaring moan, forgetting for a second where they were. Mrs. Bennet covered his mouth with her open palm and squeezed his cheeks; this soon shut him up.

"Quiet, you idiot, someone might hear you," she whispered in an unimpressed hiss. She wasn't happy, not least by the noise, but rather by what she had just read.

The young man gently dismounted Mrs. Bennet, and proceeded to wipe his member on her four thousand dollar Egyptian cotton duvet cover, something she loathed and always bit her tongue about. She winced every time he did this.

She edged forward and perched herself at the foot of the bed, being careful not to touch the sticky spot not too far away from where she was sitting.

The young man collected the clothes he had thrown in every direction, as they undressed each other a short while ago. Mrs. Bennet was more than aware of the family he came from and the wealth they possessed; she never understood why he chose to dress in clothes that made him look like he grew up in the projects. He stood out more, if anything, in her hotel wearing what he did.

Now dressed, he stood at the doorway, staring at the woman as she cranked up the television's volume. He edged closer to her as he slipped on his shoes. She didn't acknowledge that he was there, instead, was fixated on every word her husband was saying. The young man had very little interest in what he was saying; if anything, he tried to think as little as possible about her husband.

"I'll see you then," he said, trying to invoke a reaction from her; Nothing. He leaned in and kissed her neck; Still nothing. Defeated, he turned around and headed for the door.

"Go down the service elevator," she said from the corner of her mouth.

"I know, I know; don't get yourself seen," he said, like it had been previously recited a thousand times. He knew the routine, whenever he visited her suite; he was a ghost, look down, in and out and never say more than he had to if he was ever stopped. He hated all the sneaking around, but would do so much more to get the end result.

Before he let himself out, he couldn't help but take one last long look at the woman he had just made love to. Her olive skin seemed to glow as the morning light touched her body.

Mrs Bennet took no notice of him leaving; from the moment she had heard her husband's voice as her lover pounded her body, her mind was on him.

There he was, on the steps of their hotel, tearing down what had taken them a lifetime to achieve. The betrayal she felt at this moment overshadowed anything that had happened over their forty years of marriage.

She muted the TV as a single tear rolled down her numb face.

***

Benjy Costa stood across the street from the Everfield Park Hotel, gazing up as high as he could to see the top before the sun's rays stopped him. He remembered seeing the hotel in a movie he had watched as a child, in Chicago. When he and his family moved to New

York three weeks ago, he walked past the hotel and recognized it while he had been scouring the city in search of work. Benjy wasn't too sure if it was the pure nerve of barging into the Head of the Housekeeping's office that day, and shoving his resume into her assistant's hand, or just pure luck, but had managed to bag himself an interview, and today, was the day.

He had bought himself a suit specifically for the occasion. It had cost him everything he had managed to save up, which wasn't a lot, but he saw it as an investment in his future. This was only the second time in his eighteen years that Benjy had worn a suit, the first being two summers ago during his father's funeral. The suit he wore that day belonged to his father and had not fitted him well; his main memory from that day, other than burying the man who was his, was how itchy he felt and how his mother would slap his hand away each time he tended to an itch on his neck.

Benjy wasn't too sure if today was an average day for the hotel. If he got the job, would he arrive everyday to mob of press blocking half the sidewalk? They seemed to be in the middle of setting things up; a raised platform in front of the steps was still being erected.

When there was a slight break in the endless flow of traffic, he darted in and out of cars as they turned the front of the hotel into a parking lot. He found that maneuvering in and out of the press was harder than making his way through rush hour traffic.

He was greeted at the front door by a gigantic figure of a doorman who towered over Benjy's already tall frame. The tall man was a man in the twilight of his life; he looked down at the nervous Benjy and noticed the gold letterhead bearing the hotel's logo. He had seen hundreds of youngsters climbing the hotel's steps with their interview confirmation letters over his nearly fifty years of service. Back when he started at fourteen, as a shoeshine boy in the hotel lobby, there were no paperwork and meetings, just a help wanted sign written on the back of a piece of cardboard.

He looked down at the nervous young man with his large dark blue eyes and opened up the hotel for him, whispering "Good luck," as he slid past him into the vast open lobby.

Hearing the doorman wishing him luck calmed his nerves, just slightly.

Benjy waited a moment before taking another step; he wanted

to take in the vastness of the hotel's entrance. To his immediate right was the Pemberly Pub. The open plan bar opened right into the hotel's grand entrance. Even if he was unsuccessful today in getting a job, he decided he would try his luck at the bar and sit back on one of the mahogany bar stools, and sip on an ice cold beer.

Opposite The Pemberly, was the entrance to the ballroom; the doorway was abuzz with people coming and going, carrying glasses, flowers and lighting equipment. Out of the corner of his eye he thought he saw an old woman carrying a small dog; he wasn't sure if she was transporting it to the ballroom or if the pooch was part of her everyday attire.

He stepped towards the ballroom; slowly, edging closer to get a peek of what was going on inside; he could tell it was full of people, as he heard the buzz of movement as he had walked through the main doors of the hotel. There were too many voices to distinguish what was being said, but one voice could be heard over the rest. When he got to the doorway, he took a look in.

The owner of the loud, firm, authoritative voice was staring back at him. Benjy knew that he was looking directly into the eyes of Mr. Bennet. He was a minor celebrity, a massive personality and the owner of the hotel.

Mr. Bennet fully opened the door. He was tall and broad, had a thick head of hair and a well-trimmed beard. Stood next to him were two people, his assistant Charlotte and the head of the hotel's security, Alex. Alex, surprised to see this tall, lean African American man stood almost nose to nose with his employer, attempting to push Benjy out of the way.

Mr. Bennet stopped him and put out his hand to greet Benjy. "How do you do there, young man?" Mr. Bennet said, in his trademark brash tone.

Benjy froze. He hadn't expected this. He attempted to splutter out a response but nothing exited his lips, apart from the fragmented beginning of the word, "Hello".

"Arthur Bennet" Mr. Bennet continued.

Charlotte and Alex couldn't help but smirk to one another. This wasn't an unusual response to people meeting Mr. Bennet, it always gave them a kick.

Benjy extended his shaky hand and clasped hold of the

hovering hand in front of him.

"Benjy," he said in a whispered tone.

Mr. Bennet shook his hand; Benjy wasn't prepared for how tight the grip would be. When he let go, he had to stretch out his fingers to coax the blood back into circulation.

"So, you want to join the Everfield family?" Mr. Bennet gestured down to the letter in Benjy's other hand.

"I hope so," Benjy replied. He couldn't believe this was happening.

Mr. Bennet again extended out his hand, this time for the letter. Benjy gave it to him and stood anxiously as Mr. Bennet read it through. After only about four seconds, he handed it back.

"She likes horses" said Mr. Bennet, reaching in and whispering into Benjy's ear.

He winked at Benjy and walked across the lobby. Waiting for him was a Chinese man who shook his hand. The Chinese man, Mr. Hilbert, the general manager of the hotel, had noticed Mr. Bennet's interaction with the young man and with a raise of his eyebrow, "What was that about?"

"He wants to join our little circus," Mr. Bennet said whimsically as the four of them walked towards to main door; Alex lead the way, clearing the path of all obstacles. As the main doors opened, an explosion of camera flashes flooded the lobby.

Benjy turned around and headed for the elevators, past the check in desk. The concierge was to one side, at his own little station. He had spotted Benjy from the moment he entered the hotel and paid close attention to his conversation with Mr. Bennet. To be fair, there was very little that Michael didn't notice. It was in his interest to know everything that was going on, not just in the hotel, but all over the city. He had contacts in every club, theatre and restaurant in New York. You wouldn't think it, but the weasely looking man, was one of the most well connected men on the east coast.

Benjy needed the fifth floor; he pressed the button for the elevator at the far end of the lobby and stepped inside. He was glad that the elevator was empty, because as soon as he had pressed the button, he started to sweat; every pore on his body started spewing out uncontrollably. His palms were soaking; he hoped that the woman interviewing him wouldn't want to shake his hands, but he had a feeling he wouldn't be so lucky. He took deep breaths, each one louder than the last. He wiped his hands on the side of his trousers and the doors opened.

Standing in the doorway was a Hispanic girl of about seventeen, holding what looked like a feather duster. Benjy looked at the button panel; he had one more floor to go. Smiling, he moved aside to let her in; she smiled back and stepped in. The door closed and they both stood still, in silence, looking ahead. They did catch each other's eye in the front mirror; their gaze broken with the noice of the doors sliding open. The both got out, and the girl gave another smile before hurrying around the corner and skipped up to an older Hispanic woman.

Benjy looked down at the letter. He needed room four-seven-five. In front of him was room four-zero-one. He looked down at his watch; it was nine-fifty-nine. He had one minute before his appointment. He didn't fancy running around the corridors, but the thought of being late appealed to him even less. He started walking, following the corridor as it snaked around; "four- one-five"; it gave him a slight reassurance that he was going in the right direction. As the numbers crept up, so did his walking pace. When he reached his room, he was full out sprinting, running with one eye on his watch, the other on the passing doors. The door opened as he reached it. He was panting and needed a moment to catch his breath.

"Sorry, I'm late" he said, trying to normalize his breathing.

He looked up, and standing before him was an older lady in a sleek grey dress, her grey hair was in a tight, high bun; he imagined it would be too tight not to hurt.

The lady looked down at her watch. "Just on time," she said in a very thick accent. An accent he couldn't place; it wasn't American. Maybe British, he thought.

She put out her hand for him to shake, slowly he extended his, hoping she wouldn't feel the remnants of sweat that hadn't transferred to his trousers. She let him into the small windowless room he had entered the last time he was in the hotel. A small desk in the corner was being occupied by the lady's assistant; she was the young girl he had met during his last visit, who just so happened to have been arranging interviews that day.

They smiled at each other as the lady walked him past a small leather couch and through another door. They entered her office. This was a much larger room with a vast window that overlooked the street below.

"Do, have a seat," she said in a rhythmic tone. He liked her accent and understood what she was saying, but still had no idea where she was from.

He took a seat in front of her desk which stood facing the window. She sat in her chair that swiveled slightly as her slender frame barely filled the seat.

Benjy took a second to glimpse around the room, his eye happened to stop at a picture of a large horse upon a wall. He thought back to what Mr. Bennet had whispered to him.

"Beautiful," he said under his breath, just loud enough for the lady to hear.

She took her eyes from Benjy's resume and looked up.

"Sorry?" she said, putting the résumé down and giving Benjy her full attention.

"What an incredible animal," said Benjy. He knew nothing of horses and was thinking in the vaguest of terms.

"Do you ride?" she said, putting her arms on the chair rests as she sit back.

"No," he said, stringing out the word. "I'd love to one day. I've never had the opportunity." He tried to look glum. He really needed this job.

The lady remembered reading his address; she knew the area wasn't an affluent one. "I would ride daily as a child," she said gleefully, not in a smug way. Benjy could tell that these animals really meant something to the woman.

"Where was that?" Benjy asked. It just slipped out; he was meant to be answering questions today.

"Wales" she replied. "Born and bred in God's country."

"I've heard it's nice there" Benjy replied, he was just spewing out anything; he could feel his mind slowly shutting down. He was still as nervous as anything.

"Rolling hills as far as the eyes can see. Quite different to the city," she said as she took a glimpse out of the window from the corner of her eye. A buzz of traffic can be heard through the slight crack of the open window.

"Let's get down to brass tacks" she said.

Benjy had no idea what she meant but had a feeling the rest of the conversation wouldn't be about horses and hills. The lady picked up his resume once more.

"You have no hotel experience," she said bluntly.

"No," Benjy said, holding down his head.

"You have no work experience at all." She pauses slightly, continuing before Benjy could interrupt, "You haven't completed your High School education and you have nothing to show for the two years since you dropped out."

Benjy attempted to answer her before she held up her fingers to hush him.

"But, I'm going to give you a chance Benjamin," he hated being called by his full name and had given up any hope of working here.

"Thank you Mrs. ..." he had no idea what her name was. The letter he received was signed by her assistant and just said he would be meeting with the Head of Housekeeping.

"Ms. Powell" she replied. "I'm yet to find a man worthy enough to take away the name my father gave me," She said in a proud tone.

Lesbian, Benjy thought, but wouldn't dare utter it, not after just getting a job.

"But, where to put you," she said in a confused tone as she surveyed him up and down.

"I think I'll have you working down the laundry room."

He didn't like the sound of that, but liked the idea of having a job.

She passed him back his résumé. "I take it all your details are correct?" she asked.

He nodded after skimming it through.

"Excellent. Someone will call you in the next few days with your work schedule."

A smile erupted over his face. Ms. Powell gave a slight smirk for a split second and stood up.

His meeting was over and he was relieved. "Any plans for the rest of the day?" she asked inquisitively.

"The Pemberly," he replied. This was defiantly his next stop. "Now I can breathe."

She looked at her watch; she thought it was a bit early for a drink, but that was just her. She opened up her top drawer and handed Benjy a Pemberly voucher for a free drink.

"I'm sure Franky can sort you out," and with that, his meeting was over and he was back in the hallway.

As he waited for the elevator, the girl appeared once more; this time, accompanied by the older Hispanic woman. He smiled at her, expecting the same in return; but got nothing.

The lift finally arrived; Benjy stepped in and waited for the two of them to enter. The girl attempted to, but was stopped when the woman put a firm hand on her shoulder.

"We'll get the next one," the woman said and with that, the elevator seemed to slam shut.

***

The television had been off for a few minutes and Mrs. Bennet had started running herself a bath in the adjoining bathroom. Her bath was the one place in the world she felt most at ease; she would lay there for hours as the world kept going around her. The white marble with its gold flecks never changed; it had looked the same since she had it installed when they first bought the hotel. She knew every fleck by memory, and the direction they ran in.

Mrs. Bennet reached in to feel the water, it was exceptionally hot, the way she liked it.

She didn't hear Mr. Bennet return to the suite, the front door made no noise. It was only when he let out a slight cough from the bathroom doorway that she knew that he was home. She ever so slightly turned her neck to see him then turned back to the bath.

"What a morning I've had," Mr. Bennet said as he slowly walked towards his wife, kissing her gently on the side of her jaw

Mrs. Bennet said or did nothing. She stood there starring into her running bath.

"Annalise?" he whispered.

"I saw you on the TV," she said, still gazing heavily into the bath.

"This is why I'm here. I've taken thirty minutes out so we can talk."

"Wow, thirty minutes," she said as she burst into laughter, "So that what I'm worth to you." She was now facing him, looking him dead in the eye; him, not flinching as she changed the tone of her voice.

"Darling, you're worth a lifetime to me," he replied. And with that, she swung her arm, slapping him hard on the cheek just inches from his eye. The sound echoed around the whole room. "I know your upset, Annalise. So I'll let what you did slide."

She left him there in the bathroom by himself and went back and sat on the bed, sitting down on the mark the young man made before he left.

Mr. Bennet could feel his cheek starting to get hotter. He walked over to the basin and looked at his reflection in the mirror; a slight red glow, but no mark. He reached into his pocket and took out a small white container, opening it out and swallowing a pill.

Mrs. Bennet was still sitting on the edge of the bed; she wanted her husband to leave. She was in no mood to see his face, so when he re-entered the bedroom and sat down next to her, she knew he would be there for the full thirty minutes.

"You should have told me," she muttered. "You can't just break up the hotel, selling bits to the highest bidder."

"You have absolutely no fucking idea what you're talking about" he snapped back at her, "There's way more to it than that."

"It would have been nice to have been kept in the loop."

"You're not part of the loop, my dear. You're my wife, you raise my children. For the most part that's done. Now your job is to go shopping, put on your dresses, look beautiful and hold on to my arm when we're out."

"This is my home," she replied, deflated. She knew there would be no winning with her husband.

"One of them, yes." He replied. "How many homes is it that we have?" he asked her.

She stayed silent, she wasn't actually too sure of the answer. They owned a lot of property.

"You need to remember to keep out of my business." With that, he stood up, unbuckled his belt and dropped his trousers.

He pushed her back on the bed and slid up her towel. Mrs. Bennet never resisted his advances; she had stopped too long ago. She knew he wouldn't last long and would just lay there, thinking of how much damage she would do to his credit card. Spending money she knew he would never notice.

Him cumming was as much as a relief to her, as it was to him. When he was done, he buckled up his trousers and headed for the door.

"Lizzie's flight arrives in a few hours," Mrs. Bennet said with no emotion as she lay where he left her.

A smile filled his face. "Shall I send her a car?" he asked, genuinely concerned about how his eldest child would get to the hotel.

"We're taking a stretch. Jane has that daft man following her around," she said, rolling her eyes.

With that, Mr. Bennet shook his head disapprovingly then left Mrs. Bennet alone.

Her bath was now overflowing, water started to spread over the floor as she lay in bed with no energy to move.

Mr. Bennet arrived at The Pemberly and recognized Benjy sat at the bar. He stood behind him as he took a sip of beer.

"Are we celebrating? Or is this a somber party for one?" He said in his booming voice which made Benjy jump out of his skin.

Standing behind him was Mr. Bennet and his assistant, Charlotte. It took Benjy a moment to gather his thoughts.

"Celebrating," he muttered; putting his glass on the mat, trying not to spill his drink.

"I had a feeling," he said. Mr. Bennet looked up and down the length of the bar; he turned his attention to the seating area before noticing a slight glow coming from the very corner.

"Franky!" He yelled. The light extinguished immediately as a small, pink haired guy came running into view, pushing his phone into his pocket.

"Use Grindr when I'm paying you again and I'll fire you" he said sternly.

Franky nodded in embarrassment, all the patrons were now staring his way.

"I'd like you to take care of my friend here" Mr. Bennet said, patting Benjy on the back.

"I don't want to see his glass empty." He said, stirring into Franky's eyes, making sure he understood what he meant. Franky nodded his head and headed back behind the bar.

Mr. Bennet patted Benjy on the back once more and left him to his afternoon of heavy drinking. He crosses the bar, followed closely by

Charlotte.

They arrived at a table occupied by two men. One man, was dressed in a tailored pinstripe suit shuffled a deck of cards, moving the pack midair effortlessly from one hand to another while he spoke in a hushed tone to the other man, dressed from head to toe in white. The sharp contrast from his dark skin made Mr. Bennet take notice of him.

"I don't believe we've had the pleasure" Mr. Bennet said to the black man dressed all in white as he moved past the card wielding man in his late twenties.

"Chrome," He said confidently in his strong London accent.

"Chrome?" Mr. Bennet replied, confused that someone would name their child that.

"Morning Art," The well-dressed man said, leaning in to give him a hug. Mr. Bennet wasn't a hug kind of person, he put up with it for a split second before dropping into the seat next to him.

Charlotte had sat herself down in the adjoining table and was typing away on a small notepad computer she had taken out of her purse. Also placed on the table were three mobile phones that buzzed and vibrated continuously in unison.

"Three minutes Mr. Bennet," she said sternly, without looking up from her screen, as she typed away ferociously.

"You heard the lady," Mr. Bennet said as Chrome and the other man sat back down.

"So, Collin," Mr. Bennet started in a slow deliberate cadence. "You saw my little press conference this morning?"

"I sure did," Collin relied. "I was a little shocked to hear that you're selling off parts of the hotel." Collin said, expecting an explanation from Mr. Bennet.

"It's all part of the master plan," Mr. Bennet retorted.

Chrome sat in silence, following the conversation and watching Collin's hands as he shuffled the deck of cards back and forth.

Mr. Bennet was not put off by Collins rapid hand movements; he had known Collin since he was a small child and had been great friends with his father; he knew too well that Collin was incapable of keeping still. He had broken a fair few vases and ornaments at this hotel when he was much younger.

"You don't sound like a local to me," Mr. Bennet said, turning his attention to Chrome.

"London," said Chrome, proudly.

"I know the city well," Mr. Bennet said, "The wife's hometown. What brings you to New York?"

"Chrome is a musician," Collin said, trying to get a word in.

"I'm sure Mr. Chrome can answer for himself" Mr. Bennet snapped.

A grin appeared on Charlottes face, she loved it when her boss would cut people down to size.

"I'm a DJ and producer," Chrome answered.

"Are you successful?" Mr. Bennet asked. "Forgive me; I'm not so keyed up with today's music. My daughter Jane is more your target audience."

"I'm seated at a table with two Billionaires," Chrome said smugly, he was a little proud of how fast he had come up with that.

"Touché," Mr. Bennet said, taking a sip of Collin's drink.

"And how is it I can help you two gentleman this morning?" Mr. Bennet asked.

"Two minutes," Charlotte spat out without losing her typing rhythm.

"My investment company is helping Chrome and his partner set up a US base." Collin said, getting a word in, staring at Mr. Bennet as he slowly sipped from his glass.

"Your father's company," Mr. Bennet replied, placing the glass down with a thud.

"He's been dead almost twenty years Dodger," Collin said slyly.

Dodger was the name Collin's father would call him and hated anyone else using it.

"It's been mine since I turned eighteen," Collin retorted as he continued shuffling his cards.

"I'm going to be spending a lot of time in the city and need a base," Chrome interjected.

"When Collin said he knew you while we were eating breakfast and saw you on the TV…"

Mr. Bennet interrupted him, "You thought you would skip all of the procedure Charlotte and I have set up, for potential buyers to go through and jump to the front of the line." Mr. Bennet started speaking faster and faster.

"That's exactly what we thought we'd do," Collin bluntly said, he starred daggers at Mr. Bennet, Continuing to shuffle his cards, getting faster and faster.

"Because I like you," Mr. Bennet said, turning his attention to Chrome, "I'll set something up."

"Do you have anything today?" Chrome asked, not wanting to push his luck.

"Thank you gentlemen," Charlotte said; her notebook and cell phones were now packed away in her purse.

"I should have a bit of time this afternoon," Mr. Bennet said, standing up.

Mr. Bennet gave Charlotte a slight nod.

"Three, forty-five" she said without hesitation.

"How does that sound?" Mr. Bennet asked Chrome, extending his hand.

"Good to me," Chrome answered.

With that, Mr. Bennet was gone from The Pemberly. Collin and Chrome watched as he crossed the lobby and got into an elevator. The large flat screen in the corner in the bar was playing Mr. Bennett's news conference.

***

Mr. Bennet burst through the hotels doors and marched up to the podium. The awaiting photographers and news cameras burst into life when they saw him.

Charlotte, Alex and Mr. Hilbert stood to one side, surveying the sight and awestruck at how many spectators there were.

Mr. Bennet banged the microphones with his heavy hand. "Is it working?" he asked himself as his voice boomed over the crowd, not entirely due to the microphones.

"Good morning," Mr. Bennet started, looking into the crowd. "Thank you for joining me at my home for the last few decades. To many people, the Everfield is a classic part of this city's heritage; a landmark for tourists and locals alike. I've lived here with my wife, who unfortunately couldn't join me today, she's up to her neck in Champagne, crab puffs and balloons; putting the last minute touches to the annual *Bennet Ball* this evening."

The crowd gave a slight chuckle at the thought of Mrs. Bennet blowing up balloons.

"And my three children, who grew up here, running around the hallways. Some of my children are yet to actually grow out of that habit."

Mr. Bennet paused as again, the crowd let out a slight laugh, more for his benefit than anything else.

"For nearly a hundred years, the Everfield has been catering to clientele from all over the world. Guests have been returning year after year. We have members of a Saudi royal family that only stay here when visiting New York. Over the years, guests have been telling me that not only do they love the hotel as much as I do. They want to keep returning here, and also live here, like I do. They want the greatest chefs from over the world, cooking for them every night. World class gymnasiums to workout in; be around the greatest parties in the city, like the event most of you will be back for this evening."

"So it is with great pride that I'm announcing that I will be offering a few lucky people the chance of owning part of New York's history and have me as a neighbor!"

Mr. Bennet took a deep breath as the reporters leaned in closer.

"I have time for a few questions," Mr. Bennet said as he put both hands flat on the lecture.

Charlotte leaned in close to Alex and whispered in his ear, "This is going to get mad."

Alex, fully aware that the press would want to get close to Mr. Bennet, stepped forward and stood by his side…

"Are you selling rooms or suites?" shouted one reporter.

"We'll have a few apartment style suites and also a few rooms." Mr. Bennet replied, looking at his watch.

"How much will they cost?" another asked.

"Prices will vary," he said, in all honesty, he had not yet thought of prices, or even which suites or rooms he would sell off.

"What does Mrs. Bennet think about the plans?" one reporter asked.

"She supports me one hundred percent," Mr. Bennet lied, "Every business decision I make, must first go through the wife for approval. That's the secret to a long and happy marriage," Mr. Bennet said confidently.

He was in no mood for any more questions; he bid the press a good day and returned back to his hotel to see his wife.

Mr. Hilbert rushed to his side.

"When were you..." Mr. Hilbert started, before Mr. Bennet cut him off.

"In the elevator." He snapped.

Alex ran ahead to call the elevator, an elevator that went exclusively to the Bennett's personal floor. There was no waiting, the doors opened immediately.

The three of them stepped inside.

"Are you crazy?" Mr. Hilbert shouted out, as the elevator doors slammed shut. "We're a hotel, not an apartment block" Mr. Hilbert continued.

"Were doing this," Mr. Bennet said, ending the conversation.

"But why?" Mr. Hilbert asked, in a much calmer tone.

"Why? Because, this is my hotel, and I'll do what I like to it."

The elevator doors opened up and Mr. Bennet stepped out, putting his hand up to stop the three of them following him.

"Charlotte, come get me in thirty minutes; if I'm not back in the office," Mr. Bennett said as the doors slid shut.

He walked along the corridor and as he dived into his pocket for his keycard, as he felt his way through his deep pockets, his phone began to vibrate. Together with his keycard, he lifted out his phone.

A picture of Collin starred back at him, taking a breath, he accepted the call...

"Hello Collin," he answered in a hushed but familiarly brash tone. "I don't know..." he paused, shaking his head from side to side.

"I have so much on... For you, I can do thirty minutes from now... Meet me at the Pemberly and I'll come find you," Mr. Bennet hung up the phone without giving or receiving a goodbye.

He placed the phone back into his pocket, slid the card into the lock and entered his apartment, quietly shutting the door behind him.

The timing was too close for his liking; the young man had only moments ago, vacated the Bennet's apartment. When he heard the elevator doors slide open, he dove into a recess a few feet away, breathing in and held his breath, as not to be seen or heard. He waited for the corridor to once again become empty. When the coast was clear, he made his way through the snaking hallways and exited through a door to find the service elevator.

***

Lizzie Bennet could never understand why people pushed past, trying to get as close as they could to the moving baggage belt. Being less than three feet away would not routine her with her possessions any faster, she thought.

The screen above her head announced her flight's luggage was next; she waited patiently for her suitcase to appear on the baggage belt and only moved when she spotted her frayed, brown suitcase appear through the dangling rubber strips. Her bag was covered in buttons and badges, the largest a PETA logo that Lizzie had stitched right across the side.

She sincerely repeated "I'm sorry" and "Excuse me please," as she moved in and out of the other travellers. She spoke well with a calm, earthy tone.

As she walked, she rolled up the sleeves of her long bulky sweater that did nothing for her figure. Her outfit, made her appear larger than she actually was. She was by no means fat or overweight, she was of average height and had an average looking face, that was round and hid behind her large glasses that suited her. She had a mop of frizzy, untamed hair that had natural blonde highlights throughout.

She was your wholesome, girl next door who, on many occasions had been described as the marrying, not fucking type. Lizzie had no problem if men though this of her; those were not the type of men whom she would ever consider for a partner.

She took her suitcase and carried it through the arrivals lounge. As she got closer and closer to the open doors, the sunlight shining through got brighter and brighter, until it got to a point where she found herself, using her arm to cast a shadow over her eyes.

When she got outside, she was confronted by a large stretch limousine that she recognized immediately; as the car that took her to and from school each day. The driver was also the same, he was in his fifties and Russian she believed. He never spoke, no matter how much she and her siblings banged the glass separating them or sang annoying, repetitive songs for a journeys entire duration.

The driver got out of the car and held out his hand to take her suitcase.

"Thank you, but I'm fine," she said, smiling and making her way to the trunk of the car. He followed her and before she got to the rear of the car, he had opened the trunk using his keys.

She slid the suitcase in and shut the lid herself as the driver stood back and let her be, knowing that she wouldn't allow him to help.

When she shut the lid, she could hear a sound coming for the back of the car. She knew the sound immediately as her sister singing. Lizzie would be the first to admit it, her sister could sing, but sharing a room for so many years as a child had made her less appreciative of her gift than others would be.

She walked to the door and reached in to grab the handle. The singing had stopped and was replaced with a shuffling sound and a loud "Ouch" and "Get off me, you fat oaf" from her mother's distinctive English accent.

Lizzie chuckled to herself as she opened the door, expecting to see her mother but instead, she was confronted a large camera that sprang towards her as she attempted to get in.

"Move out of the way," Mrs. Bennet barked as the camera retreated from Lizzie's view and left room for her to get in.

Lizzie kissed her mother on the cheek as she climbed over her; she was sat right by the door. Her sister Jane was seated in the seat next to Mrs. Bennet and a man holding the camera had retreated all the way down the other end of the car, filming Lizzie's entrance.

"What's going on?" Lizzie asked, laughing, as the driver shut the door behind her. She sat down in a seat next to her sister. Jane and she hugged then Lizzie buckled up.

The man was wearing a scruffy pair of blue jeans and a white T-shirt that barely covered his stomach. He bent down on to the floor and panned slowly through the Bennet women.

As the driver lurched forward, the man was sent lunging forward into the carpet, he held out his arm to stop the camera from making contact with the floor.

"Careful Buster, you nearly broke Mr. Hitchcok's camera." she called down to the driver in a gleeful tone. Mrs. Bennet saw him raise his eyebrow in acknowledgement in the mirror as he fully pulled out into the road and started their return journey back into the city.

"It's James" the man in his thirties said, dusting himself off as he sat back down, making sure his camera was in one piece.

"I could care less what your name is young man," Mrs. Bennet bluntly said before turning her attention to Lizzie.

"How was your flight, Darling?" she asked her eldest daughter.

"It was fine," Lizzie replied as she unzipped and reached into a small pouch she had over her shoulder that looked like it would snap at any moment. It was in stark contrast to the top of the range cell phone she switched back on.

As Lizzie waited for her phone to fully boot back up, she ran her fingers through her hair, getting caught up in the knotted mess.

"We really must do something with your hair," said an unkind voice. Jane spoke in a very slow deliberate way, pronouncing each and every syllable.

From about the age of thirteen, Jane started speaking with a crackled, vocal fry that annoys her mother, even to this day.

She was wearing large dark sunglasses, as was her mother. Jane's hair was immaculate and dead straight; it continued past her long thin face and down over her shoulder. Her makeup, of what Lizzie could see, was as always, perfect and flawless. Jane always had a good complexion and Lizzie couldn't understand why she would want to cover it up.

"I will, before the ball," Lizzie said, not taking her sister's comments about her hair seriously.

Her phone had now fully booted up; she had no messages and wasn't expecting anyone to contact her. Jane and Mrs. Bennet watched as she placed her phone back into her tiny purse, barley large enough for her cell.

"What's going on with your nails?" Mrs. Bennet asked in a concerned tone.

Lizzie looked down at the fingers and could see nothing wrong with them. She had always bitten them and this had infuriated Mrs. Bennet, who had tried everything to prevent it when Lizzie was a young girl; even, for a short time, bringing in a therapist to speak with her daily until Mr. Bennet found out and put a stop to it; this went on for almost six months.

"I see you're still biting your nails," Mrs. Bennet said in her surly tone; it was a way she spoke with to everyone. Lizzie never took it personally.

Lizzie looked at her nails once more and shrugged it off; it wasn't something she ever thought about.

"We must get them sorted before tonight," Mrs. Bennet said, in what was to her, a pleasant tone.

"If I have time," she wasn't that bothered what her nails looked like; as long as they were reasonably short, she was happy.

"We have plenty of time," Jane said, looking down at her twenty thousand dollar watch. Mrs Bennet took a look at her equally expensive time piece.

"I was thinking maybe Buster would be alone in picking me up, and you both would be at the spa." Lizzie said, making fun of them a little bit.

"Don't be silly dear, I wanted to see you first," Mrs. Bennet said seriously.

"First?" Lizzie asked. She was joking about them going to the spa. "Are you dropping me back beforehand?" Lizzie asked.

"No time." Jane said, without looking at her watch. "When's the last time you even got a treatment?" she asked as a matter of fact.

Lizzie had to think; it would not be within the last week, like her sister or mother, or even in the last few month.

"Probably last time I was in the city," she had been dragged along that time too.

"Blimey, darling" Mrs. Bennet said, taking off her glasses to look Lizzie in the eyes. "You need to start taking care of yourself."

Jane was nodding along in agreement, "Mom's right."

"Imagine how your father and I would feel if we got a call one day saying…" Mrs. Bennet took a second to think; …you'd dropped dead from stress."

"I'm not going to die of stress, mom." Lizzie said, reassuring a serious Mrs. Bennet.

"College is stressful," Mrs. Bennet stated to Lizzie, "I don't for one second imagine you're drinking or going out. Stanford is stressful"

"I go out," Lizzie said defensively.

"The library doesn't count," Jane sneered from behind a magazine she took out of her obnoxiously large Fendi purse.

The rest of the drive consisted of Mrs. Bennet and Jane, quizzing Lizzie on her daily routine and which products she used, neither of them happy with the fact that she shopped in the dollar stores. Mrs. Bennet had convinced herself that Lizzie had lost the credit cards her father had given her.

"Yes, one is for emergencies, Lizzie," Mrs. Bennet said calmly. "But we gave you one for daily use. How are you surviving, Darling?" Mrs. Bennet asked in a concerned way.

Lizzie wasn't in the mood to tell her mother that she had taken out student loans so she could pay her own way, and would repay them after graduation.

They had just pulled up outside a tall unassuming brick, Uptown building. *The Lucas Family Treatment Facility*; an exclusive, members only spa, only a few blocks away from the hotel.

Mrs. Bennet wasn't done interrogating her daughter about her finances. Lizzie kept looking over at the man with the camera, not to keen about talking about money in front of a man she had only just met. Mrs. Bennet and Jane both noticed this.

"Just ignore him," Jane said to reassure Lizzie. "Just pretend he's not there."

"That's what I do," Mrs. Bennet snapped, giving him a look as she got out of the car.

Mrs. Bennet went up to the door and rang the intercom. The door was never kept unlocked.

"Lucas family treatments," said an upbeat voice almost immediately.

"Annalise Bennet," Mrs. Bennet replied without thinking.

Jane, Lizzie and James were all stood behind her. Buster had gotten back into the car and would wait until they were inside; before returning to the hotel for a coffee and await a call to pick them up.

The door, a solid piece of black opaque glass, gave a high pitched buzz and opened. It opened up into a large white open space, filled with light. A small desk at the other end had the clinic's name and logo above in red on the wall. Mrs. Bennet led them across the waiting room. James bobbed up and down, whizzing in and out of them, filming the location and their entrance.

"For Christ's sake, will you stop moving around?" Mrs. Bennet spat at him, as he nearly bumped into her.

The receptionist, a petite red haired girl stood up as they approached and held out her hand for Mrs. Bennet to shake.

"Mrs. Bennet," she said affectionately. "Lizzie, Jane," She said equally as warmly. She wasn't sure whether to greet James or not.

"Just ignore him," Mrs. Bennet said bluntly.

"Can I get you ladies some champagne before your treatments?" The receptionist asked politely, sitting back down.

"No, thank you," Lizzie answered for them, before her mother or sister could get a word in.

The receptionist sensed that this is not the answer Mrs. Bennet would have given.

"How about I put a bottle on ice? To have while you're inside?" she said while she wrote on a pad on her desk.

Mrs. Bennet smiled, "Excellent idea."

"We've had many guests already today, who will be at your ball later this evening." The red haired said to Mrs. Bennet. "The whole city is talking about it."

Mrs. Bennet smiled, "My husband and I do try our best to put on a great event."

The receptionist laughed, "We all know who the real driving force behind it is."

Mrs. Bennet looked confused, looking at the receptionist for clarification.

"You, Mrs. Bennet," She laughed, Mrs. Bennet gave a slight chuckle.

"Still lots to do." Mrs. Bennet told her, wanting to get to her treatment and not speak to this girl all afternoon.

"The usual?" the girl asked Mrs. Bennet, who nodded. She asked the same to Jane, who again nodded. When she turned her attention to Lizzie, she froze. It had been such a long time since she had been here that she wasn't sure what she wanted, "Lizzie, what can we do for you today?"

Lizzie was equally as stumped. She hated these kinds of places and could barely remember what services they offered. There was no brochure or lists on the desk in front of here.

"A facial, maybe," Lizzie answered; saying the first thing that came into her head.

"A facial?" the receptionist asked.

"No, I think she's joking" Mrs. Bennet interrupted, laughing. "She knows she can't have a facial this close to an event."

"I do?" Lizzie said quietly to herself.

Mrs. Bennet looked Lizzie up and down and noticed she was twiddling her fingers.

"Let's just go with a mani-pedi to start with," Mrs. Bennet said determinatively; this treatment would do wonders for her self-confidence, she thought.

Lizzie looked at her nails, there was nothing wrong with them in her eyes, but she didn't have the energy to argue.

"Excellent," the red haired woman said; it had not accrued her to ask James if he was having a treatment done. She doubted Mrs. Bennet would foot the bill for him or he himself could afford it. "If you head into the robing room, we'll have the champagne all ready for you." The girl stood up and gestured to a door just beyond the left side of her desk. The door had a small *woman symbol*, the door mirroring the ladies, to the right, had a sign indicating the men's.

Lizzie pushed the door open and was followed in by Jane and Mrs. Bennet. James attempted to enter too, but was stopped, with a raised eyebrow from Mrs. Bennet.

"No chance," she muttered before slamming the door shut.

James lowered his camera and shrugged at the girl behind the desk. "Why don't you have a seat." she said, pointing to a white couch near the front door.

He started walking across the room when he heard the door open behind him.

Jane had appeared, looking for him. "Put on a robe and meet us in the treatment room." She said without properly making sure he was there, before hastily disappearing once more.

James turned to look at the receptionist who pointed with her long finger, towards the men's room.

Mrs. Bennet, Jane and Lizzie sat down on benches in the minimal dressing room. It had individual long lockers; each with a fluffy white robe and slippers inside. None of the lockers had locks on them which Lizzie noticed.

"Don't be daft, Lizzie. No member is going to steal, here," Mrs. Bennet said as she hung up her coat.

"Didn't Bernie Madoff go here?" Lizzie asked, as she pulled of her sweater, not seeing her mother's dumbstruck reaction.

Jane seemed more interested in feeling the robe, rubbing it over her skin and face than getting involved in the conversation.

They all started to undress, down to their underwear. All three women were in great shape, even Lizzie who had no interest in revealing her body to the public. All three of them lived active lifestyles; Mrs. Bennet probably getting more exercise than her daughters combined, having numerous ways of elevating her heartbeat.

Jane notices the quality of Lizzie's underwear paled in comparison to that of hers and her mother's.

"Mom, I think someone needs to visit Carine Gilson's" Jane said, pointing to Lizzie's heaped underwear.

"Darling, at least shop at Victoria's Secret when you're by yourself. Will you do that for me?" Mrs. Bennet said as compassionately as she could.

Lizzie felt like rolling her eyes. She nodded in agreement so they would move off the topic of her Target panties, which fitted and felt fine to her. She put on her robe and waited for the others to get unchanged.

Lizzie couldn't help but notice her mother's breasts and how perky they were; they were firmer than hers and didn't move when they were freed from the bra.

"Less than a year old," Mrs. Bennet said grinning, as she copped a feel. "Feel them," Mrs. Bennet said seriously. Lizzie had absolutely no interest in touching her mother's breast; but Jane, on the other hand already had a good feel of them.

"Who did these?" Jane asked, as she dipped down to look under the breasts.

"Dr. Bernstein," Mrs. Bennet said with a smile on her face. "He's truly a wizard when it comes to understanding the female body."

Her mind wandered to her pre-surgery consultation where the thirty-five year old doctor drew over her breasts, explaining the procedure they were minutes away from undergoing. As he cupped her breast, she put her hand over his, making it impossible for him to pull away; if he had tried. She leaned in and kissed him, marker-pen smudged over his crisp pink shirt. He pulled down his pants and bent her over the desk.

"Mom," Jane was repeating, trying to get her mother's attention.

"Yes dear?" she said, zoning back into the room.

"You will have to introduce me to him," Jane said, as she juggled her already firm, well rounded breasts.

"I don't think so, sweetie," Mrs. Bennet said. Thinking how

hard his desk was banging against the wall. "He specializes in the mature women." she consoled Jane, who look put out by her refusal of an introduction. "There are a few who would do you wonders," she said, thinking of an obese fifty year-old who sweated profusely while standing still; she had walked out of that appointment without even shaking his hand.

"I think you look fine," Lizzie said to her sister.

"Fine?" Jane sneered, looking her naked body up and down, angling herself to get a better look in the full length mirrors on the walls.

"She's joking, darling. Isn't that right, Lizzie," Mrs. Bennet said, passing Jane a robe.

With all three of them robed up, they exited the dressing room.

If Mrs. Bennet at Jane had issues with Lizzie underwear, they would evacuate the building if they saw what James possessed. He sat down and took off his holy socks and pulled down his shabby jeans. His underwear was tatty and sweaty. He emptied the contents of his jeans into the locker; his cell, his wallet and keys. The last item to leave his pocket was a small bag of white powder that didn't enter the locker straight away.

He continued to undress, putting the remainder of his clothes away. He reached into his wallet and took out a UCLA student ID which was ten years out of date; he took that and the white powdered bag over to a basin. He poured out a bit of the powder; he had become good at judging how much he needed. He formed the coke into a line using his card. It never occurred to him to look around to make sure the dressing room was empty. He leant over, bare-ass in the air and snorted his drug of choice.

He let out a brief energetic sound, which made the red haired girl look up from her desk.

He put the bag and card away in the locker and slipped on his robe. He loved the feeling it had against his body, particularly the way it rubbed against his hairy chest. He spent a moment rubbing the robe up and down his chest and stomach. A need to masturbate overwhelmed him; as tempted as he was to flip on his camera and review some previous footage he had taken, he put on his slippers, tied up his robe, picked up his camera and entered the treatment room.

The women were all there when he arrived; not waiting for him, they had started their treatments ten minutes ago.

"Where the fuck have you been?" Jane demanded, ushering him over to film her as a Filipino woman started to slather mud all over her face.

"Why is he filming you Jane?" Lizzie demanded, she had not been told anything about this before she returned home for the summer.

"I'm filming for a…" Jane started, before being shushed by the Filipino, to be quiet.

"Filming for what?" Lizzie asked her mother.

"While your sister pursues a career in the music industry, she wants to document it for a reality show?" Mrs. Bennet said in a very bored tone as a short Asian man massaged her feet.

"What network is this going to be on?" Lizzie asked her mother, who had no idea and shrugged.

She asked again, this time to James who ignored the question.

"I'm filming," he finally answered, annoyed that Lizzie was ruining his shot.

Lizzie asked again, this time in a more serious tone.

"Has my sister and family signed releases? Do you have a permit to shoot here?" Lizzie asked.

"What are you, a lawyer?" he asked.

"Not yet," She answered, "I'm studying Law at Stanford."

"Just ignore him," Mrs. Bennet muttered from behind her glass of Champagne.

"Like any man, if you ignore them, they'll soon sod off," Mrs. Bennet said, as she downed the remainder of her glass. She put her glass down next to Lizzie's full one.

"Why aren't you drinking," Mrs. Bennet demanded. "That glass alone probably costs over seventy dollars."

As much as Lizzie hated waste, she really wasn't interested in having a drink, particularly being this early on in the day.

"Is Max here yet? He's coming tonight, right?" Lizzie asked, wanting to get away from talking about alcohol, Mrs. Bennet took hold of the glass and gulped; shaking her head at the same time.

"I don't believe so." Mrs. Bennet said as she let out the smallest of burps.

"Why? He said he was going to come." Lizzie said.

"We've not spoken."

"I saw him two weeks ago; he stayed with me at the dorm for a few days. Does he not call you?"

"Of course not, I'm his mother," Mrs. Bennet laughed as she knocked back the remainder of Lizzie's glass. "He called Charlotte and cancelled a few days ago" Mrs. Bennet said quietly, "Too busy surfing."

"Shame," Lizzie said to herself as she looked down at her toes; secretly pleased that she was having them done.

Chapter Two

"Well, what do you think?" Mr. Bennet asked Chrome as they walked around a large living area with a sunken horseshoe shaped sofa; large enough to sit twenty people. A projector on the ceiling played a muted music video on a screen that stretched over the entire wall with crystal clear quality; a black rapper was surrounded by nothing but piles cash as scantily dressed women, that gyrated over him as he performed directly into the camera.

Chrome took a moment to look from Mr. Bennet to the screen and back again; he wasn't sure if Mr. Bennet was intentionally playing the video of his business and producing partner, or it was just a coincidence.

"I love it," Chrome said as he walked around the pool that started inside and proceeded to fill most of the balcony; large enough to fit sixty people dancing. Chrome looked into the water and took a step back, the bottom of the pool seemed to have no solid bottom; he could see the street far below.

"A glass bottom," Mr. Bennet said; as Charlotte let herself into the apartment.

She could see her boss and Chrome out on the balcony smiling; the viewing was going well, she thought.

She put down her purse on a small table by the front door, next to a small Buddha statue, which she lifted up, looked over at a distracted Mr. Bennet and placed in her bag.

Chrome put his arms on the railings and looked out over the city views as the wind blew into his face. He looked down and saw a limo pulling up outside the hotel. He could see Buster get out of the car and open up the door. James was the first to exit, followed by Jane, Mrs. Bennet and then Lizzie. Chrome was staring at Jane; his eyes immediately went to her, even from this height he could see her beauty.

"Beautiful view," Chrome said, not speaking of the city's skyline.

Mr. Bennet looked down at what Chrome was looking at; Mr. Bennet smiled when he saw his family get out of the car. "Lizzie," he said under his breath.

"My family," Mr. Bennet said proudly, "Well, most of them. My son is in California."

"Who's the brunette?" Chrome asked as Mr. Bennet tried to get a better look at Lizzie.

"Jane, my middle child; She's a performer too; been singing since she was, this big." Mr. Bennet gestured down to his knee.

"She any good?" Chrome asked, trying to pay attention to Mr. Bennet, only managing to look him in the eye when the Bennet women had walked up the steps and entered the hotel.

"I think so," Mr. Bennet laughed, "Of course, I'd say that."

Chrome walked back into the suite and sat down on the couch; he really liked how soft it felt as he dropped down into it; he could imagine himself and Jane screwing on this couch.

"Custom built for this suite," Mr. Bennet said, following him back through.

The thought of having young musicians living in his hotel really didn't appeal to Mr. Bennet, but he felt something was different about Chrome. Getting Charlotte to find out everything Google had to offer about him, including his net worth and music calibre, made him think differently about him; he was yet to really make it big in America, Chrome and his partner were the people the music industry were all talking about; they were on the verge of cracking the states.

"You said your family lives here, in the hotel?" Chrome enquired as he imagined bumping into Jane in a corridor at night.

"Myself, the wife and Jane, yes." He knew where this was going; Jane was the key to this sale.

"Why don't I let you try the place out for a few weeks; get a feel for the hotel and what it can offer you. Do you have plans this evening

Chrome?" Mr. Bennet asked as Chrome shook his head.

"Come to my Ball, this evening, as my guest. Meet my family." Chrome began to smile; an introduction to Jane is something he would be very interested in.

"Great," Mr. Bennet announced as Chrome stood up. "Charlotte?" he called, looking around for his assistant; who as going through the cupboards of one of the three bedrooms. When she heard her name being called, she ran back to the living room.

"Chrome will be staying in this suite for a while as my guest, please ensure Alex gets him a few keycards sorted, and place the room off the booking system."

Charlotte opened up her purse, taking slightly longer to locate her cell and started typing away, nodding with each word she wrote as Mr. Bennet continued to speak.

"I've also invited Chrome to the ball this evening. Please add him the guest list," Mr . Bennet barked as he took another look around the suite; a suite he had great fondness for.

"Is it okay if I bring a plus one?" Chrome asked.

"Do you have a girlfriend, Chrome?" Mr. Bennet asked.

He slept with many women at any one time, but no one in particular had his heart. "Nah;" Chrome said is a cool tone. Mr. Bennet stared deep into Chrome, trying to read if he was lying. "I mean, I'm not seeing anyone, I date. I meet women."

Annoyed, Mr. Bennet was ready to leave; he had given him the use of one of his most expensive suites and an invite to one of New York's most exclusive annual parties, in exchange for what Mr. Bennet saw was an arraignment for Chrome to get to know his daughter; instead he wants to bring someone else to the ball. "Charlotte, Set it up," Mr. Bennet said then left, without announcing his departure.

Chrome turned to look at Charlotte. "Don't mind him," She said, "He's got a busy day." Chrome nodded, thinking nothing else of it. Before Chrome left, Charlotte took down his contact information and told him the keycards would be ready for pick up this evening from the Ball.

***

When the Bennet women walked into the lobby, it reminded

Mrs. Bennet of a school play she had once seen, performed by children with learning difficulties; a chaotic mess with no clear direction. Her husband was soliciting business from someone who insisted they join them at their child's school production. Ever the great actress, she had managed to shed a tear during an inaudible rendition of Sondheim's 'Send in the clowns'; a song she recognised by the music alone.

Jane gave her mother air kisses and tried to do the same for Lizzie; who out of her element, ended up bumping her nose into Jane's cheek instead.

Lizzie had thought Jane was acting oddly during the short ride back from the spa, she had insisted on not speaking; instead texting her input into conversations.

She stomped off through the lobby towards the elevator that goes exclusively up to the Bennet's floor. Lizzie had always noticed Jane had the power of getting strangers to move out of her way; something she had managed to sustain from an early age and takes full advantage of.

It surprised Lizzie when James failed to follow her sister, instead turned his attention on her. "No," Lizzie said, pointing him in Jane's direction. "I've not signed a release, so no footage you have of me can be used. You're only wasting your time, following me around."

James took the hint and followed Jane across the busy lobby. He on the other hand, doesn't have Jane's gift of parting crowds.

"You really don't like him, do you?" Mrs. Bennet said in her brash British tone.

"Neither do you!" Lizzie returned, walking her mother to the entrance of the Ballroom; already being guarded by Alex and his team, checking everyone entering and leaving.

Mrs. Bennet walked directly to the front on the line, bypassing all the suppliers delivering boxes and crates of all sizes for her ball. She let Lizzie go up to her room, and entered the ballroom without acknowledging the security team.

The vast Ballroom was still being prepared for the evening; tables were yet to be laid, lighting rigs still needed construction around the stage, and the bar was yet to be stocked.

Mrs. Bennet had very little control over the planning and preparation of the ball, or any of the hotels events; her husband's office took care of these. Still, she would go down to the front line to see what was going on and attempt to put her stamp on things.

She surveyed the ballroom and noticed someone placing a huge swan ice sculpture on a table near the bar. She stomped over to him and stood, staring at him.

"Hello?" He said, slightly unnerved by the tall Mrs. Bennet; wearing a large coat in summer with dark sunglasses.

"What are you doing?" She asked.

"Delivering this for tonight," He replied, pointing at the ice sculpture that was starting to drip down onto the table.

"Are you crazy?" she asked, looking at her watch. "The Ball doesn't start for four hours."

The man stood there and shrugged his shoulders, "Do you work here?" He asked.

"No." She snapped at him. "Do I look like I work here?" The man looked her up and down and didn't know what to say.

"I'll take care of this, Mrs. Bennet" said Alex from behind her; jogging through the ballroom to join them. He had heard Mrs. Bennet's raised voice and entered the ballroom; he didn't want to scare or distract the other suppliers and contractors.

"Where's my husband?" She demanded, pruning her lips and looming over the already tall Alex.

"He's just gone into a meeting," said a familiar voice from behind her. Charlotte had just entered the ballroom looking for Alex.

God, Mrs. Bennet thought. She hated being around her husband's inner circle.

"Would you tell him, Lizzie is back at the hotel, when he gets out." and with that, she was gone.

"Perhaps we should ask Pierre, if we can borrow his freezer," Charlotte suggested to the delivery man; pointing him in the direction of the kitchen doors.

When the man had vanished, Charlotte turned her attention to Alex. "So, how much of an inconvenience would it be to amend the guest list?" she asked slyly, knowing she would evoke a negative reaction from him.

"It would inconvenience me greatly and has a possibility of having a detrimental impact on your health; if you were to tell me that the guest list needed changing."

"Oh," she said, thinking in a comic way.

"Are you referring to the guest list that was locked two hours ago?" He asked her; his face fixed in a serious way that contrasted a fun lilt to his tone.

"That very list." She said, handing him a yellow post-it-note with, Chrome plus guest, written on it.

"Chrome, plus guest? What the fuck is a Chrome?" He asked, as if it were a joke. "We have five members of Congress, two Senators and a Governor coming tonight. If this 'Chrome, plus guest', comes to the hotel, wearing a turban; I'm pointing them in your direction; and telling them you think you're the reincarnated Mohammed who enjoys hot lesbian sex while doing shots of Tequila." He said, thinking of the headache this could cause if anything was to go wrong.

"It is what it is" She said, unable to give any explanation. Alex knew full well that she was merely the messenger, doing Mr. Bennet's bidding.

They both took a moment to look around the ballroom and how much work was yet to be done. "You're going to be right up to the cloth this year," Alex winked at her, as they both stared the empty bar with a wall of Moet Champagne boxes stacked in front of them.

"Where are the bar staff?" She asked, annoyed; this year, they hired no agency staff and kept everything in house. Partly to save money, but mostly in an attempt to make things run smoother.

The ice sculpture delivery man had now returned, looking very sombre.

"Shall I try and find you a pair of hands to move the swan?" Charlotte asked.

The man shook his head, "He won't take it."

"What do you mean, he won't take it?" Charlotte asked sarcastically.

"He told me that I could, fuck right off and take my poxy swan with me." A look of terror appeared across the young delivery guy's face, as another drop of water fell onto the table.

"On that note, I'm off," Said Alex. He began to walk off and tuned once more to Charlotte, "No more changes to the guest list, please" Alex said, winking at Charlotte.

Charlotte looked at the man who was doing nothing but stare at the sculpture; "Let's get him in the freezer, shall we?" she said reassuringly to the man.

Together, they walked towards the kitchen.

The beer from The Pemberly had only recently finished entering his system when Benjy received a call from Ms Powell; he would be working his first shift tonight. He was just about to turn onto his block when he felt his pocket buzz with fury. He stopped outside the decayed ruins of a burnt out car to take the call; most of the waiting staff had come down with food poisoning and he would be required to step in.

Benjy wasn't confident to be working the ball that evening; partly because he was a little drunk and partly because it would be such a huge event for his first day.

He decided he wouldn't have time to go back home, even though he could see the front door of his building from where he was stood. He turned around and walked the way he came; his stomach full of nerves and beer.

***

Mr. Bennet stepped into his tux trousers, holding onto Charlotte's shoulders for support. She often dressed her boss and didn't mind, every time he made her do something demeaning or directed a sexist comment her way, she would pick out something in his hotel to stash in her purse; she was trying to remember when there was a day that went by when she didn't extend her collection. Over the five years she had spent being his shadow, Charlotte had managed to accumulate a great trove of goodies; her apartment and bank were full of reminders of how much she hated her boss. There was a vase on a table on the seventeenth floor that was going through her mind as his stubby hands dug into her shoulder.

Charlotte looked over at the clock on the wall behind Mr. Bennett's desk, the ball started nearly twenty five minutes ago. Mr. Bennet and his family were never there to greet guests as they arrived, instead they would have the guests greet them.

"Mrs. Bennet and Lizzie should be on their way." Charlotte instructed Mr. Bennet, as she buttoned up his shirt, trying not to touch his greying chest hair.

"And Jane?" He asked her.

"She will be arriving about thirty minutes after you all arrive."

Charlotte reminded Mr. Bennet.

Mr. Bennet's office door swung open. Mrs. Bennet and Lizzie entered in their evening dresses.

Mrs. Bennet looked stunning in her sleek pale yellow Chanel Couture gown. Lizzie had not done much to her hair, but it looked slightly more tamed. She was wearing a floral gown she had bought from a thrift store three summers ago for less than twenty dollars.

This was the first time Mr. Bennet had been in the same room as his daughter for months; when he saw her enter behind his wife, he almost pushed Charlotte over to give Lizzie a hug.

"Don't you look beautiful," Mr. Bennet said as he kissed his daughter on the cheek. Mrs. Bennet raised her eyebrow, not believing a word her husband was saying. Mr. Bennet chose to ignore Mrs. Bennet's sigh and kissed her hand; "Stunning." he muttered to his wife.

"Are we all ready?" Mr. Bennet asked his daughter and wife. As they headed to the door, Mrs. Bennet let out a slight cough; only loud enough for her husband to hear. Mr. Bennet gave his wife a look.

Lizzie headed over to Charlotte, a girl she knew from high school; "A scholarship girl" Mrs. Bennet would always mention if Charlotte's schooling ever came up in conversation, which was quite often, considering the amount she had spent educating her own children, at the same school; one expense the Bennet's would never brag about is the amount they spend trying to keep their son, Max, sober. Promises in Malibu should now have a wing bearing their family name, Mrs. Bennet often thought to herself.

As Lizzie and Charlotte caught up, Mr. Bennet walked over to a huge portrait of his wife that stood over his desk, her steely eyes looking over his daily dealings. He pressed the frame on one corner and it slowly swung open, revealing a large safe, almost the same size as the picture that hid it. He typed in a code into the electronic keypad then unbuttoned his shirt; around his neck was a small key on a gold chain that he used to finally open up the safe.

No one actively looked at what Mr. Bennet was doing, but everyone knew. Mrs. Bennet walked over to and sat upon a long leather couch that stretched an entire wall of her husband's office.

Mr. Bennet took out a small black velvet clad box, placed it on his desk and relocked the safe using the same security procedure that opened it, but in reverse.

"My darling," Mr. Bennet called over lovingly to his wife, a tone his associates would swear blind that he was incapable of producing.

Mrs. Bennet looking surprised to be called out; she stood up and appeared to glide over to her husband. "Yes?" She giddily said as she took hold of his hand.

Lizzie paused her conversation with Charlotte and looked over at her parents. Mr. Bennet, still holding on to his wife's hand, reached for the box on the corner of his desk and presented it to her.

"A little token of my appreciation," He said as she took hold of the box for herself. Mrs. Bennet held her breath as she slowly opened it up; Lizzie and Charlotte took a few steps forward to get a better look.

Mrs. Bennet sincerely gasped as she opened it up; this prompted Lizzie to take another step forward so she could see the box's contents.

Mrs. Bennet was a woman with many beautiful possessions; jewellery, art, cars, property all over the world and even a private jet. It was well known that it took a lot to take Mrs. Bennet's breath away and make her stop in her tracks. So when Lizzie stepped to her motionless mother's side to view what had captured her attention, she too let out a gasp that even shocked her father.

"What do you think darling?" Mr. Bennet asked her as he slowly walked towards his wife; "May I?" Mr. Bennet asked; prompting Mrs. Bennet to pass him the case. Lizzie stepped aside to let her father step behind his wife.

Mr. Bennet moved his wife's hair from her shoulders and slowly reached in to kiss her shoulder and neck; he put his hands on each side of her waist; guiding his wife to walk towards the free standing mirror that Charlotte had brought in earlier.

Still kissing her, her perfume filled his nostrils; the smell took him back to a beach on a private Caribbean Island they vacationed on last summer, where all Mrs. Bennet wore was the perfume he smelt this evening; they lay naked on the sand, watching the sun set with a rum filled coconut.

Lizzie and Charlotte waited, holding their breaths for the Bennets to turn around. Charlotte had yet to see the gift; Mr. Bennet always bought his wife a present on the night of their annual ball; always a piece of jewellery for her to wear to the event.

Mr. Bennet slid aside Mrs. Bennet's hair as he placed something around her neck, he clasped the back and put his wife's hair back to the way she originally had it. He stepped back and stood by Lizzie as his wife took a moment to look at herself in the mirror.

Charlotte looked down at her watch; she should be down in the ballroom by now. As soon as she saw Mrs. Bennet turn around, she would make a move.

Each year, Charlotte received a dress to wear for the ball; this year Mr. Bennet had bought her a green Dolce and Gabanna gown that went out at the hips, hugged her body tight and flattered her curves. Even though tonight wasn't a night for her to enjoy herself. She liked that for one evening, she looked like she belonged to the world of the Bennets.

Mrs. Bennet's eyes were fixed on her chest; she stared into the mirror for what seemed an eternity. She slowly turned around, wanting to catch everyone's reaction.

Slowly, she twisted her body, her neck and chest seemed to be the last part of her to face them. The three of them stared in awe as she stood before them. Mrs. Bennet stepped forward, the lunar light from the sky shone directly into the space she entered; she appeared to glow as she stood before them.

Lizzie didn't know what to say; she had seen nothing like it in her life. Being born into a world of luxury; objects and gestures of extreme wealth didn't faze her, but this stopped her in her tracks.

Mr. Bennet enjoyed seeing his wife happy; this he could tell, truly made her happy. The necklace she wore wasn't the lightest piece she owned, but wasn't uncomfortable. It sat on her chest and around her neck like a cashmere sweater, not digging in to her skin in the slightest.

The necklace had a pattern of twelve pink and blue oval shaped diamonds, large enough that you could make out their shape from across the room.

"How many carats?" Mrs. Bennet asked in hushed tone.

"Seventy Two." Mr. Bennet replied as he buttoned up his tux jacket, "Each." He concluded.

The three women all looked at him.

"What?" Lizzie asked, making sure she heard him correctly.

"They're all between sixty four and seventy two carats." He said with a smug look across his face.

Mrs. Bennet placed a hand on her chest to feel them, looking down as she passed the diamonds through her fingers.

"Neil Lane made this personally," Mr. Bennet said as he held out his hand for his wife to take. She stepped forward in her seven inch red Louboutins and firmly clasped onto her husband.

"Wait till Jane sees it," Lizzie said as they left Mr. Bennet's office; "Dad, you'd better get Alex to follow mom around all night," she joked.

Mr. and Mrs. Bennet laughed, "Alex has a busy night," Mr. Bennet said. "I have two of NYPD's finest instead," he said in a serious tone.

"What?" Mrs. Bennet said as they waited for the elevator doors to open.

"Darling, I wouldn't let you take a shit, by yourself with that around your neck." He said with a smug look on his face, "If only you know how much I paid for it." He concluded the topic as he guided Mrs. Bennet to step into the elevator with his hands placed on her waist.

As the four of them waited to reach the lobby, Mr. Bennet reached into his inside pocket.

"I have a gift for you too…" Lizzie looked up, "…Charlotte," he said. Everyone waiting to see what he pulled out from his pocket.

Charlotte knew it wouldn't be something good and it wasn't; he passed her a yellow piece of paper with five more names for her. "A few late additions to the guest list," he said, not realising or caring what a huge inconvenience he had just presented Charlotte with.

Charlotte took the paper and read through the names. "Wasn't he in prison?" She asked concretely, pointing to one of the names. Lizzie leaned in to read the names.

"For insider trading, yeah," Mr. Bennet replied, "It's not like he killed his wife." The silence was filled with Mr. Bennet's chuckle.

The elevator doors opened. As they stepped out, Mrs. Bennet pruned her lisp, and exhaled as she noticed two uniformed policemen talking with Alex; her husband wasn't joking.

Mr. and Mrs. Bennet gave a wave to the waiting guests who applauded as they saw them exit the elevator. Lizzie wasn't about to wave, her parents never expected her too. Jane would have used two hands if she were here.

The four of them walked to the front of the line that snaked half of the lobby. They stepped through an airport style metal detector.

Charlotte slyly passed Alex the note as she walked past him, whispering "Sorry", giving him an apologetic face, "I'll make it up to you."

The two police officers greeted Mr. Bennet and he introduced them to his wife, who reluctantly shook their hands.

The Bennets, Lizzie and the two officers entered the ballroom; as they did, a spotlight shone in their direction, following them as they walked their first few feet. They got the same reception from their guests that they got in the lobby. The already quite full ballroom applauded their entrance; they had come in mid swing. People at the bar were shooting back vodka, some sat in the many circular tables that surrounded those who were dancing on the central dance floor. As the claps died down, the ball guests went back to what they were doing; they would all wait their turn to get their meeting with Mr. Bennet. The night had only just started.

Benjy had spent his first thirty minutes working for the Everfield collecting glasses. Being his first shift, he had no uniform to wear; he was given a tux that was ordered in, especially at short notice for him. His instructions for the evening were to pick up any used glasses and not let those currently in use to run out.

They were a small team this evening, made up entirely of people brought in last minute due a bad batch of Sushi prepared for the original staff's lunch; they all ended up returning the fish less than an hour later.

He had only met Franky earlier that afternoon, who largely left him alone and spent his time on his phone, presumably on Grindr. Franky wasn't too thrilled about the guy he'd been pumping full of beer all afternoon working with him. This evening would be the first in which he would be in charge of running the bar at one of Mr. Bennet's events; even if it was due to a technicality.

In the first five minutes of guests arriving and getting their drinks, Benjy had collected three trays of empty glasses and taken twelve more drink orders.

On his third trip, he returned to the bar with a full tray of glasses; he almost dropped them on the floor in front of him; standing with Franky behind the bar was the girl he had seen earlier. She noticed what happened and giggled; sliding the tray across the bar and taking it to the dishwasher one handed.

Benjy took a second to centre himself, this is not the impression he wanted to make. The girl replaced the empty tray with a full one. Benjy attempted to pick it up; the glasses shook as he began to lift it. The girl ran around to his side of the bar and placed her hand over his, pressing the tray back onto the bar.

"Charlie" She said, holding out her hand.

"Benjy," he replied. He could smell alcohol on her breath.

"Well, Benjy. Why don't you keep to collecting the empties and taking orders," She said, picking up the tray of Champagne glasses one handed; she disappeared into the crowd, the last thing Benjy saw of her was her ass that seductively swung from side to side.

"You've got no chance," said a pink haired Franky, who's head was less than inch from his; with his feet off the ground, Franky was supporting his weight with his hands as he leant over the bar.

"Yeah, says who?" Benjy asked, in a jokey way.

"Her mamma," Franky replied in a hushed tone, worried that she may hear them talking about her.

Benjy looked around the ball.

"She's not here, idiot." Franky joked, throwing Benjy a bar towel, gesturing him to mop up a pool or beer in front of him. "If it were up to me, you could fuck her all night long, but everyone knows her mamma don't let her out of her sight; got her a job here just to keep an eye on her." Franky talked as he made a full bar's length worth of cocktails, throwing shakers, fruit and glasses up in the air; all while talking to Benjy.

Charlotte came up behind Benjy and took one of the completed cocktails. Before leaving, she turned to a motionless Benjy.

"Why are you standing around, talking?" Charlotte demanded from him.

"It's my first day," Benjy replied, spluttering out his words.

"Do you want it to also be your last?" She quipped as she took hold of a napkin.

"No." Benjy said, taking the bar towel once more and wiping down the area he had just cleared. Charlotte nodded her head and walked away; smirking as she took a sip from the glass .

Charlotte found the Bennets and passed the glass to Mrs. Bennet, who drank it in one go and threw it down onto a passing occupied table without looking; making a full glass of red wine spill into the lap of a woman wearing a crème dress; the woman's husband stood up and was pushed pack down just as fast by one of the officers.

The Bennet women followed Mr. Bennet aimlessly around the Ballroom as he met his guests; Mrs. Bennet loathed shaking so many people's hands; she complained the entire time in sly, offhand comments to Lizzie. After less than five minutes of walking around, Mrs. Bennet was starting to feel the downside of walking around on seven inch shoes. Her slender frame towered over all those she met.

After the press conference Mr. Bennet gave this morning, everyone wanted to talk to him about purchasing one of his suites. It was Charlotte's job to hand all those interested, a card with a special web address to register their interest. She was finding that following Mr. Bennet's conversations were quite difficult; a DJ on the stage was pumping loud music into the ballroom.

Everyone was staring at Mrs. Bennet's chest; if they hadn't noticed it by themselves, Mr. Bennet made sure to point it out to them. Mrs. Bennet was growing increasing tired of following her husband around. She leaned in to his ear, "Me and Lizzie are going to have a sit down," before turning around, taking hold of Lizzie's hand and walking over to their reserved table. The two officers, surprised when Mrs. Bennet did a one-eighty, and bolted away, sprang to life and followed her across the ballroom.

Lizzie and Mrs. Bennet took their seats at their table. Charlie had seen them sit down and made a B-line for them, still carrying half a tray of Champagne. As she stepped up to the table, the two overzealous officers cut her off from Mrs. Bennet.

"For God's sake" Mrs. Bennet shouted, loud enough over the music that those in the surrounding tables looked over at what was going on. "Take a step back," she demanded of her shadows; shooing them away to stand behind her.

"Is that bubbly you've brought us?" Mrs. Bennet asked Charlie, who took a moment to digest what just happened.

"Yes." Charlie said, putting the tray down on the edge of the table. She handed Mrs. Bennet and Lizzie a glass each. Lizzie initially refused but changed her mind when she heard her mother mumble something under her breath as she took a sip of her own drink.

Lizzie took the glass and put it to one side, "Thank you." She said, smiling as Charlotte left.

Mrs. Bennet slowed down with her drinking, taking smaller sips; she could feel it going to her head. She looked around her ball; all the people were having a good time as she sat being guarded.

"You should go up and have a dance," Mrs. Bennet suggested to Lizzie as she starred into the dance floor. Lizzie shook her head and took a tiny sip of her drink. She took out her cell and started skimming a Law essay she had to read over the summer.

Mrs. Bennet spotted her husband once again; he occasionally popped in and out of view while greeting guests. "Put that away, dear" Mrs. Bennet instructed her daughter who was engrossed in her phone. After spotting her husband, she decided to keep drinking at the same pace; she took hold of Lizzie's glass and started to knock it back.

"A lovely ball you have put on again, Annalise," said one of three women, all about the same age as Mrs. Bennet, who found themselves standing in front of her table. Mrs. Bennet stood up and gave them all air kisses. All the women kept their eyes fixed on Mrs. Bennet's chest; the neckless was something that everyone in the ballroom was talking about. People were walking and dancing past her table just to get an up close glimpse of it.

Mrs. Bennet returned to her seat and made idle small talk with these women, people she didn't really care for. They were all the wives of Mr. Bennet's business associates.

Mrs. Bennet exhaled in relief on their exit and shifted her body to face her daughter. "Pigs, the lot of them," Mrs. Bennet sneered inches away from Lizzie's face. "You couldn't have swooped in on them?" Mrs. Bennet called over to the officers standing behind her; who both chuckled.

Lizzie was in no mood to contradict her mother; she nodded in agreement, hoping she would move onto talking about something else.

"The whole town knows that Marjorie and her husband are broke," Mrs. Bennet laughed to herself, referring to the woman who initiated the conversation. "They sold their townhouse and are now slumming it in some twenty-thousand square feet rented uptown apartment."

Lizzie could really care less; she forced herself to look interested in the probably untrue rumours her mother insisted on sharing. Mrs. Bennet proceeded to point out other guests who were going bankrupt. She rhetorically asked Lizzie how half of the people she saw got invites, Insisting that Lizzie must know who in the room was screwing the help and whose husbands were secretly gay; Mindless gossip Lizzie had absolutely no interest in.

Mrs. Bennet was just about to scold Lizzie for once again being on her phone when she felt her cell begin to buzz from her purse. She read her message, hiding it from a disinterested Lizzie. "I'll be back in a moment, Darling," Mrs. Bennet said to her daughter before she put her hands on the table to help her stand up, Lizzie nodded without taking her eyes from her screen.

Mrs. Bennet felt the two officers close in on her as she stood up. She turned around and stared down at them. "I really hope you don't think you're following me to the restroom." Mrs. Bennet snapped at them.

"Sorry Ma'am." One of the officers replied, "We've got our orders not to let you out of our sight."

"Not me," she said as she started to undo the clasp of her neckless. The two officers were dumbstruck, both unsure what to do and what was actually happening. They both stood there, waiting to see what she would do next.

Mrs. Bennet took the neckless off and began putting it around the neck of a surprised Lizzie, who immediately felt uncomfortable having it around her.

"There!" Mrs. Bennet said angrily, staring them down before disappearing off into the crowd.

Lizzie looked back and gave a wave to the two officers who stood directly behind her. "You'd might as well take a seat." Lizzie said to then, "I'm not going anywhere," as she continued to read about tort law.

Mrs. Bennet tried to navigate herself through the crowd; being who she was and almost seven feet tall, many people attempted to stop and talk to her. She politely excused herself and continued to make her way across the ballroom.

She made her way to the corner of the ballroom and outside the main kitchen entrance. This kitchen wasn't in service this evening; the canapés were prepared and being served from a smaller kitchen on the other side. She took a breath and pushed the door open.

The kitchen was dark and cold; lit only by the neon light of the emergency exit signs and the small glass door fridges that were placed throughout. No one had been in here for two days while the ball preparations were ongoing. The music could still be heard from the ballroom but was muffled by the oak door that separated them; her footsteps echoed on the tiles as she slowly began to walk around.

"Over hear," said a familiar voice. She turned towards a dark corner where she could make out their outline. The man she had been screwing earlier in the day stepped out of the shadows.

"What are you doing here?" She asked him as she walked slowly towards him.

"Don't worry," He said as he stepped forward and put his hands around her waist "No one saw me." He leaned in and kissed her passionately.

***

The two officers had refused Lizzie's invitation to sit with her; instead, leaving her to sit at the table by herself. Lizzie was starting to feel uncomfortable as the ball guests began to stare in her direction, to get a look at her mother's neckless.

She was still reading her essay, trying to ignore the stares when she got a text message from her sister Jane; 'Tell Dad it's time,' is all it said. Lizzie replied, asking for clarification but a presumably annoyed Jane told her to just do it.

Lizzie put her phone back in her purse and stood up. She could feel the two officers stepping into her personal space. Without saying anything to them, she began to walk into the crowd.

The ball guests seemed to part out of her way as she walked through them, looking for her father. It took her a few minutes, but eventually she managed to track him down; he was in deep conversation with the hotel's manager, Mr Hilbert; Lizzie caught the tail end of their conversation about the impracticalities that moving guests for room-to-room would cause.

"Lizzie," Mr Hilbert said, leaning into kiss both of her cheeks. The officers saw Mr. Bennet and kept their distance.

"Lizzie dear," Mr. Bennet said as he turned to face her. His eyes darted directly to the neckless around her neck. "Where's your mother?" He asked her in a concerned tone.

Lizzie shrugged her shoulders, she hadn't said to her where she was going to. As Mr. Bennet attempted to walk off to find her, Lizzie stopped him. "I got this text from Jane," she told him, "She said, it's time?"

Mr. Bennet looked down at his watch; he was shocked that he had been in the ballroom for nearly an hour. "You guys, go take a seat." Mr. Bennet said to Lizzie and Mr. Hilbert, "You're going to want to see this," he said with a smirk on his face.

By the time Lizzie and Mr. Hilbert made their way back across the ballroom and returned to their table, Mr. Bennet had ascended the steps at the front of the ballroom and was standing on the stage with a microphone in his hand, overlooking his guests.

"Can I have your attention please," he said into the microphone. His voice was barely audible over the music; many guests had noticed him on the stage but the DJ, who shared the stage with Mr. Bennet hadn't.

"Turn this shit off!" Mr. Bennet shouted at the DJ, after crossing the stage to stand directly in front of him.

The DJ did what he was told and plunged the ballroom into silence. This caused everyone to stop what they were doing and look up at the stage.

***

Mrs. Bennet was deeply involved with the young man in the kitchen. Her dress had been slid right up and her panties pulled down to the floor. When she heard the music stop, her eyes burst open. Her young lover had no intention of stopping, instead he moved from kissing her neck to kissing her on the lips to muffle her loud moans of pleasure.

***

"I'd like to thank each and every one of you for coming tonight," Mr. Bennet started when the initial post music speaking had died down. "The Annual Bennet Ball is now in its twenty fourth year; the guests and atmosphere get better with each year." Mr. Bennet said as the crowd began to cheer. "My wife, who I've temporarily misplaced, would..."

"Perhaps you should call Saks!"

Mr. Bennet was interrupted by a female voice from the back of the room. He strained to see who had called out, but had an idea.

The ball guests parted to reveal Collin, standing at the entrance, wearing a lime green tuxedo. He had entered, arm in arm with an older, tall woman with short, spiky platinum blonde hair; she was wearing a fitted white suit. She was the owner of the voice who had interrupted Mr. Bennet.

Mr. Bennet began to laugh as she came slowly into focus, as she and Collin began to walk towards the front of the ballroom. They were followed into the room by Chrome and another black man who was wearing dark rimmed black sunglasses, a chunky gold chain and a sombrero. He was also wearing low riding blue jeans and a white T-shirt with, 'Bitch had those bruises when she arrived' in a blood-stained inspired font.

Mr. Bennet recognised the inappropriately dressed man as the person from the music video that was playing when he showed Chrome around one of his penthouse suites earlier in the day.

"Who shot the DJ?" shouted the sombrero wearing man who was now standing behind Collins with a martini he had snatched from a table, as he walked in.

A taken-aback Mr. Bennet continued to speak; "I'd like to introduce my daughter, Jane to the stage. Thank you." Mr. Bennet threw his microphone at the DJ in the corner, stomped off the stage and slinked off to the back of the room to re-join Lizzie.

The ballroom lights all shut off in unison. The hiss from a smoke machine pierced through the silence as a slow beat started coming through the many speakers. A singular spotlight shone on the centre of the stage as Jane seemed to rise from the floor.

She was scantily dressed and now had hair extensions that went down to her midriff. She stood there in a stage full of fog as the beat increased in pace.

An explosion of light filled the dance floor as Jane began to dance a highly intense, expertly choreographed routine.

James, her camera man had appeared out of nowhere and was now in the front of the stage filming Jane's performance.

As the introduction built up towards the first verse, the audience held their breath with anticipation; everyone asking themselves, *will she be any good?*

Chrome was one of those hoping she could sing. He was still standing at the front, directly in front of the stage and was mesmerised by her dancing. He too held his breath as she lifted up the microphone and began to sing.

A shudder went through his body as she opened her lips, goose pimples covered his arms. He felt as if he was at a Jane Bennet concert and she was singing directly at him.

"She's good," said Chrome's sombrero wearing friend, who pulled Chrome back into the room.

Mr. Bennet and Lizzie were both captivated by her performance. They both knew that she could sing, but impressed she had put time and effort into something.

***

Mrs. Bennet's lover paused when he heard the singing from the ballroom. "Is that Jane?" He asked her.

"Don't stop," she demanded, thrusting her hips, hoping to restart him.

"Don't you want to watch her?" He asked, slowly getting back into the rhythm of things.

"It's being recorded," She said, "Carry on. I can watch it another time!"

With that, he continued with the momentum.

***

Bang.

Jane slapped her thighs, passing her microphone up her body slowly and continuing to sing, when the mic finally reached her mouth.

Mr. Bennet at times had to look away. Lizzie too, was finding her sister's performance unsuitable. The crowd, however usually unaccustomed to such a display, couldn't keep their eyes off her.

When she finished singing, the ballroom remained silent as Jane stood in an empty spotlight. She panted and tried to catch her breath when the crowd erupted into applause and cheers.

During her performance, Jane had noticed Chrome and played up to him; purposefully dancing near him and locking onto his eyes.

Mr. Bennet rushed to the front to rescue his daughter from the crowd that would gather around her; he had forced Lizzie to join him down the front.

Jane hugged her father and Lizzie as she stepped off the stage after taking her bows.

Collin and the older woman had left to go to the bar mid-performance and left Chrome and his friend by themselves. They got to the side of the stage before anyone else to join the Bennets. Chrome began to clap slowly. "That was amazing." he told Jane.

Charlie had appeared out of nowhere and Chrome took two glasses of champagne; one for himself, the other he gave to Jane.

"Thank you," Jane said, as she took a sip of champagne while she padded herself down with a small towel.

"Darling, this is Chrome," Mr. Bennet interrupted, introducing Jane to him. "Chrome is thinking of purchasing one of the penthouses."

Jane really took a shine to him at that moment; initially she thought that he would be someone who she could fuck later that evening. "It's nice to meet you," She said, as she got closer to him.

Jane turned her attention to the sombrero wearing man who now had their back to them, he was standing with Charlie; drinking glasses of champagne one after another.

"Fitzy," Chrome called to his friend, who on swinging around, had two glasses in his hands. Unfortunately for Lizzie, she was standing just a little too close to Fitzy and ended up getting the contents of his glasses thrown all over her dress.

Lizzie let out a short squeal as she felt the two officers pounce and drop Fitzy onto the floor.

She was soaked; the Champagne had managed to cover her from head to toe.

"Ok that's enough," Mr. Bennet called to the officers, who both helped Fitzy up from the floor.

"Jeez," Fitzy said, as he had two feet back firmly on the ground. "You spilled my drink!" He said to an unimpressed Lizzie. He, like Chrome was English, but the charm of his accent was lost with the way he spoke and his attire.

Lizzie looked him up and down before storming off to get changed.

Fitzy leaned in close to Mr. Bennet, "God, what's her deal? Do you know where the bar is?"

Mr. Bennet was never speechless but all he could muster was to point him in its direction.

"You've got one hell of a set of pipes on you," Chrome said, trying to get people to forget what just happened. "You had much studio time?" he asked Jane.

"None."

"I'm working on a track at the moment and would love to have you drop by and sing backup," Chrome said to Jane who looked very excited.

She let out a girlish squeal; a noise that Mr. Bennet had never heard his daughter make before.

Chrome handed Jane a card, "Drop by around ten." As Jane took hold of the card, he kissed her hand. Chrome grabbed Fitzy by the arm and pulled him into the crowd.

Mrs. Bennet opened the kitchen door and looked around; the ballroom was now full of music and people dancing and having a good time. She made her way to the bar where she was confronted by the tall blonde woman who entered with Collin.

"He's a bit young for you, isn't he?" Mrs. Bennet abruptly said to the woman as she looked Collin up and down.

"You don't remember my son, Collin?" The spiky haired woman said to Mrs. Bennet.

Mrs. Bennet leaned in to embrace Collin. "My lord, you've grown!" she said to him.

"I'm not a little boy anymore." He said to her.

"No, you're most certainly not." Mrs. Bennet said to him, as she tried to make out the outline of his bulge.

"Where's that neckless everyone keeps talking about?" Collins mother asked Mrs. Bennet.

Mr. Bennet put her hand on her chest, "Oh, Lizzie has it," Mrs. Bennet remembered.

"You'd trust your child with something that valuable?" The woman sneered at Mrs. Bennet.

"I trust my children with everything," Mrs. Bennet snapped back at her. "Lovely seeing you dear," Mrs. Bennet said to Collin, kissing him on the cheek. "Excuse me," Mrs. Bennet said before leaving them without a drink and re-entering the crowd.

Chapter Three

When Lizzie woke up the next morning, the first thing she noticed, wasn't the sunlight that filled her childhood bedroom, but the smell coming from her champagne soaked dress that she had placed on a chair at the other side of the room.

Later on that day, she would call the laundry service to get it dry cleaned. She thought it not a good idea to tell her mother or sister out of fear that it would come back to her with a slash down its front.

Mrs. Bennet and Jane would lead anyone to believe that she was channelling the just rolled out of bed look, based on the way she presented herself; they would never believe that when she stepped out in public, it was a drastic improvement. If Lizzie did come down for breakfast looking the way she did, Mrs. Bennett would surly have a heart attack.

Lizzie climbed out of bed and found her comfy slippers that had moulded itself to the shape of her feet over the years. She crossed her bedroom and turned on the kettle she had in the corner of her room. She felt dehydrated after the alcohol she drank last night; not a lot to other people's standards, but plenty for her.

Lizzie switched on the radio and Carol Kings Tapestry quietly filled her room as she undressed for her morning shower.

***

Jane had been one of the last to leave the ball that evening; basking in the praise people gave her for her performance. It was only when Franky told her that the bar was dry, she decided to call it a night.

She saw Chrome a few more times that evening, mostly from across the ballroom as they caught each other's eye.

When Jane woke up at eight, after only four hours sleep, she flung the duvet off her and ran into the bathroom. She turned on her shower and began to undress, studying her flawless body in the mirror until the steam from the shower made it impossible.

***

Mr. and Mrs. Bennet left the ball at a reasonable time; they never stayed until the very end. The Bennets first made a trip to Mr. Bennet's office to put the neckless back in the safe; Mrs. Bennet had retrieved the neckless from Lizzie's room when she discovered that she had left and wore it, walking around chest first, the entire night.

When they returned to their bedroom, Mrs. Bennet was almost at the point of passing out; she had been drinking at an alarmingly high rate that evening, even for her. She was still annoyed with her husband for the press conference he gave and for not consulting her with his decision.

Mr. Bennet decided to end his night by having sex with his wife; Mrs. Bennet lay there and let him get his end away, falling asleep before he climaxed. When he was done, he curled up in bed and he too fell asleep, leaving his wife uncovered.

The first thing she did in the morning was to put on her sweats and head down to the gym. She started each day with a two hour workout; a mixture or cardio and weights. For a sixty-four year old woman, she was in the best shape of her life and didn't know anyone within twenty years of her, who could keep up with her on the treadmill.

Mr. Bennet wasn't much of a morning person, he started each day with three aspirins; whether he needed them or not, washed back with scolding hot black coffee that Charlotte delivered to his room promptly at seven-forty five.

The day after the ball was no exception; Charlotte let herself into the Bennets' suite dead on time, just as the clocks all started to chime.

She arrived with hot coffee in one hand and morning papers in the other. She had marked every mention of the Bennets' private and personal lives for his inspection. After such a big day for Mr. Bennet and his family; the press conference in the morning and ball in the evening, each local and national paper had mentioned them multiple times.

***

Jane had no idea what outfit to wear today, she walked into her extensive walk in closet and paced in endlessly; discarding jackets, tops and sweaters as fast as she had taken them off the rail for inspection. She had managed to pick out a pair of panties and bra; even that was a huge decision.

As dedicated as she was to choosing something to wear, she kept getting distracted by E! News; she often daydreamed about them running stories about her, it made no difference to her whether they were true or not or even if she was being portrayed in negative way; being associated with Chrome was one step in that direction.

***

It had been so long since Lizzie spent any time in New York and her parents' hotel, that she had no idea what to do. She had received no invitation to join anyone for breakfast and no afternoon plans to speak off. Apart from seeing her mother for five minutes last night, after she left the ball, she had not heard from any of her family.

She was showered and dressed, and sat on her bed, flipping through the extensive list of books that made up her summer reading list.

***

Mrs. Bennet had been working out for over three hours; the harder she hit the punch bag, the more her endorphins rushed through her body. It was her husband she envisioned she was laying into; every hit and kick, harder and more satisfying than the last.

When she was done, she returned to her suite to find Mr. Bennet had long gone. She ran herself a bath and poured herself a vodka martini in the bar in her suite, sipping it as she soaked in her bubbly tub.

***

Jane had finally decided on an outfit, a white Chanel pant suite; she would look sophisticated for Chrome. After meeting James in the lobby, she would give Buster a call to drive them to the studio.

Before leaving her room, she opened up a drawer of her dresser. Inside was filled with large bags of white power. She rummaged through and found herself a smaller, manageable bag to carry and put it in her purse. She had in her possession, an extreme amount of drugs that didn't belong to her.

As Jane left her suite, she entered the Bennets' private floor that housed her parents and Lizzie's and her suites, Mr. Bennet's office and a large communal room that was never used.

She waited the thirty seconds it took the elevator to plunge from the top to the bottom of the hotel; waiting for her to get out was James, camera at the ready.

The lobby was abuzz with last night's guests who stayed the night at the Everfield; Mr. Bennet made back a large amount of his ball costs from his friends staying at his hotel.

One person who had stayed at the hotel last night, was Franky. Now, back behind the bar, he had found a hotel guest on his dating app and entered his room at the crack of dawn, after he had finished at the ball. This was something he did a few times a week; he was one of the hotel's most frequent guests, regardless that he's never paid to stay a night there in his life. He kept a clean change of clothes in his locker for such occasions.

Jane waited outside the front of the hotel for buster to drive around and pick her up; it had never, nor would it, occur to her to go down to the parking lot and get in the car from there.

She waited next to the old doorman that opened the hotel door for her as his wife; equally as old as him, brought his lunch, like she did every day.

Buster pulled up and Jane entered the car, followed by James. The people outside the hotel took great attention at the camera that followed Jane, as did most people who saw them wandering around.

Jane passed Buster the card Chrome had given her and off they drove, into the slow stream of traffic that seemed endless as she looked up at the traffic ahead of her.

"Where are we off to today?" James asked Jane as she took off her sunglasses and put them in her bag, careful not to reveal too much of its contents.

"You know, you fucking idiot," Jane spat at him as she zipped up her Michael Kors purse.

James shut down his camera and placed it on his lap. "Jane, listen," he started as Jane was about to shout at him for turning off his camera.

"If this is going to work, you need to speak to the camera, no one wants to see you wandering around by yourself. You need to tell your fans were you're going and why you're going there. They want to get to know you. Look into the lens and speak to them, let them get to know you, the real you."

Jane took a moment to think before saying anything. She liked how James mentioned her non-existent fans to her. In her mind, there were many people, who would love to watch her everyday life with many networks scrambling to air her show, especially if she hooked up with Chrome and managed to get him to produce her album.

"Pick up your camera," she said; she knew he was right, but didn't want to give him the satisfaction by mentioning it.

James turned on his camera once more and began rolling.

"So, last night I met Chrome and Fitzy after I performed at my Fathers ball and today, I'm meeting Chrome at the studio. He's working on a track and invited me along."

She noticed that Buster had pulled up; without saying anything he turned off the engine, got out of the car and let her out.

"Were here," Jane said giddily, still in her valley girl drawn out tone.

James got out first, so to get a shot of Jane exiting the car and her first seeing the studio. They were outside what looked like an old factory, made entirely from red bricks.

By the entrance door were plaques with the name of the buildings tenants, Jane cared less for them except for one; *DeBourgh Studios*.

Buster drove off and parked within view of the building, they were overlooking the Hudson river and Jane had never been to this part of town before.

She walked towards the front door and it slid open before her. She stepped into the reception area where a large black security guard was seated behind the desk; Jane could hear a quiet TV playing under the desk in his direction.

She ignored him and proceeded to walk towards the lift. A sign showed that *DeBourgh Studios,* was on the fourth floor.

"Excuse me ma'am," called over the security guard, he had switched off his TV when he noticed her.

"Ma'am?" he called again, as Jane didn't stop and pressed the elevator button.

"I'm here to see Chrome." She snapped at him, as the numbers above the elevator slowly began to count down from six.

The security guard was up out of his seat and walking towards her with a clipboard in his hand.

"Name?" he asked her.

"Chrome," again, snapping at him.

"No Ma'am. Your name," he asked, getting ready for an argument; Jane was refusing to look at him as she waited directly in front of the elevator. Jane turned to the man and took off her sunglasses; she had returned them to her face after getting out of the car.

"Jane Bennet." She snarled at him, expecting him to know the answer to his own question.

The guard looked down his sheet and appeared to tick her off his list. He turned his attention to James. "You, young man, are not on my list." The guard was standing directly in front of James; blocking his shot of Jane.

"You didn't ask my name," James said to the guard.

"There really isn't any need; Miss Bennet is the last to sign in." The guard said in a serious tone, the elevator was almost here, two more floors to go; it screeched and wined as it came hurtling down to the ground floor.

The security guard took a step towards James. "I'm going to have to ask you to stop recording, Sir. This is a private premise and you don't have permission to film or even be here." The security guard pointed to the front door.

James stood still, not moving as the guard edged closer to him.

"I'm going to have to ask you to leave, sir." The guard demanded of James as they were now inches away from each other; the guard ruining any chance of James using his footage.

"I have an appointment with Chrome." Jane said, trying to reason with the guard who didn't want to engage with her.

"Yes Ma'am, you; Not him" The guard told her, hoping she would drop it and let him be.

Jane turned away from the elevator door and walked the three or so steps to face the guard, who turned around to face her; stood in the middle of the two of them.

"I don't care who you think you are, Mr rent-a-cop on fifteen dollars an hour. You're letting him up too." Jane said to him without blinking, her voice getting louder and more high-pitched.

"Okay," said the guard.

"Okay?" Jane asked in a confessed tone. "Okay…" She repeated, calmly, rather smug with herself.

She span around on the spot and let out a squeal. Standing in front of her in the open door of the elevator was Chrome.

"Sorry, I never thought to add your friend to the list," Chrome said with a wide grin in his London accent.

Jane was embarrassed and wished Chrome hadn't seen her throw shade at the guard.

"Going up?" He asked her, holding out his hand to beckon her forward.

Jane got into the elevator and didn't say anything during the long four floors up. It opened into a room with couch, speakers and a mixing board.

Sat down, waiting for Chrome to return, was a black girl with a beehive over a foot tall.

"Chrome, Baby, are we ready to get started" The girl said as she stood up, all six feet of her in barefoot. She was a lot thinner than Jane, who placed her purse down on a couch as the girl wrapped her arms around Chrome; kissing his cheek.

"Monika," Chrome said to her as she let go, "Meet Miss Jane Bennet, Heiress to the Everfield hotel."

Monika looked Jane up and down then wrapped her arms around her. "I've never met an Heiress." Monika said.

"Really?" Said Jane, after she was finally let free. "Most of the girls I went to school with were," she said in a serious way; not quite believing that this girl was yet to meet someone who would one day inherit a share of a large fortune.

"A drink, Jane?" Chrome asked her as she sat on the arm of the couch.

"I'm fine." She said, not really knowing what would happen next.

Chrome smiled at her as she walked across the small room and sat on a large swivel chair and faced the girls, with his legs open.

"How about I play you the track?" Chrome suggested; Jane and Monika nodded their heads.

Chrome swung around to face the mixing board, and after a few buttons were pressed, a heavy beat started to fill the room. Chrome tapped along with his fingers on his knee; watching the girls' reactions as they listened.

"Wow Chromy," Monika said as the track finished playing.

Jane didn't know what to say, "It sounds great," she said after Chrome and Monika waited for her input.

"There is still a lot more work to do on it, but it's getting there. That's why I have you lovely ladies here today. How about we jump into the booth and see what we can do?"

Monika ecstatically leaped up and raced into the booth before Jane had even digested what Chrome was saying to them.

"It'll be okay" Chrome said reassuringly to Jane as she slowly got up. As she passed him, he leaned in and whispered into her ear; "You look beautiful in that outfit."

Jane smiled the widest as she had in the longest time as she entered the booth.

Monika sat on a stool with her headphones already on and doing loud mouth and throat warmups that included a lot of raspberry sounds.

Jane shuffled over to her stool and placed on her headphones.

"Can you hear me?" Chrome asked them through their headphones.

"Loud and clear," Monika said breathily, looking directly at Chrome.

Jane gave him a gentle nod. She was nervous; this was her first time stepping into a professional studio.

"I'm going to play the rack a few times and I just want you to riff, make up whatever words of sounds u think go with the music. If it's any good, I'll keep it." Chrome was upbeat and ready to go. He opened an energy drink can and drank it in one.

"How about we go Jane first, then you Monika, then together?" Chrome suggested to them.

"Sounds good to me," Monika said as she took a sip of water.

Jane wished she had accepted the drink now; her throat started to feel very dry. She took a deep breath and waited for the music to start. Just before it did, Chrome told her to breathe and relax.

Monika smiled at her as the heavy beat started to fill her ear drums. For the first ten seconds, Jane listened to the beat; trying to familiarise herself with it. Chrome and Monika didn't take their eyes off her; she didn't look at either of them but could feel both of their eyes on her. Without her knowing, James had also joined them in the booth.

A high raspy voice started to fill her ears; she looked up to see Monika, singing into the microphone. She was staring directly at Jane, unblinking, as she seemed to propel the track forward.

After a few seconds, Jane gulped a breath, slowly breathed in and out and opened her mouth.

She started to zone out Monika and was able to project her voice to the wooden ceiling above. Monika stopped singing when she heard Jane sing; harmonising where she could and letting Jane take the lead. A final note from Jane fulminated around the booth.

Jane looked up and saw Monika with her eyes and mouth wide open. Chrome was slapping his hands onto the mixing desk, furiously euphoric at Jane's final note. As the track slowly bounced to a conclusion, Monika took off her headphones.

"What the fuck was that note?" She asked her as she clapped her hands.

James was whizzing around the room, trying to find the best angle to film from.

"You need to come back here and hear what you did," Chrome instructed Jane, her entire face was flush and was still getting her breath back.

Jane slipped off her headphones and jumped down from her stool; looking over at James, she saw he had a huge grin across his face.

"Was it okay?" She asked him, as she followed Monika out of the booth. Without time for James to reply, Jane was receiving a monster of a hug from Chrome.

"That was unbelievable. Was I right when I said she could sing?" He asked Monika.

"You were right, as you always are." She beamed at him.

"Shall we give it a listen?" Chrome suggested as they both sat down. He turned his back to them and the music started to fill the room.

Jane listened intensely; feeling embarrassed when she heard the emptiness and when Monika stepped in. She sounded good, she thought as she listened to her voice. When she heard her own voice kick in, she hated it; she had started off so wobbly, she thought. Jane forced herself to listen. She did sound good singing with Monika and waited for her note. She knew it was coming. Chrome and Monika stared at her, to see her reaction to hearing the powerhouse ending.

Jane braced herself for it, holding her breath as it filled the room.

It shocked her to hear the note that she produced. Monika wrapped her arms around Jane and squeezed her tight.

Over the next two hours, Jane and Monika recorded more for Chrome as he sat and watched in awe as Jane sung, and how well she and Monika sang together. They gave him plenty of material to shape into a song.

Monika had plans later that evening and left Jane and Chrome, who were by now drinking vodka shots.

"It was nice meeting you," Monika said to Jane, hugging her before stepping into the elevator.

Chrome moved over to the sofa and sat down beside Jane, close enough that their bodies were touching.

Chrome noticed James in the corner, filming them. "Why don't you give us a bit of time together?" Chrome looked at Jane, making sure she was okay with being left alone with him.

"I think we've got everything for today." Jane said to James. "Wait in the lobby and we can head back into the city soon."

James mumbled something to himself before placing his camera on a table to collect later; he grabbed his backpacked and went down the elevator to wait in the lobby.

Jane got up to find the ladies' room, taking her purse with her. She locked the door and opened up her purse, taking out the small bag of coke and prepared herself three lines.

As if in unison, James too was snorting his own cocaine in the restroom downstairs. It had been many hours since either of them had their last hit.

Jane returned and tiptoed over to Chrome, who was at the mixing board, listening to Jane's first take; still unable to get that final note out of his head.

He turned around when he sensed her standing behind him. She unbuttoned his plaid shirt and ran her hands down his washboard abs. He took hold of her, by the wrists as he kissed her passionately, leaving her scrambling for breath. In less than thirty seconds, they were both naked and Chrome had lifted Jane onto the mixing board, sitting her on her pants suit to make it more comfortable for her. Jane held back her head and waited with anticipation for his long, hard, dark member to enter her.

Chapter Four

James waited for over an hour for Jane to come down and before they left, he returned upstairs to retrieve his camera and equipment. He had purposely left the camera rolling after his banishment.

When he was back in the budget room that Jane had managed to persuade her father to let James use; he began to go through that days footage, cataloguing it and making copious notes.

Finally, when he got to the final recordings of the day, he sat back and watched Jane being ravaged by Chrome.

He knew he could sell the footage now and make some serious money. Chrome may not be a big name in America, but in Europe, he and Fitzy were huge. The British tabloids love a good sex story and with a video, he could add a few zeros. For the time being, James would sit on the footage and add it to his collection of Bennet sex tapes.

On his desktop, he had a special folder for the Bennet family's sexual indiscretions. He had been following Jane around for nearly three months and had amounted a trove of footage; mostly her shopping or eating quinoa salads, but even so, he was lucky to catch something he shouldn't.

He rendered the Jane and Chrome studio sex file and dragged in into his folder, first opening it up to see its contents.

It already had a file with Jane's name in the title. Her first sex tape, a tape he filmed with her full backing.

He thought back to the three years previously when he first met Jane. James had not long graduated from USC film school and was flying back to L.A from New York when they first met. He was on the east coast taking meeting with a Broadway producer who wanted him to write the book for a musical; they had read a spec script he had sold for half a million dollars to Paramount and flew him first class to meet them.

Jane and him were sat next to each other on the flight, Jane had spotted him pre-flight in the bar with a wallet full of cash; so wasn't put off when he began to speak to her mid-flight.

Jane was very emotional this time in her life; her parents had kicked her out for her excessive drug taking and put her on a one-way flight to stay with her brother to clean herself out.

Jane giggled at his lame Jokes and acted humbled when he told her how attractive she was. She had heard it so often through her life that it meant nothing to her anymore. For the entire flight, they drank champagne and swapped contact information before they reached LAX.

Jane liked the idea of hooking up with an up and coming filmmaker who would help her become a star, and James was a red-blooded man who wanted to do untold filth with her.

They began to date and Jane quickly ran through his money after her parents cut her off.

When James saw his bank balance start to reduce to nothing, he started gambling the remaining money he had; hoping to make more before he blew the rest of his cash.

He had managed to persuade Jane into filming a sex tape to make some cash for them; someone he went to collage with had a successful porn site.

At this point, his world really was starting to look bleak; the tape got lost in the crowded internet; Paramount wouldn't return his calls after the movie went into turn around, and Jane left him to return to her parents after the money and drugs disappeared.

His hopes of one day of winning an Oscar seemed impossible as he lay in his bed alone, clutching onto a bottle of JD. After almost two and a half years of dodging his texts and emails, James finally managed to get back in communication with Jane; only after threatening to expose the tape she filmed to her family. They reached a compromise where he would film her pursuit of a recording career; having exclusive rights to her life and shop the series around, giving him his big break.

As he lay back in his desk chair, watching Jane sucking on Chrom's dick as he beat off, he thought that his life wasn't so bad. When there was a knock on his door, he was forced to pause his computer and buckle up his pants. It was room service, bringing him his free meal; a rib-eye steak. He thanked the girl and wished her a good night before continuing to watch Jane and eat his dinner.

Chapter Five

When Jane arrived back at the Everfield after her recording session with Chrome, she saw Lizzie alone in the Pemberly eating a sandwich; she thought nothing of James scurrying off to his room.

Jane sat down at Lizzie's table; it took Lizzie a few moments before she realised she wasn't alone. This had been the first time all day Lizzie had seen a member of her family and was pleased when she saw her sister.

"You look happy. Have a good afternoon?" Lizzie asked Jane, as she closed her book and placed it on the table.

"Yeah, I did actually. Was just in the studio with Chrome," Jane replied, taking off her sunglasses.

"Nice," said Lizzie who was glad to see her sister interested in something other than shopping or her hair. "Was his friend there?" Lizzie asked, worried about Jane being in a confined space with someone she considered an idiot.

"Who, Fitzy?" Jane laughed, "No, just me, Chrome and this Monika girl, a little touchy feely for my liking."

"Mom is a little touchy feeling for your liking," Lizzie joked.

"True, true," Jane laughed, agreeing that their mother, who wasn't one for body contact.

Lizzie took a sip of her coffee, stirring the dregs and downing the last mouthful.

"You Irish up your coffee?" Jane asked Lizzie as she looked

around the bar to see who was working.

Lizzie laughed, "No, just humble filter with sugar and cream."

Jane spotted Benjy three tables over and waved her arm in the air to get his attention.

"Good afternoon Miss Bennet, Miss Bennet" Addressing both sisters.

"Dry Martini, hold the olive and lime instead of lemon." Jane gestured to her sister to order her drink.

"Oh, just an ice water with a lemon wedge, please."

Benjy started to turn when Jane stopped him "Wait, She'll have the same as me."

"No, no thanks. Just the water," Lizzie protested, as Benjy stood there, unsure of whose order to fulfil.

"If you like your job, you'll listen to me. Sho'," Jane snapped at Benjy as she sent him off to fetch them their drinks.

"No Jane," Lizzie pleaded, pointing to her book.

Jane picked up the book and scanned the cover, "Big sister, you've been here roughly twenty four hours. I'm not going to allow you to spend the little time you have left in the city reading these books."

Lizzie tried to take the book off Jane but she kept it out of reach. "I'm here for the summer; there is plenty of time for me to have a drink with you."

"There's also plenty of time for you to study too." Jane reasoned with Lizzie who was unable to come up with an adequate comeback. Jane looked around the room and noticed she had a direct unobstructed view of an open roaring fire the other end of the Pemberly. With one swift move, she threw the book across the room, landing it smack dead in the middle of the yellow flames.

"Jane!" Lizzie exclaimed, bolting out of her chair and running across the quiet bar.

She got to the fireplace and knew it was too late to attempt to fish it out. When she returned to her table, Benjy had returned with two martinis and a water. He put them down and began to clean the adjoining table as Jane's phone began to buzz hysterically, the sound bounced around the Pemberly.

"Are you crazy," Lizzie snapped at Jane as she sat down, going for the water before Jane knocked it over, spilling it all over the hardwood floor.

"Oops," Jane said unapologetically as she read her text message.

"I'm so sorry," Lizzie said to Benjy who got down on his hands and knees and began to mop up the water.

"Darling sister," Jane sang to Lizzie.

"What?" Lizzie asked as she reluctantly accepted the Martini from Jane.

"What's with the tone?" Jane asked, smirking as she took a sip of her drink.

"I wonder!" Lizzie said as she took a tiny sip of her drink and smirked when the drink touched her taste buds.

"Good right," Jane smugly said to Lizzie as she reread her text. "I got a message from Chrome."

"Weren't you just with him?" Lizzie asked.

"Yes, bless him," Jane joked. "He's invited me to the Lydia Lounge tonight."

"Isn't it really hard to get in there?" Lizzie asked her sister, "Even for someone like you."

"Us dear sister, us, but yes; I've never been. Chrome knows tonight's secret password."

Benjy slowed down clearing up the broken glass, listening intensely at their conversation from under the table.

"Is there a secret knock too?" Lizzie joked as she took another, longer sip from her drink.

"Don't be so facetious Lizzie." Jane told her sister.

"Wow, such a large word for such a…"

"You really want to finish that?" Jane dared her sister with her perfectly shaped eyebrow raised. "You walk up to the doorman, say *Austin* and boom, you're in."

"As simple as that?" Lizzie asked Jane.

"As simple as that."

"Let me know if it works will you?" Lizzie said to her sister as she watched the remaining part of her books hard cover disintegrate into the ashes.

"No need Lizzie, because you're coming with me." Jane said seriously.

After Benjy finished wiping up the water and collecting the glass into his bar towel, he got up and scrambled out of view unnoticed as Jane tried to persuade Lizzie to join her out that evening.

As he returned to the bar, he passed Franky the towel of broken glass.

"What's this?" He asked Benjy as his hands were filled with a sodden towel filled with shards of glass.

"A little present," he joked as he noticed Charlie in the hotel's lobby. "Excuse me" He said to Franky as he ran out of the Pemberly.

Benjy entered the lobby and walked over to Charlie who was talking to a girl with at least seven colours in her hair.

"Hey," He said to Charlie, interrupting her conversation.

"Hey" She said to him back, copying his easy breezy tone. "Do you know Kitty?" She asked him.

"No." He said, smiling at the girl's crayola hair.

Kitty wore the regular Everfield uniform but stood out more than most employees. Apart from her unusually eclectic hair, she had deep purple lipstick and unusually thick eyeliner. She worked at the Everfield's flower stand in the lobby, selling mostly Roses and Tulips. She had attempted to sell Lilies before Mrs. Bennet banned them from the hotel. Kitty and Mr. Hilbert, the hotels manager had never known someone to be so against a flower before.

"Do you have plans tonight?" Benjy asked Charlie, feeling obliged to ask Kitty too.

"Depends" Kitty said to Benjy, winking at him.

"On what?" Benjy asked her.

"On whether you can top the amazing night we have in store. Now show us your cards, dark chocolate," Kitty jested with Benjy.

Benjy took a moment to get over Kitty's abruptness.

"I was planning on going to the Lydia Lounge." He said confidently.

Kitty roared with laughter, "You're not from around here, are you?"

Benjy shook his head. "Chicago."

"It doesn't matter where you're from my brown friend, only an outsider would suggest going to such a place."

"What's wrong with the place?" Benjy asked cautiously.

"Nothing, or so I assume." Kitty said as she set her enchanting gaze on him, without blinking. "There's no way you're going to take a dump in that place, never mind order a drink."

"I can get us in." Benjy said confidently.

"Get us in where?" Franky said over Benjy's shoulder.

"Lydia Lounge," Kitty said in an amused tone.

"Shut the front door!" Squealed Franky as he spun Benjy around, noticing his rock hard shoulders, lingering too long on his frame.

"Keep your fingers to yourself fairy boy, I don't think you're his type. Are you?" Again, Benjy was spun around.

"No, no. Sorry." Benjy said, glancing over at Charlie.

"No need to apologise," Kitty said to Benjy as he tried to face all three of them. "Well, you win, Hershey Bar. Trying to see you talk the four of us into Lydia Lounge beats pizza and Liam Hemsworth any night. I guess we're going out tonight, girls." Kitty said to Charlie and Franky.

Benjy smiling, "I guess we'll meet you outside the Everfield at eight"

"Sounds good to me," said Franky.

"Eight is fine," said Charlie. Although she was looking forward to a quiet night in, she was intrigued to see what adventures tonight would bring.

***

Jane, Lizzie and James got out of their cab less than a block from The Lydia Lounge. Lizzie had managed to persuade Jane to take public transport as a requirement of her joining her. James pulled out a small hand held camera from his pocket and started to film the huge line in front of them.

"All these people know the password?" Lizzie asked her sister. She was very cold and wearing a dress that revealed way too much skin. Prior to leaving the hotel, Jane had chosen her outfit, applied her makeup and restyled her hair.

With only the limited time Jane had, she thought she did an amazing job at transforming her sister. Although she was nowhere near her level of hotness, Lizzie looked good, she thought.

"Don't be silly, Lizzie. Every night these poor sods try their luck to get in, hoping they'll change their policy. It's sad if youu ask me." Jane marched forward, turning around to see if they were keeping up with her.

"Put that camera away, you daft sod." Jane scolded at James, who retreated the camera back into his pocket. "Just keep up and don't say a word."

The three of them walked directly to the front of the line, past all the people waiting out in the chill.

After less than ten seconds in front of the doormen, they were allowed in.

Benjy, Franky Charlie and Kitty arrived just as Lizzie, Jane and James entered the club. Only Benjy seemed to noticed them get through security.

"Look at that line!" said a shocked Franky, "Do we have to line up?"

"No. Let's just walk to the front." said a confident Benjy.

"You sure, Benjy?" said an unsure Charlie.

"Yeah… What's the worst that could happen?" Benjy asked them.

"We don't get in," said Kitty sarcastically. "Lead the way then," she instructed him.

Benjy took a deep breath and began to bypass the line, sheepishly followed by the other three.

They all looked nothing like the leggy blondes and muscular men with chiselled look that they were passing, in line. Kitty wore black ripped cargo pants and a vest, Franky, a yellow catsuit, Charlie a simple black dress and Benjy the black trousers and shirt from his uniform.

All eyes followed them as they walked towards the heavily guarded front entrance. The crowd seemed to stop making any noise as they passed them.

The three of them stopped at the end of the line as Benjy walked alone up to an almost seven foot Latino doorman, who was twice as wide as he was.

He took a breath before approaching him.

Charlie, Franky and Kitty stared in disbelief as Benjy beckoned the Latino giant to lower his head to Benjy's level. They saw Benjy whisper something into his ear then him returning to his original height. For what seemed like a minute, the Latino giant didn't move; the only movement coming from his eyes as he looked over at Benjy's group.

In one swift moment, he unclasped the velvet rope and stepped aside for them to enter.

In shear disbelief, Franky, Charlie and Kitty rushed forward and followed Benjy through the archway door.

"How did you get us in?" Charlie asked as she jogged to his side.

"It's simple," he said, "I told them I was with two of New York's most beautiful women. How could they refuse to let you in?" He said, winking at Charlie.

"What am I, chopped liver?" Franky asked Benjy bluntly.

"Funny, they weren't too interested in you," Benjy said as Kitty patted Franky on the back.

"You choose the club, next time," Kitty whispered into his ear as she squeezed his ass.

They exited a red velvet tunnel and were transported into a club that resembled the inside of a castle. Solid blocks of stone lined the walls; they looked up at an almighty high ceiling. The velvet walkway opened up directly into the dance floor. The club was packed and no one made any notice of them entering.

Just off the dance floor was a VIP section that was raised slightly and cordoned off.

Benjy spotted Lizzie, Jane and James enter the exclusive section.

"A VIP section in a VIP club?" Benjy asked the group.

"How else will the super-rich and powerful feel any better than the regular rich and powerful?" Kitty asked Benjy as she grabbed Charlie by the arm and dragged her into the centre of the dance floor; leaving Benjy and Franky on the outskirts, looking in.

"Wanna dance?" Franky asked Benjy, seriously.

"I'll sit this song out," said Benjy as he looked around the majestic club that looked like it was transported out of middle England.

Chrome clapped his hands when he saw Jane, Lizzie and James at the entrance of the VIP area. He told the doorman to let them in.

"Here's the girl with the powerhouse pipes," said Chrome excitedly as he took hold of Jane's hand as they entered his section.

"Fitzy, come here boy" Chrome called over to the black man sat in the corner, clutching a bottle of Moet, sat between two model looking women.

Fitzy got up, leaving the girls behind and swagged over to

Chrome.

James had his camera out, filming the club and Jane's reunion with Chrome.

Fitzy stood in front of Jane, Lizzie and James, drinking from his Champagne bottle. He was wearing a white t-shirt with, 'I didn't steal your car, but I stole your daughters V plate' written down his front.

Lizzie shuddered as she read what his t-shirt said. She was so out of her element; she wasn't one for loud music, and being around Fitzy made her feel uneasy.

"You remember Jane, from last night? I played you that wicked track we were working on today." Chrome gestured towards Jane, who was forced to accept a kiss on her cheek from Fitzy.

"And this is her sister..." Chrome went blank.

"Lizzie," said Lizzie politely. She closed her eyes, bracing herself as she, expected a kiss from Fitzy also.

She opened her eyes to discover Fitzy staring at her. "How many sisters do you have, darling?" Fitzy asked Jane.

"Just Lizzie," Jane said, smiling at her sister.

"Impossible, I remember your sister from last night. This frumpy, ugly girl in that awful dress," Fitzy said, confused.

"Yeah, that was me," Lizzie said smiling, realising she had to put up with this idiot.

"No." Said Fitzy, "She was wearing this fat ass bling around her neck and ran off when I spilt my drink down her."

"Still me," Lizzie said, trying to reassure Fitzy that they had indeed met last night.

"Damn girl, you look hot. I'll put last night down to you being on your tidal flow, didn't recognise you without a drink down your dress." Fitzy continued to look Lizzie up and down, trying to sneak a peak of her rear.

Lizzie didn't know what to say. She turned to her sister, "Buy me a drink."

"People usually buy me drinks, but sure." Jane smiled at Lizzie.

"Ladies, ladies, take a seat," demanded Chrome. "I'll get a few bottles and get this party started."

Fitzy returned to where he was sitting; Lizzie heard him tell the two girls he was with to "Shove off." Lizzie saw the two girls get up, one of them taking a Champagne bottle from the ice bucket on her way out.

"Keep it," Fitzy called after them, "It's the last time you'll be drinking this horse piss." Other patrons in the VIP area were looking over at Fitzy as he flung a jacket one of the girls left into the dance floor below; skimming Kitty's shoulder, she looked up and but couldn't see anyone.

Lizzie and Jane sat down where the two girls departed and waited for Chrome to return. Fitzy sat down next to Lizzie, really close. James remained standing, hovering over their table with camera in hand.

In a far corner of the VIP section, Lizzie notices a man sat alone, doing a card trick; Shooting a continuous flow five feet into the air and looping it back into his other hand, seeming to defy gravity. She recognised the man from her parents' ball last night.

"Lizzie? Lizzie?" Fitzy was trying to get her attention.

"Sorry, I zoned out," she said apologetic, before realising who was calling her name.

"You like this music?" Fitzy asked her.

"It's not what I'd choose to play," She told him.

"What would you…?" Fitzy started to ask.

"…Champagne. Champagne for you, Champagne for you, Champagne for you," Pointing at Fitzy, Lizzie and Jane; stopping when he saw James standing there.

Chrome placed a fresh ice bucket onto the table as a waitress brought over four glasses.

The waitress popped open a bottle and poured them drinks, Fitzy stared at her ass the entire time. Jane and Lizzie both noticed. After they had their glasses, Jane dragged Lizzie into the centre of the VIP area and joined the dozen or so people dancing.

Chrome followed, along with Fitzy.

Jane ended up gravitating from dancing with her sister to dancing with Chrome; very quickly grinding on his front.

Lizzie was stuck with Fitzy, who made his best to talk to Lizzie. She pointed to her ears, "It's too loud, I can't hear you," only half lying to him.

With her back to Fitzy, Lizzie managed to cut in and dance with her sister and felt a cold liquid roll down her back.

She span on her feet and looked at a shocked Fitzy with his empty glass.

"Lizzie girl, it wasn't me. I swear," pleaded Fitzy.

Lizzie turned to her sister. "You wanna go?" asked Jane.

"No, no. Its fine," she said to Jane.

"It wasn't me. It was this joker." Fitzy pointed to a wide shouldered Football player type. "Dude," Fitzy called over to the wide guy, who was caressing the ass of his five foot Chinese date. "You need to apologise," demanded Fitzy.

"Fuck off, puny man," said the well-built man in a thick Russian accent.

"Fitzy man, just leave it. You're okay, right?" Chrome asked Lizzie.

"Yeah, what's one more alcohol soaked outfit. By the end of the week, I'll be able to give the Pemberly a run for its money," Lizzie joked.

"You need to believe me. It wasn't me." Fitzy pleaded with Lizzie. "Seriously dude, say sorry to the lady," again, Fitzy called over to the Russian.

The Russian took his hands off his girl and squared off to Fitzy.

"Go away, little man," said the Russian angrily as he shoved Fitzy hard, sending him flying. When Fitzy managed to find his feet, he walked back over to the man.

"Fitzy, leave it man," shouted Chrome, trying to grab hold of his friend's arm.

Before Chrome was able to hold Fitzy back, he sent the Russian tumbling backwards; pushing him into another guy, who looked like the Russian's twin. The Russian recovered from his push and gave Fitzy a hard push, knocking him onto the floor.

"Back down, man," Chrome instructed Fitzy.

"My old man would be spinning in his grave, if he saw me walk away right now." Fitzy returned to his feet and ran over to the Russian who lunged his fist into his face, knocking him to the floor and out cold.

When Fitzy eventually woke up, he found himself slumped up in the back of a police car; his wrists cuffed together.

He saw Lizzie, Chrome, Jane and James standing outside the car, speaking with two officers. Behind them, he could see the Russian guy, talking and joking with a police officer, re-enacting his punch and pretending to be a crying Fitzy. Fitzy slumped back into his seat and closed his eyes as the pain from his jaw started to sink in.

Chapter Six

Jane, Lizzie and James sat on the cold rock hard benches opposite the booking desk at the eighteenth precinct police station, as Chrome paced up and down in front of them, trying to get his lawyer on the phone.

"Seriously Phillip, what would happen if Fitzy shot someone? You need to pick up your fucking phone. Call me back when you get this," Chrome was shouting down his phone.

"Keep it down, or you're out," said the bored desk sergeant from behind his newspaper.

"Sorry," said Chrome in a hushed tone as he slumped down on the bench next to Jane.

"What's the point in having these high-priced Manhattan lawyers if they don't answer their phones?" Chrome said irately.

"Lizzie's a lawyer," said Jane as she rubbed his hand.

"You're a lawyer?" Chrome asked her; confused that she hadn't mentioned it before.

"What? No," said Lizzie trying not to raise his hopes too high. "I'm a first year student at Stanford; Studying Law."

"So you can help?" Chrome asked her, turning his body to face Lizzie.

"C'mon Lizzie," Jane said as she studied her makeup in her compact.

James stood up and took out his camera, ignoring the signs that prohibited recording and began to film their conversation.

"Now's not the time," said Lizzie to James as she tried to sho' him away.

James looked at Jane who nodded her head, prompting him to put his camera away.

"Cheers," Chrome said to Jane. "Fitzy's first American album is about to drop and I don't need any proof he was in here. I'm gonna need your footage from the club to be deleted."

"Of course, anything you need," said Jane who snapped her fingers at James. "Delete it." She ordered him.

"I don't need any type of bad publicity," Chrome said as he thought of the footage being played on TMZ and Wendy Williams. As the thought of bad publicity flooded his mind, another thought entered; vacant partly due to vodka and partly due to Champagne. "We have a flight tomorrow, first thing. He has to be on the Jet." Chrome remembered.

"Wait," Lizzie called out as James started to press buttons on his handheld camera.

"Did you record what happened at the Lydia Lounge?" Lizzie asked James.

"Yeah, everything," said James who handed over his camera to Lizzie.

She looked down at the small LED screen and pressed play. It was muted and played out the altercation, recorded in plain view.

Lizzie handed James back his camera. "Head outside, record a copy onto your phone and send it to me," She instructed him.

"I don't have your number," he told her.

She gestured for James to hand over his phone, which he eventually did. Lizzie saved her number and handed it back to him. "Quickly, go outside."

Lizzie waited for James to leave before she got up and stood directly in front of the sleepy and docile looking policeman. Lizzie coughed to get his attention.

"Yes Ma'am?" he said to her as he looked her up and down. "Restrooms aren't open to the public," looking back at his paper.

"I don't need the toilet," Lizzie snapped at the policeman.

"Then what is it that you do need?" He asked her, completely laying his paper down to get an unobstructed view of her.

Lizzie took in a breath and swallowed it. "What I need," Lizzie said, keeping calm, "Is information regarding…Fitzy."

"Who?" The desk sergeant asked as he looked over at his computer screen.

Lizzie turned around and looked at Chrome.

"Fitzgerald Darcy," whispered Chrome.

Jane whispered his full fame, laughing at it.

"Fitzgerald Darcy," said Lizzie confidently to the increasingly annoyed policeman.

"Mr. Darcy," said the police officer, "Let me see." He started to type away on his computer. "Drunk and disorderly, battery and resisting arrest," the sergeant read out; signalling each charge on his fingers.

"Are you sure you didn't miss out being black, to his list of crimes?" Lizzie asked the officer in a serious manner.

The desk sergeant without flinching locked his eyes on Lizzie's and commanded her full concentration.

"I don't know what you're insinuating, but we have dozens of eyewitnesses saying your friend Fitzy, pushed the victim, and was only hit in self-defence."

"That's a lie, and resisting arrest? He was out cold?" Lizzie questioned the man. "And he's not my friend," Lizzie continued.

"Why do you care?" asked the desk sergeant who was beginning to realise he wouldn't get back to his paper any time soon.

"Because what you're doing is wrong, and illegal; that's not what happened," Lizzie began speaking louder and faster.

"We have a pile of statements refuting your interpretation of events, Miss…"

"Bennet, Lizzy Bennet. Any proof? Surveillance footage from the club?" Lizzie enquired.

"Too dark," he said to her confidently as he smirked over at Jane and Chrome; "didn't catch anything."

The desk sergeant picked up his coffee and started to take a slow condescending sip from his 'world's greatest cop' mug.

"That's no problem," Lizzie said calmly as she smiled glowingly at him. "We have footage of what happened tonight."

"You have footage? Of the incident," spluttered the police officer as he digested what Lizzie was telling him. "Of the altercation involving Fitzy… um, Mr Darcy, I mean?"

Lizzie's phone made a beeping noise. She opened James's text and began to play the grainy video.

"Yes, we have video evidence." Lizzie handed the officer her phone.

His face dropped as the video played out. "That could be anybody!" he said, trying to reassure himself.

"I can get a clearer video if you like?" Lizzy said confidently as she gestured for her phone back. "We haven't had much time to prepare. Not to worry, when it comes to the trial, we'll make sure we have a copy worthy of such an event. I wouldn't worry about all the media interest that this arrest will bring, you've covered yourselves, right?"

Lizzie got her cell phone back by reaching in and snatching it out of his hand. "Jane, Chrome, we've wasted enough of this officer's time. Up you get."

Chrome and Jane reluctantly get up from the benches.

"First, I'm just going to take a note of this helpful officers badge number," Lizzie leaned in to get a better look at his badge. He attempted to cover it when he noticed what she was doing.

"I've got it." She said smirking as she turned around.

The three of them began to walk towards the door.

"Don't turn around," Lizzie whispered as they got closer and closer to the door, each step made Lizzie question her methods.

"Wait," called over the sergeant just before they were about to walk out the main doors.

"Yes," said Lizzie under her breath.

Lizzie turned herself around slowly. "Yes?" she asked him all confused.

"Let me make a call and see what I can do. No Promises." He said in an unbothered tone, like he was doing himself a disservice by doing them this favour.

"Why don't you take a seat?" He advised to them as he picked up his telephone receiver.

Fitzy insisted on hugging and kissing Lizzie many time on the cab ride back to the hotel.

"You have no idea how much you helped me out tonight, Lizzie girl." Fitzy said, truly sincerely to Lizzie.

"Maybe learn to listen to people," she snapped at him after managing to put her purse between them.

"I will, from now on, I swear," Fitzy mimicked crossing his heart to Lizzie.

When they arrived back at the Everfield; the five of them squeezed out of the cab. Lizzie and Fitzy stared at the stars, and passing cars, while Jane and Chrome engulfed each other's faces on the steps of the hotel. Once Chrome felt he had removed all of Jane's lip-gloss, they parted ways and wished each another a good night.

Benjy, Charlie, Franky and Kitty reached the hotel just as the Bennet's group retreated into the warmth.

"I've got to make a move," said Franky, who was ferociously messaging someone on his app.

"Have fun," winked Kitty, as he ran up the Everfield steps. "I'm going to have a coco from the Pemberly, wanna join me Charlie?" Kitty asked her as she was half way up the steps.

"I'll be there in a minute," she called out to her as she cupped her hands.

"You have a good night?" he asked her when they were alone.

"I did," she said to him, her cheeks going red, not entirely due to the cold chill in the air.

"Was this your first time to a New York club?" she asked him.

Benjy nodded his head. "My first time at any club," he told her. "I don't get a chance to get out much.

"Well, every other club from now on is going to be shit in comparison," She joked with him.

"Yeah," he said laughing.

As he was laughing, she leaned in and pecked him on the cheek. His body froze in the millisecond that the kiss lasted.

"Welcome to New York, Benjy Costa," she said to him as she made her way up the steps.

He followed her with his eyes as she walked up the remainder of the hotel steps.

"Welcome to New York," Benjy muttered to himself as he began the long walk home.

Chapter Seven

Mrs. Bennet sat on the end of Jane's bed as her daughter proceeded to empty her closets contents into six suitcases she had positioned all around the room on the floor.

"When was the last time you were in London, darling?" Mrs. Bennet asked, as she passed Jane a scarf with a foxes head still attached to it, Mrs. Bennet gave it a sniff before screwing her face and throwing it into a nearby suitcase.

"Maybe three years ago," Jane answered her mother as she tried to remember, her face was hidden by sunglasses; she was trying on multiple pairs in the mirror.

"You'll have fun. I do miss the shopping in Knightsbridge." Mrs. Bennet told her daughter, "make sure Chrome takes you to Hibiscus, they do the best foie gras ice cream I've ever had."

"Ice cream?" Jane asked her mother, making sure she heard her right.

Mrs. Bennet nodded her head, "as silky and smooth as your hair, my dear."

Jane started to stroke her hair, smiling to herself as she threaded it through her fingers. "It is smooth," she told her mother, through her mirror.

"Almost finished packing?" Mrs. Bennet asked. She got up and started to inspect the suitcases. "How long are you going for?"

"Six days," Jane told her as she came out of her closet with two armfuls of hangared clothes that she threw into an empty suitcase.

"Why are you going again?" Mrs. Bennet quizzed Jane.

"Why not?" Jane said matter-of-factly, "Fitzy is releasing his album in Britain."

"But arn't you seeing that Chrome chap?" Mrs. Bennet asked her.

"They're joined at the hip; Business partners."

"You sure they're not other partners too?"

"What? No?"

"I remember this one time I dated a black man..." Mrs. Bennet started.

"Mom, really not interested." Jane bluntly told her.

"Just remember Jane. One black man in bed is euphoric, two black men in bed with you is stratospheric. Don't brush off the idea, dear." She instructed her daughter, "Don't brush it off."

"I'll keep it in mind," Jane told her mother as she started to zip up her Louis Vuitton luggage set.

Mrs. Bennet was still circulating around Jane's room; peering into jewellery boxes and opening up drawers. She attempted to open up the drawer where Jane kept her enormous stash of coke when Jane re-entered the room with another armful of clothes. They fell onto the floor when she saw her mother reach towards the drawer handle.

"Mom, can you help me pick these clothes up?" Jane asked her, stopping her mother.

Mrs. Bennet looked at her watch, "You know what, Jane. I've got to run." She told her daughter as she picked up her bag from the bed and put it in the crook of her arm.

"Safe flight," she called over to Jane as she opened up the door. "Remember darling, if you do see your Aunt and Grandmother. Do walk on by." Mrs. Bennet said seriously as she shuddered, imagined Jane bumping into her mother and sister in Selfridges.

Once she was alone, Jane opened up her coke filled drawer and packed the clothes she had dropped over them, doing her best to hide them.

It took her a further forty minutes to fill the remaining suitcases. When she was done, she picked up the telephone on her nightstand and called the front desk.

She had without meaning, called the phone of Michael, the hotels Concierge.

Michael had spent the entirety of his morning culling his rolodex; something he often did when restructurers and producers weren't playing ball. He'd wait for them to notice the lack of business that the Everfield was sending their way and wait for them to offer better discount rates, which they always did.

"Everfield concierge desk," Michael said as he picked up the phone, his face looked more like a rodent when he spoke on the phone.

"I need a car to the airport," Jane instructed him as she reapplied her lip-gloss in her vanity.

"I think Buster is about to about to pick your mother up from…" He had to stop himself before he revealed her mother's location; discretion was something he prided himself on. "Bloomingdales," he said, thinking of were Jane may believe her mother may be. Instead, Mrs. Bennet was in a hotel room across town, being fucked by her younge lover.

"Well, tell him to take me to the airport first, I need my bags brought down."

"You're off on a trip?" he asked her as he began to message Buster to stay at the hotel and bring the car around.

"Yeah, London," she told him.

"I see. Which airport shall I tell Buster to drop you off at?" Michael asked her.

"I don't know," She told him, "Chrome and Fitzy had to leave first thing on their jet. You think daddy will let me take his?" She asked her.

"He's currently using it I'm afraid, Miss Bennet." He told her apologetically. "He's on his way to the hotel in Toronto."

"When will he be back?" She asked him, she knew that it wouldn't be until later this evening, and she was right.

"You'll just have to book me a commercial flight then," She told him. "Don't you dare put me in business," she told him bluntly. "I'm ready to go. Oh, and book James a seat too. Put him in coach." And with his instructions, she hung up the phone.

Michael signalled a bellhop to go to Jane's room, and began to call his contact at Nelly Airways.

As Jane waited impatiently outside the hotel steps for Buster to bring her car around, she notices Fitzy running towards her, holding a bouquet of flowers.

"What are you doing here?" She asked him, surprised he wasn't over the Atlantic right now.

"Over slept," Fitzy told her bluntly. Jane tried to read his signature white t-shirt with defamatory writing scrawled across his chest.

Today's shirt had, *Why pay for sex, when you can steal it.* Unlike Lizzie, Jane liked Fitzy's taste in t-shirts.

"So, where's Chrome? He messaged me when he was at the airport!" Jane asked him.

"He should be almost home now."

"He flew without you?" she asked, even she would think twice before flying off alone, without her travel companion.

"It always happens. There's no waking me up if I'm wrapped up in a comfy bed, especially if I have the company of a woman."

Jane looked down at the flowers he was holding. "Are those for me?" She asked him.

"What?" He noticed what she was looking at. "No, sorry; for your sister, just to say, thank you, for helping me out last night."

"I helped too," Jane said, fluttering her eyelashes as she eyed up the bouquet he was holding.

"Have you seen Lizzie?" He asked her, ignoring her intention of getting the flowers from him.

"No." She said bluntly as Buster pulled up and got out of the car, helping the bellhop carry her mountain of bags to the car. She knew exactly where she was; she had been in the library all morning.

"Here's my ride," she told him as Fitzy began to climb the hotel steps. "She's not in," she called after him. He stopped and turned around.

"You said you hadn't seen her," he said to her as he slowly walked towards her.

Michael appeared through the hotel front doors, carrying a piece of paper.

"You going uptown?" he asked her.

"Possibly, why?" She said to him suspiciously.

"Can I get a lift?" he asked, diving into the car before Jane was able to get an answer. James followed Fitzy into the car with his rucksack over his shoulder.

"Miss Bennet," Michael called down at her as she was about to slide into the car. She got in and waited for him to come to her.

"Your ticket," he said, passing her the boarding pass. "JFK" he told her as she shut the door and slid down the window.

"First class?" She asked as she snatched the ticket from him.

"Would I book you anything else?" He said with a glint in his eye as Buster pulled off into the stream of traffic.

While she was reading over her flight information, ignoring Fitzy, her phone began to ring.

The name Max peered across her screen. Cautiously, she pressed the accept button.

"Max?" She said, confused why her brother was calling her.

"How are you?" She asked, as Fitzy sat staring into the mirror, attempting to seem uninterested in her call.

"Just on the way to the airport… London," she said, still skimming her booking information.

"Cunt!" she screamed out.

"No, Max. Not you… That idiot Michael at the hotel booked me an aisle seat. If my flight wasn't in fifty minutes, I'd turn around and do a Naomi…Actually, I don't wanna scratch the screen," she said as she took her cell phone away from her ear and examined the perfectly polished gold that covered the back of her iPhone.

"When are you coming back to the city? You missed me perform at Daddy's Ball."

She tried to remember the last time she had seen her brother. Jane noticed that Fitzy averting his gaze from her.

"When are you home next? I've met…" She stopped herself when she realised who was sat next to her.

"Don't go," she pleaded as he was about to hang up. "We all miss you. Lizzie's home for the summer… Okay, try." She said before hanging up.

"You have a brother?" Fitzy asked as she put her phone back into her purse.

"Yes," she said to him bluntly. "Buster, pull over here." She called to the front of the car.

The car sharply veered out of the road.

"Uptown, as requested." She said to him smugly, as she opened her door and made room for him to pass.

"Thanks for the lift," he said as he exited to car.

As soon as the door shut, they were back in the heavy New

York traffic, en route to the airport.

Chapter Eight

As Jane waited at the airport bar, cocktail in hand, it reminded her of the last time she flew from this very airport alone. She was nineteen and had just been evicted from her parents. It was in this same bar that she had met James; except this time he was the one having problems to affording a bottle of water.

When she took her aisle seat, she was sat next to a fat balding man in his late twenties. No matter how wealthy or successful he presented himself, she would consciously suppress the feeling the three vodkas had given her, as she waited to board the plane. She could think of nothing worse than getting caught up with another James.

The man, who identified himself as Simon, trying to shake her hand as they took off and was full of flu. His nose was red and he coughed and spluttered from the moment he sat down.

The passing air hostesses gave Jane a sympathetic look every time they passed her. There were absolutely no seats for her to move to; nut, it didn't stop her from asking every time she could get one of their attention.

Instead, they made sure her glass was constantly full with a mixture of Vodka and Champagne; letting her get drunk, hoping the copious amount of alcohol she was consuming, would stop her from complaining about the man. that she insisted had Ebola.

Jane chose to ignore his attempts at starting a conversation with her. He did pepper in, "I'm sorry," every time he sneezed, spreading his germs throughout the cabin.

Jane had never been so relieved when they touched down at Heathrow.

Michael had arranged for someone at the airport to meet her to help her with her baggage on arrival. It still didn't make up for her shitty seat, she thought.

As soon as she hit the cold London air, her chest exploded into a coughing fit.

Simon, the man who was sat next to her on the journey, passed her by, still sneezing and wheezing, riding a mobility scooter, that he was now driving on the main road; he had attached his suitcase to the back with some green string.

***

Benjy enjoyed the contrast of working at the Pemberly and down in the hotel's basement, doing the endless laundry the hotel seemed to produce. Franky had requested that Benjy work at the Pemberly permanently after the Bennets' ball, but Ms. Powell had not allowed a full transfer, instead allowing Benjy to split his time between the two departments .

The endless heat from the mountain of industrial washer dryers, Irons and steamers made the basement uncomfortably hot; air-conditioning had yet to reach this floor.

Benjy lifted and pushed a heavy trolleys of laundry up and down the length of the hotel, past the furnaces that kept the hotel above the right temperature. He removed his sweat soaked shirt and threw it in his locker, getting the attention of the dozens of women and girls he worked with. He could see them prodding and winking at their friends as he past them.

When he returned to the trolley he was pushing, he found Charlie was in the ironing station next to him. At first she didn't recognise him, but when she did, she averted her eyes as he spoke with her. She had never seen a man wearing so little clothes, this close to her before. She had seen semi naked men in the movies and on TV, but never in the flesh.

"What are you doing after work?" He asked Charlie, who still had issues looking at him full on. She did her best to look directly into his eyes.

"Nothing," she said, wanting to look down at his torso for more than a fleeting second.

"I finish in twenty minutes, if you wanna grab a bite to eat." Benjy suggested, knowing full well that she was embarrassed. He thought it was cute and smiled throughout their awkwardly staggered conversation.

"Me too," She replied, starting to notice everyone else looking at them.

"Well, shall I meet you outside, by the steps? After our shift?" He asked; he was thinking of taking her to a burger bar he had past while walking to work.

"Sounds good to me," said a blushing Charlie.

"Charlie Tyson!" Shouted a booming voice from behind Benjy's back; Charlie's face dropped and no sign of flirtation was anywhere to be seen. She took a step back as her formidable mother marched towards them.

Benjy had remembered seeing her during his interview and how she had refused to get in a elevator with him. Franky's voice could be heard swirling around his head, who had given him the stark warning of not to expect any alone time with Charlie.

Charlie's mother appeared next to them and began to yell at her in Spanish as Benjy stood there, watching the shrunken girl next to him, on the verge of tears, getting an almighty earful from her mother.

"Go and see what needs doing at the back," Miss Tyson concluded, in English, as she pointed to the back of the basement. Benjy watched as Charlie left him alone with the red faced, Latino woman. She looked around at all the people staring in her direction, "Get back to work," she yelled at them before turning her attention onto Benjy. She took a step forward into Benjy's space, forcing him to step back; he could feel his ass was almost sat on the edge of the laundry trolley.

Benjy tried to say something but was struck down with one finger firmly pressed against his lips.

"Now, you listen to me," she snared at him. "I know exactly what boys like you want with girls like my daughter."

Benjy tried again to say something but again got the same finger against his lips; this time squashing his lips against his front teeth. "You, my boy have no chance with spending any time with Charlie."

He looked down at the protective mother in front of him; looking her in the eyes, noticing how youthful they looked; she couldn't be older than her mid thirtys, but had not aged well at all.

Without declaring the conversation was over, Miss Tyson turned around and followed her daughter towards the far end of the basement.

Benjy stood there for a moment or two, getting his breathing back to a more normal rhythm. He looked around and the other workers still glanced over to him, averting their gaze whenever he saw them.

A Filipino woman in her sixties slinked over to Benjy with a pile of folded shirts, "Don't take it personally. She's just looking out for her daughter; doesn't want her to make the same mistakes that she made." Without stopping, she was gone.

After his shift, Benjy waited outside the Everfield. He had hoped that Charlie would be able to get away from her mother. He waited for twenty minutes and tried to ring her cell phone without any luck. He gave up on the possibility of sharing a meal with Charlie that evening and began his long walk home.

It took Benjy almost two hours to walk home most nights. He arrived home to find his morbidly obese mother asleep in a large chair, in front of the TV, while his four year old brother played with a pile of pizza boxes by her feet.

They had not long lived in their shabby apartment, but it looked as if they had been there for decades. Food and drink stains had already ruined the carpet, mostly around his mother's chair, while a visible cloud of cigarette smoke that lingered on the ceiling.

The first thing he noticed as he walked through the door was the stench of shit that filled his nostrils. He could tell that his brother's diaper hadn't been changed since he left early in the morning. He lifted him up and carried him in to the bathroom and stripped him off, quickly bathing and redressing him.

"All clean," He said as he let his brother run back towards his mother's feet to continue playing with the pizza boxes.

Benjy did his best to tidy up the place; he was constantly surprised by the number of dirty plates, bowels and food wrappers that littered the apartment, considering how immobile his mother was.

It took him over two hours to finish tidying up the mess and settle his brother down for the night.

Benjy's mother had awoken twice since Benjy had been home, both times requesting that he make her something to eat; requests he always complied with.

When it was around ten o'clock, Benjy retreated to his bedroom and tried in vain to call up Charlie. He stripped down for bed and put his phone onto charge. Sat up in bed; he could hear sirens screeching nearby from the world outside. Benjy spent each evening escaping to a different world; reading a car magazine; he'd eventually fall asleep with the magazine resting on his chest.

Chapter Nine

Jane was standing in the middle of her obscene amount of baggage as Chrome's car pulled up in front of her. She was in the midst of coughing and spluttering, blowing her nose into her handkerchief when she realised he was stranding in front of her.

"Chrome," she said in a gasp, as she stuffed her sodden cloth into her pocket. Her cheeks were red and puffy and her hair, frizzed and out of shape.

James was seated cross-legged on the floor as he changed his camera's battery; he bounced to life, camera rolling, when he realised Chrome had arrived.

"You look...jetlagged," Chrome said to her as he ferociously tried to think of a way to say she looked like a hot mess. Jane reached into hug him, he hesitantly embraced her too.

"Let's get you to my pad, your chariot awaits." Chrome gestured to the pink limousine behind him. The car's driver began to load Jane's bags into the trunk as Jane stepped in.

She was taken aback when she saw a tall, blonde woman with fake breasts and lips; seated in the back of the car. Jane got a head rush as she took her seat; breathing heavily, catching her breath as James sat next to her.

The blonde woman, already annoyed when Jane entered the car, appeared to be furious as James got in, wielding a camera.

"Chrome?" The blonde woman called out through the open

door. "What the fuck is this?" she demanded, as James took his seat. Her voice was shrill and slow and gave Jane a headache; each word she said, sent a painful pulse racing through her brain.

After helping the driver with Jane's bags, Chrome returned to the car and took his seat next to Jane. He couldn't help but stare at her pale skin as the car started to move.

"Chrome?" The woman again called out, this time much louder and shriller than before.

James couldn't help but stare at her large breasts that bulged out of her extra small tank top.

"Look all you want," she called out at him, "But, no one as ugly or fat as you is ever going anywhere near these," she pulled down her top and exposed her breasts for James, his camera zooming in.

"Now, you've had your look. Get that fucking thing out of my face." She straightened out her top and turned his attention to Chrome, "Who is this fool?"

"Tabatha!" Chrome said sternly at the girl's actions, "My sister," he told Jane.

Jane looked confused; she was white and Chrome wasn't. He picked up on this, "We're both adopted," he told to her, "with the amount of fake tan she wears, sometimes she's darker that me" he joked, shooting Tabatha a wink as he squeezed Jane's knee.

"Ha ha," Tabatha said sarcastically. "But seriously, who is this bint?" she demanded of him.

"This is Jane Bennet," said Chrome, ignoring the bint remark. Jane wasn't too sure what a bint was but knew it wasn't a compliment. She felt too weak and tired to argue with this girl, who was baiting her to snap back.

"I don't feel too good," Jane said as she threw up between her legs. Vomit proceeded to splash everywhere and caused Tabatha to scream as she felt warm specks of chunks spray on her bare legs and strapless white stilettos.

"Dirty fucking bitch!" Tabatha yelled at Jane who was still heaving.

James sprang into life when Jane initially threw up, pushing into Tabatha to get the best shot he could.

Chrome held Jane's hair as she hurled, looking around in vain for something to contain the mess. He stroked her back as she concluded being sick.

"I'm so sorry," muttered Jane as she passed out in his lap.

"She's buying me new fucking shoes," said Tabatha as she leaned forward and wiped her shoes on Jane's skirt.

Jane woke up alone the next morning in a bed and room she did not recognise. Her head was pounding, mouth dry and eyes crusty. She reached for a bottle of water that was placed on her bedside table. As she opened the bottle to take a sip, she noticed her pile of suitcases and bags that were neatly stacked in a distant corner of the modern and sleekly designed room.

The only clue she could work out, of her current location was the noise from the window a few feet away. She was too weak to get up; her arms buckled as she strained to lift up her body to catch a glimpse of the hustle and bustle she could hear from the street below.

She longed for someone she knew to be sat on the edge of her bed, even James she thought to herself, as she sipped slowly from the water bottle.

Lizzie was reclined in her aeroplane seat as she watched her plane track its progress across the Atlantic on the screen in front of her. She was less than three hours away from London and had slept through the majority of her journey.

Her book, over nine hundred pages of Law research, lay heavy on her lap; she had dipped in and out of it between bouts of sleep, but found concentrating on anything impossible, as her mind wandered back to how scared her ill sister must be.

She had volunteered immediately to come to Jane's side. Her mother had told her merely in passing in the hotel's lobby, on her way to get her hair done, that Jane had fallen ill. Mrs. Bennet had thought nothing of them going to Jane's side. "They have the NHS there," Mrs. Bennet had told Lizzie, "It's free healthcare; she'll be fine." And with that, Mrs. Bennet exited the hotel in pursuit of a hairdresser in Chelsea to give herself a new hairdo.

Lizzie had marched into her father's office, interrupting him during a tense-looking meeting with a man she recognised. He was at their ball, arriving with Chrome, Fitzy and another woman; she also remembered seeing him briefly at the *Lydia Lounge*, playing with a pack of cards.

"Daddy, we need to talk," said a distressed Lizzie. "I just spoke to Mom and…"

"…Lizzie!" Mr. Bennet said in an alarmed tone as she burst through his office door, "Would you, and Mr. Hilbert mind giving me a few moments with my daughter?" Mr. Bennet asked of the two men seated in front of his desk.

The hotel's general manager, Mr. Hilbert gestured Collin towards the office door. "My office is next door," The soft spoken, Chinese man said to Collin, "I have a bottle of Chivas Regal Royal salute. You ever tried it?"

Collin ignored Mr. Bennet and Hilbert, and stopped Lizzie from reaching her father.

"Lizzie Bennet?" Collin asked her.

"Yes?" she said quizzically, "Do I know you?"

"We knew each other, a long time ago, when we were children."

Lizzie looked at him, she couldn't recognise any of his facial features, even if she did know them in adolescence.

"Collin," he told her.

"Collin Williams," she said slowly as she remembered him; his features starting to familiarise itself once more, "we were with you in Aspen when…" she stopped herself.

"…When my father died" he finished for her in not the glum way you would expect someone would, when speaking about the death of a parent, but in a blasé kind of way. "A long time ago."

"How are you doing?" She asked him, putting her hand on his arm in a sympathetic, motherly way.

"Like I said, a long time ago," he told her, "I'm running the company; we're more profitable than ever."

"That's good to hear," Lizzie said smiling; she was glad that the sudden passing of his father at such an impressionable age, hadn't caused too much of an unsettled beginning to life. The billions he inherited would have helped too, she thought.

"You don't live in the city, do you?" he asked her.

"No, I'm just here for the summer. I go to college in California."

Collin looked at her pale skin and wouldn't have believed her, if he knew it not to be true.

Mr. Bennet tried on countless occasions to interject, but

was unsuccessful until Collin took that split second too long to say something else.

"Lizzie, it sounded important. The reason you wanted to speak with me," Mr. Bennet final managed to say.

Lizzie looked at her father and almost forgot why she was in his office. "I'm sorry to disturb," she said as she looked at all three men.

"It's no problem at all," said Collin; his perfectly-aligned, sparking white teeth glistened as he smiled at her.

"How about that Scotch?" Mr. Hilbert asked Collin.

"Sounds good to me," without looking at him. "It was nice getting reacquainted," he said to Lizzie as he left with a smile on his face.

Mr. Bennet sank into his chair as soon as they were alone.

"Daddy? Are you okay?" Lizzie asked concernedly.

"Yes, yes," said Mr. Bennet as he tried to gather his thoughts. "Just one of those days."

"How are you?" He asked her as he sat up and looked up at his daughter.

"It's about Jane…"

"…Yes, I heard she wasn't too well."

"I want to fly to her, to London."

"By yourself?" He asked her, unsure about the idea of Lizzie flying alone.

"Yes, by myself," she didn't like that her father still saw her as a little girl.

"It's probably just a bug, Twenty-four hour thing. She'll be fine by the time you get there." Mr. Bennet said, trying to reassure her.

"Maybe so, but I want to go," she said stubbornly.

All Mr. Bennet could see was a six year old Lizzie, who would stamp on her feet and demand that they take in any stray dogs they would see when out and about. He was unable to refuse her requests even then.

"Okay," he said to her, Lizzie's face beamed with joy. "I'll get Charlotte to book you a seat."

"Thank you, daddy," she rushed over to his side and wrapped her arms around him.

Mr. Bennet reached across his desk and pressed the intercom, that buzzed as the button was pressed, making Charlotte enter almost immediately.

"I'd best get packing," she said as she let go of her father. She skipped across the room, saying a quick, "hello," to Charlotte as she left.

***

Lizzie was gently awoken by a stewardess who asked her to buckle up to land. She looked through her window as the London skyline slowly came into focus; it had been nearly three years since she last visited England. Lizzie's early childhood involved frequent journeys on Concord.

Lizzie managed to manoeuvre through Heathrow with ease; she collected her small tattered bag and stepped into the cold, overcast and dreary London afternoon.

She threw her bag over her shoulder and edged towards the curb. The front of the arrivals entrance was packed with cars; a steady stream of taxi cabs passing by.

She raised her hand, with the aim of getting one of them to stop.

"You'll never get a taxi that way," said a familiar voice from behind her shoulder.

She took a deep breath and turned around. Fitzy was standing there with Tabatha; to Lizzie, a mystery big breasted woman, wearing a mini skirt and extra small white blouse.

"Welcome to London," said Fitzy, who leaned in, open armed, to give Lizzie a hug. Lizzie was too tired to stop him and stood there as he wrapped himself around her. He was wearing his trademark white t-shirt with wildly offensive slogans. Today's read: *School is for kids, send the goats and put the children to work (they made this top!).*

Lizzie shook her head as she read his t-shirt, "How many of those tops do you have?" She asked him angrily, almost not wanting to know the answer.

"Umm…" he said, as he looked down at his t-shirt, "I couldn't even tell you, I make them myself. I think of a slogan, text Fat Steve and he sends them to me."

"Do you re-wear them?" She asked, not thinking he did, she couldn't remember seeing him wearing the same top twice.

"God no," he said, thinking she was crazy. "At the end of the day, I throw them away!"

Lizzie again shook her head, thinking of all that waste.

"I'm guessing you've worn that outfit, at least three times this week," Tabatha sneered from behind her large dark sunglasses.

Lizzie took no offence at what she said to her; she had heard it so many times from her mother and sister. She could never understand why people wore sunglasses on overcast days and inside; every time she had asked Jane or her mom, they had never given her an answer. Instead of answering the woman she had no interest of talking to, she turned to Fitzy, "Where's my sister?"

Lizzie followed him and Tabatha to a nearby waiting limousine.

"Where are your bags?" Fitzy asked her, shocked when she gestured to the small bag over her shoulder. "We'll have to get you an outfit or two while you're here," he announced as he let Tabatha and Lizzie get into the car.

As Lizzie sat down, she noticed the seats were covered with dozens of magazines; all of them bearing Tabatha's face.

"Let me move these, out of your way," said Tabatha in a blasé manner.

Lizzie noticed that she wore close to no clothes in the pictures. She thought it was quite pathetic of her to have left them out, deliberately for her to see.

"It's me," Tabatha said to an uninterested Lizzie.

"Yes, I thought so," she said, truly not bothered.

"I'm a model." She told Lizzie, as she played with her long blonde hair, twirling it between her fingers.

"What do you model? Gloves?" She asked her.

"No!" she knew that Lizzie wasn't taking her seriously.

"She models her boobs, mostly," said Fitzy, as he stepped into the car and sat close to Lizzie's side.

Tabatha reached for a bottle of champagne that sat in an ice—bucket; she opened it and poured just herself a glass.

"Share the love," said Fitzy, who poured himself a drink, "Lizzie? Can I tempt you?"

"Oh, no thank you," she said as she turned her phone off aeroplane mode. Her father had messaged her twelve times during her flight; each message sent her phone into a craze of noise before she put it on silent.

"Someone's popular," said a snide Tabatha as she sipped on her glass slowly, leaving remnants of lipstick on the rim.

"It's just my father," Lizzie told her as she put her phone away in her jeans pocket.

"I don't have a father, I'm adopted" said Tabatha bluntly.

Lizzie didn't quite know what to say to her in response.

"Perhaps, you have a mother instead?" Lizzie came up with, trying her best not to smile.

Her retort made Fitzy giggle and choke on his drink.

"Yes," Tabatha said, not impressed with what Lizzie said.

"Tabatha, is Chrome's sister," Fitzy said, turning his body to face Lizzie.

"Really?" Said Lizzie, without thinking.

"Really!" Said an annoyed Tabatha.

Lizzie couldn't imagine the soft spoken, polite Chrome being related to her; she could imagine Fitzy being her brother, them both brash and without tact.

Tabatha took the bottle off Fitzy, topped up her glass and poured another and gave it to Lizzie.

"No camera crew?" she said sarcastically from the corner of her mouth as Lizzie reluctantly took the glass from her.

"I left mine at home," Lizzie joked. She placed the stem of the glass between her legs.

Tabatha moved seats to sit next to Fitzy, practically on his lap.

"So," Tabatha said to Lizzie, leaning in so close, "You hail from New York?"

"Born and bred," said Lizzie. She hated being grilled, particularly from people she didn't know.

"With a silver spoon between your lips?"

Lizzie really had no idea how to answer her; her families wealth never came up in discussion and most of her classmates at Stanford had no idea of the world she grew up in.

Tabatha waited for a response that didn't come, "Yet, you choose to dress like you grew up on a council estate? I had to work hard and earn every penny I got! Hard work, my love, hard, bloody work."

"Yes, standing in front of a photographer with your breast out for everyone to see certainly is hard work. I can't imagine the amount of blow jobs you have had to give to get where you are!" said Lizzie who took a sip of her drink, not knowing where what she has just said, came from.

"I'm not a sex worker!" screamed Tabatha.

Fitzy bit on his knuckles, trying to fight off his laughing.

"Aren't you?" asked Lizzie seriously, not blinking, looking her dead on in the eyes. "You don't sell sex? Every time you have your picture taken, you're not selling an orgasm to some forty-five year-old?"

"I'm not a prostitute," said Tabatha, getting herself worked out.

"You may not be a prostitute, but you're most certainly selling sex! One semen filled tissue at a time," A jet lagged Lizzie blurted out.

Lizzie felt the car pull up; she looked around and saw a swarm of paparazzi waiting outside the car.

"Where are we?" Lizzie asked as the driver got out of the car.

"Tabatha has a shoot, we're just dropping her off." Said Fitzy, who put his empty Champagne glass down.

Tabatha followed the silhouette of the driver as he walked around the car. She lunged for the door and locked it before he got there. She was red-faced after her verbal altercation with Lizzie.

"Can you pass me my coat?" Tabatha asked Lizzie.

She looked around and noticed a mound of fur on the seat next to her.

Lizzie picked it up and recoiled as she passed it to her. "Is that real?" She asked Tabatha, whose eyes lit up when Lizzie took notice of it.

"Yes. Three-thousand pounds from Selfridges, You like it?" Tabatha said to Lizzie who looked deeply unimpressed as she wrapped herself in the brown moleskin coat that had gold detail sewn into it.

"Do I like it?" Lizzie let out a laugh, "You're truly a vile human being. I prefer my fur coats on the poor helpless animals, not on a hanger." Tabatha said nothing; she was stunned into being silent.

The driver tried repeatedly to open the locked door.

"We better not keep you; there are men everywhere that need relieving. How else are you going to pay for the skin from the kittens out there?"

Tabatha seemed like she could cry, she wasn't used to anyone speaking to her like that.

After a moment, Tabatha centred herself, unlocked the door and stepped out to the awaiting photographers.

As soon as the door shut behind her, Fitzy burst into a fit of laughter and a slow applause.

"God, girl. No one's ever spoken to her like that in her life! Brava." Fitzy wiped away the tears of laughter as the driver got back in the front seat.

"Next stop, Rosings?" The driver asked Fitzy.

"Yes," he said as he ceased to clap. "She was pissed!"

"She doesn't seem like a very nice person," said Lizzie, who couldn't help but smirk at her argument.

"She's not," Fitzy agreed, "I should know, we were once engaged."

"You were engaged?" She asked slowly, "to her?"

"We all make stupid mistakes when we're young," he said to her, justifying his previous relationships.

Lizzie couldn't help but think that Fitzy was still making idiotic choices and couldn't realistically blame his age.

"I can't believe you called her a prostitute!" Fitzy said, still laughing.

"I did not!" She giggled, "I called her a sex worker."

"That sex worker sells a lot of magazines. She's a big name here in the UK. You've been in the country less than thirty minutes any what an enemy you've made!"

Lizzie shrugged it off; she could care less who Tabatha was, and what she thought of her.

Chapter Ten

Mrs. Bennet took slow sips from her wine glass as she sat alone, looking around the quiet and dark New Hampshire restaurant, that she visited whenever she stayed at the lake house. She liked the lake house, but this had been the only time she had visited in nearly two years.

"Would Madam like to order?" said an Italian waiter who came up to her table.

"Not yet," she said, dismissing him away as she cradled her glass.

She kept looking around the room, tapping her index finger on her glass impatiently

"Where is this boy?" she muttered under her breath as she worked her way through the chardonnay; the waiter had brought her the remainder of the bottle.

As she searched for the base of her glass, a young man walked through the door; the same young man she has been sleeping with in New York. He looked around the small place and spotted her hiding in the corner, finishing off her glass of wine. She looked up as he began to walk towards her with a grin across his face.

"You're late," she snapped as he sat down next to her in the corner, kissing her neck as if that would suffice.

"I'm sorry," he said; after he had finished with her neck, "Beautiful perfume," he took in another nostril full.

"It should be; it's a thousand dollars a bottle," she told him as she pointed to the wine.

He poured her another glass and poured himself less than half, the remaining amount.

"You drank the whole bottle?" he asked her.

"You were late!" she snapped.

He took the wine glass out of her hand and put it upon the table, then placed her cheeks between his hands. "I said, I was sorry," he pulled her face forward gently, and leaned in to kiss her, on the lips.

Slowly in the dark corner, they locked lips; passionately kissing like the lovers they were.

Mrs. Bennet couldn't remember the last time her husband kissed her like that. It was intimacy like that kiss that made her to continue running back to the man seated on her right.

The waiter once again returned to the table, looking down over them as they broke off their long embrace. "How about a little something to cleanse the palate?" he said with a grin from ear to ear.

"I'm not that hungry," said Mrs. Bennet, she had felt off all day; not eating, throwing up. She thought she may have what Jane had.

"When's the last time you ate?" The young man asked her.

"Oh, this morning, I think." Mrs. Bennet had to think long and hard about it. She had first thrown up while at the gym into the pot of a large synthetic tree; she had held onto the large burgundy pot for dear life as she expelled chunks of last night's meal of a martini or two and watermelon balls.

"Jane has taken ill and I fear I may have what she has," Mrs. Bennet finished off her wine.

"You need to slow down," he told her.

"You're not my father," she spat at him.

"No, you're right, I'm not. But I do love you," He laughed, as he too finished off his wine.

"How about we go back to the house, and find something to eat there?" He said, winking at her as he slid his hand higher and further up the inside of her thigh .

He gave out a small gasp when he realised she wasn't wearing any underwear. "I guess we should get the check then." He took out his wallet and removed two credit cards and mimicked conalingus between their V-formation.

"Behave yourself," she said as she slapped his hand away from her nether region.

After returning his cards to his wallet, he pulled out a fifty and threw it onto the table and helped her up out of her seat.

Oblivious to their surroundings, the other diners that sat in their dimly lit tables, waiters scurrying around with drinks and plates and the small bell that chimed, announcing that the front door opened; Mrs. Bennet was unaware that while she was having help to put on her coat, that an old acquaintance had entered the restaurant.

"Annalise?" a woman's voiced echoed through the restaurant; it caused some of the diners to overt their concentration from their food, "Annalise Bennet?"

Collin's mother, the brash, spikey haired blonde woman who Mrs. Bennet had last seen at her ball was standing in the doorway.

The young man dropped his hands from her coat and dashed to the restroom within a split second. By the time Mrs. Bennet slowly turned around, she was alone.

"What are the odds?" said the spikey haired woman as she walked towards Mrs. Bennet, flinging her coat at a passing waiter. "I don't see you for fifteen years, then twice within a fortnight... I do fear, that the powers what be, are making our lives intertwine once more."

"I fucking hope not," she muttered under her breath. "Hello Veronica," Mrs. Bennet greeted her, with a nervous grin. She spotted a young man behind her, a boy she had never seen before, but much younger than her lover.

"My God, wasn't that... forgive me, It's been so long. I can't remember his name." Veronica asked Mrs. Bennet.

The young man unfastened his top few shirt buttons and splashed water in his face in the restroom, "She saw nothing Max... everything is fine," he tried to reassure himself.

"Breath... breath," he repeated over and over in hushed tones, while he inhaled deeply, clutching onto each side of the basin.

Maybe she didn't even see me, he thought to himself. Max couldn't even comprehend what his life would be like if people found out about their relationship. As much as he wanted to go out into the restaurant and rescue his mother, he found no motivation at all to move from the spot where he stood.

He looked around the tiny bathroom; the small window was

hardly large enough for a house cat to fit through, the only way out was back the way he came.

He was brought back to reality when his phone began to ring. He scrambled inside his pocket for his cell; 'Mom,' appeared on his screen, along with a picture.

"Yes?" he said, cautiously.

"I'm in the parking lot," Mrs. Bennet said, before ending the call.

Max re-buttoned his shirt and dried his face with a towel.

"Straight out," he told himself, "Don't stop, just get out!"

He unlocked the door and slid out, opening the door as little as possible as to reduce the squeak.

He re-entered the restaurant and immediately spotted Veronica; she was sat in the same table he previously took up. As he was about to look away, she made eye contact with him, smiling as he began to walk her way.

"My, my Maximillian, haven't you grown up!" She said, forcing him to stop and engage in conversation. "You're the mirror for your father when he was your age," she told him as she got up out of her seat and gave him a kiss on the cheek.

"Hello Aunt V," he said, placing the biggest grin he could across his face.

"We missed you at your parent's Ball," She said as she retook her seat without any intention of introducing the man she sat with.

"I live out on the west coast, something came up," he told her, not sure if she believed what he was saying, or not.

"I just came back from L.A, I'm going to be working out there from October. We should catch up properly, over drinks, sometime," she said, rather than suggested. "Oh sorry, you don't drink anymore, do you?" she asked him, just as a waiter turned up with her drink order and removed two empty glasses from the table.

"Everything in moderation," he told her as he began to edge towards the door.

"Listen, I mustn't keep you from your mother," she told him, giving him permission to leave. "I'll see you, real soon," she told him as he began to walk away.

He left the restaurant and got out into the parking lot as fast as he could. It took him a minute to find his mother, who was bent over a bush. The closer he got to her, the louder he could hear the sounds of her vomiting. She held her stomach as she threw up.

"Are you okay?" he asked her, putting his hand on her shoulder.

He attempted to rub her back, but she shrugged him away. "Don't touch me," she told him between bouts of sick.

"Did she see us? What did she say to you?" he asked her concernedly.

"No… She didn't see us. Our secret is safe," she said to him, raising her voice. "No one knows we're fucking, don't worry." By now she had finished throwing up.

Max spun her around to face her and held onto both of her arms, pushing them against her sides.

"You want to shut your mouth?" he hissed at her. "We were almost caught… Okay, we just have to be more careful from now on." He said to her, his grip getting tighter as she tried to wriggle free.

"We're in the middle of fucking nowhere," she snarled at him, "Let go of me," she demanded of him; he eventually loosened his grip. "There can't be another time, this is it; it has to end."

"You want to give up what we have?" he asked her, almost daring her to say no.

"No, I don't want to…" she told him as she looked directly into his eyes; she could see every contour of his face; the moon shone brightly on him, in the cloudless sky.

Max's face was completely white, every pixel of colour had vanished from his face when Veronica had called out his mother's name; he too, felt that he could vomit at any moment.

He reached into his pocket to call their car to pick them up, "Lets head back," he told her.

She nodded, without saying anything. He attempted to put his arm around her, she again shrugged him off. "Not now, Max," she told him as they made their way back around to the front of the restaurant.

Chapter Eleven

Lizzie had to wait until the next morning to see her sister; Jane had slept through the entire day. She refused Fitzy's offer of joining him on a night out; instead, Lizzie spent her evening binging on Downton Abbey; months before it was due to air in the states.

After showering and eating a cereal bar she found in her purse, Lizzie crept along the corner and knocked on the door she was told was her sister's.

"Hello?" she heard her sister say faintly from behind the door.

Lizzie gave the door a good push and it creaked open. As she entered the bedroom, she saw her sister throw a newspaper to the foot of the bed when she saw her sister. She left the door open to let the air flow through the stuffy room.

"Lizzie?" Jane asked, "What are you doing here?"

Lizzie noticed that Jane really didn't sound like her usual self; her voice was much deeper and naisely.

"I was in the neighbourhood," Lizzie joked as she shut the door behind her and walked towards her sister; giving her a half-heartedly hug as to not catch what she had. "How are you feeling? Lizzie asked her, as she poured her a fresh glass of water from the jug on the night stand.

"I'm ok," Jane took a sip of water and swiped the paper onto the floor when she noticed Lizzie paying attention to it.

"What's this?" Lizzie asked as she reached across the bed to retrieve the paper, laying across Jane's legs and making them go numb.

Lizzie unfolded it and stared at the pictures in front of her and laughed to herself.

"Why are you laughing?" Jane asked her.

"Isn't that Chrome's sister?" Lizzie asked, pointing to a picture of Tabatha who was wearing a fur bikini with, Sex Worker, written on her torso in what looked like blood, "Tabatha?"

"Yeah, you met her?" asked Jane.

"Yeah," said Lizzie who was distracted by another picture on the same page. Fitzy had his arms around two blonde women; he was covering their naked chests with his arms.

"She certainly made an impression on Tabatha," said Chrome's voice from the open doorway.

Both girls turned around and saw Chrome wearing a suit and holding a bouquet of freshly cut daisies. He walked over to them, smiling at Lizzie as he passed her and sat on the side of the bed next to Jane, putting the flowers into her water jug. He reached in to kiss Jane, but she turned her head.

"You'll get ill," she told him as he put his hands on the side of her face and turned her head to face him; kissing her on the lips, ignoring her feeble attempts to protect him from infection.

"You're looking nice," Lizzie said to him after he and Jane finished kissing.

"Fitzy's album drops today; he's on his thirtieth interview this morning, alone. I can't stay too long. I just wanted to drop in and see how your sister is doing," Chrome said as he noticed the paper in Lizzie's lap.

Lizzie noticed him looking at the paper, "I'm surprised he was up before noon," Lizzie said self-righteously.

"May I?" Chrome asked, as he gestured for the newspaper. Lizzie passed it to him and watched his facial reactions carefully as he read the article and looked over the pictures.

"This isn't the real Fitzy," said Chrome as he passed the paper back to Lizzie.

"Looks pretty real to me," Lizzie said as she turned her nose up at what Chrome said.

"It's all for show, just a persona that he puts out to the world. He's been rapping since he could talk; he's spent his whole life in pursuit of what he has today. You know the first thing he bought when he got his royalty cheque from his first album?"

"I don't know?" said Lizzie, who all she could think about was drugs, alcohol, women or a combination of all three.

"A house, for his mum. They grew up living in his grandma's house, sharing a room with his mother until he was sixteen. Every penny he spends is only spent after he makes sure his mum is taken care of. Have you googled him?"

"No," she said, she had tried to think about him as little as possible.

"He's a global superstar and incredibly wealthy; the only market he is yet to break is America."

These were things that Lizzie kind of knew; she had never heard of him until recently and had the view that he was someone with much wealth.

"He has a foundation which gives huge amounts of money to charities all over the UK; he did an Open University degree in marketing while he flipped burgers and we wrote his first album. He has an incredible work ethic; what you see in the papers and when he's out in public is all calculated by him, each fragrance launch or album or tour is planned out to the tee, every t-shirt he produces is planned out months in advance. He keeps a diary outlining the daily, weekly monthly and yearly goals he has. I really think that if you got to know him, he'd surprise you."

Lizzie really didn't know what to say; she sat there digesting the amount of information she had just been given. The silence was interrupted by Chrome's phone that buzzed erratically.

"Excuse me," he said as he answered the call.

Lizzie and Jane gave each other a look as they watched Chrome pace the room.

"Sorry about that," Chrome said as he sat back on the bed.

"Everything okay?" Jane asked.

"Yeah, just got offered a DJ set at a party Oprah Winfrey's throwing."

"Oh my god," said Jane who looked excited, when she heard Oprah's name and the thought of her maybe getting to meet her.

"I turned it down." He told her as her face dropped.

"Why?" asked Lizzie, she was a huge fan and couldn't

understand why anyone would turn down Oprah.

"It's the day after we get back to New York and I'd rather spend the day with you," Chrome said as he gazed into Jane's eyes.

"Aww," said Jane and Lizzie in unison.

Chrome smiled widely to their reaction, "I think I'm blushing," he told them. He looked at his watch and bolted out of the edge of the bed. "I've got to go," he told them. As he was about to lean in and kiss Jane, he turned to Lizzie. "You wanna come and see Fitzy perform later? He's going out live on a Lunch Time chat show."

Lizzie began to shake her head, although she wouldn't mind; she didn't want to fly all this way to look after her sister and abandon her for some boy.

"No, not this time," Lizzie said apologetically, "I should stay here and look after Jane," she said, smiling at her sister.

"Go," barked Jane, sounding the most well she had all morning. "I'll be fine," she told her, "I feel better already, better than I was."

"I don't know," said Lizzie who was contemplating it, but really didn't want to leave Jane.

"It will just be for a few hours, right?" Jane asked Chrome.

"Yeah, two hours, max."

"Okay," said Lizzie who didn't usually fail to peer pressure.

"Excellent, I'll send a car to pick you up in an hour." Chrome gave Jane a last kiss before leaving them alone.

"Are you sure you'll be fine?" Lizzie asked Jane, knowing full well that is was too late for her to change her mind.

"Yes, go, have fun," Jane said giggling. "Have you spoken with Mom, I can't get hold of her."

"She's at the lake house; the signal is still so inconsistent there," Lizzie told her.

"I have no idea why Dad still has that house, if you can only use your cell two percent of the time, it doesn't make sense," Said Jane.

"The views there, are beautiful," said Lizzie who would rather look over the lake than read Perez Hilton, unlike her sister.

"You'd better get ready," said Jane as she looked at Lizzie outfit.

"I am ready," said Lizzie who re-examined her outfit and was still satisfied with what she was wearing.

"Lizzie, you need to change," Jane instructed her.

"Blimey, you are feeling better," Lizzie said with a glint in her eye.

Lizzie got up and gave her sister a hug and retreated back to her room in search of an outfit that would pass the Jane test.

Lizzie managed to find something to wear, something that Jane actually thought she looked good in; she wore a lilac blouse with a tight fitting skirt that emphasised her curves. She had just finished curling her tangled hair when her car arrived.

She passed James as she got into her waiting car; he was outside in nothing but a pair of ill-fitting shorts, smoking a cigarette which he extinguished with his bare feet. Lizzie gave him a half-hearted wave as she drove off, feeling him stare at the back of her head.

"Where are we going?" Lizzie asked the driver, who greeted her by name when she exited the Georgian townhouse.

"The London Eye, Ma'am," the driver said in a charming cockney tone.

Lizzie's face lit up, the London Eye was one tourist attraction she had always wanted to see up close. She imagined herself standing in a pod, looking over London as daylight started to extinguish on a cool spring evening. It was the wrong time of the year for that to happen, she would just have to wait for the right season.

As they were stationary at a red light, the driver passed Lizzie a *'Man without fault launch event,'* Access all areas laminate that had her name and picture on it, a picture she didn't recognise and was sure it had been Photoshopped.

"We're about two minutes away," said the driver as he put the car back in gear and continued with their journey.

A huge stage stood at the base of the eye, with two large pictures of Fitzy's face either side; a large banner with *'Man without fault'* and today's date sprawled across the top of the stage, connecting the two pictures.

A large LED screen that played clips of Fitzy's music videos, pictures of his album cover and some of his quotes repeated on a loop to the large awaiting crowd. The front of the stage was full of journalists, photographers and rows of cameras, with a huge amount of cheering fans standing behind them.

The driver pulled up and pointed Lizzie in the direction of the side of the stage where there was a large congregation of security guards who were going through a small line of people also with A.A.A passes around their necks.

Lizzie got out and the car drove off; she had no idea how she was getting back or even where she and Jane were staying.

She took a slow stroll over to the side of the stage, passing dozens of excited teenage girls that wore T-shirts with Fitzy's face and replicas of his trademark white T-shirts. She was surprised by the number of older people, mostly women who were carrying banners and wearing his face on their chests.

Lizzie joined the small line that was about five people deep, she waited less than a minute to be processed. The security guard smiled as he read her name around her neck; Lizzie was too busy looking up, as the pod glided over her head.

"Thank you, Miss. Bennet," said the security guard, who waved her forward.

Lizzie didn't realise that she had gone through security; she stepped forward into a small pool of fans that surrounded the front half of the stage.

Lizzie retreated back and stood at the rear, sipping a bottle of water she took out of her purse. After ten minutes of making small talk with the other guests, who would ask her which competition she had won; Fitzy was introduced onto the stage by Chrome, who winked at Lizzie when their eyes met.

From the moment they got a glimpse of Fitzy entering the stage, the crowd erupted into deafening cheers. A startled Lizzie looked up and saw Fitzy, strutting across the stage wearing not his white T-Shirt, but a black T-shirt with his albums name in white writing.

"Who's ready to get their hands on my mother fucking new album?" Fitzy shouted into the microphone, making the crowd cheer louder than before.

He walked over to a table on the side of the stage, put his microphone in his back pocket and grabbed two stacks of CDs which he threw into the air into the excited crowd. He did this three more times, frizby-ing copies of his record as far as he could. Those that he hit with his flying CDs were excited to get their hands on it.

"Anyone get hit? Do I get anyone?" He asked the audience ecstatically.

Cheers of "Yes" and "Me" echoes through.

"Good!" he shouted at them, "You can't sue my ass; you all signed away your rights, before being let in," while laughing, again he continued to throw albums into every corner.

"Who wants to hear a song? I wanna hear you cheer before we start the music. This track is called *Censure*."

The crowd started to really increase in volume, people walking by and those in their cars directed their attention towards the mass of noise.　　　"I want everyone in London to hear the love and praise you all have for me." The music quietly started to play over the crowd, building in pace and volume. "I want the Prime Minister, across the river," Fitzy pointed over to the Houses of Parliament, "I want him to stop what he's doing, to look out his window and hear what he's missing out on. The power we have at this very moment."

Lizzie was captivated by the hold he had over the crowd; If he so wished, he could get them to march down to Westminster and burst into the Commons. They hung on every word he spoke and were hypnotised as he performed for them. All of them had their phones out, recording him and taking his picture.

His performance intensified as he fed off their energy, which in turn pumped the crowd up further. With each song he shared with them, they craved more from him, chanting his name whenever there was silence.

"What do you think?" said Chrome who appeared out of nowhere next to Lizzie.

Lizzie, who couldn't take her eyes off the stage, was surprised when she saw Chrome next to her.

"Hey," she said to him, "He's great, he really, really is," said Lizzie, not meaning to sound so surprised, "This is incredible."

"You think this is good, you should go to one of his concerts," he told her as they both watched him picking girls from the main group to come and join him on the stage.

He was joined on stage by five stunning girls who all took it in turn to receive a hug from him.

"How you bitches doing? Enjoying yourself?" he asked the excited group of fans next to him.

They were all fanning out, not believing how close they were to him. Some took it upon themselves to touch parts of his body, one going as far as grabbing his crotch and giving an exaggerated satisfied face to the crowd at large.

"Later baby, later," he told her as he ran his fingers through her long blonde hair, "My mamma is watching. She don't wanna see me nail your ass on this stage. Coz that's what's gonna happen if you keep doing that." She finally let go, after Fitzy managed to step back.

"I have one last song to share with you guys and I'm gonna sing it to one of you lovely ladies."

The five girls on the stage all looked at each other, excited and then confused.

"A little competition," he said with a glint in his eye. "If anyone has ever been to one of my concerts, you all know what's coming up!"

"Boys, set it up," he shouted out. Three stage hands ran onto the stage, one pushing a cart, with fifteen bottles of ketchup and a cup of straws, another with five hula-hoops and the last carrying five pairs of large, novelty scissors.

"You girls ready for a little competition? Not only do you get to sit on my lap while I sing my last song, but you also get this…"

A fourth stage hand came out onto the stage, carrying a huge naked picture of Fitzy, with him holding his album, barley protecting his modesty.

Fitzy took a marker pen out of his pocket and signed the picture across his chest.

"You girls wanna win what I'm offering?" he asked them; they all looked enthusiastic about the prize, but kept looking at the mini obstacle course that was laid out in the front of the stage.

"Are these girls actually gonna do this?" an astonished Lizzie asked Chrome who clapped his hands along with the crowd.

"Yeah! Why wouldn't they?" he said blaséily, "The crowd loves it, the girls get the chance to get something out of it. Each one of them thinks that if they win, they're gonna go home with him; look at the way they're looking at him. Every girl in the audience is jealous and all the guys wish it was them, standing where Fitzy is."

Lizzie looked around, Chrome was right; all the girls were smiling, but resented those on the stage.

"Girls, you stay there for a moment," Fitzy instructed them as he walked to the front of the stage. He picked up a pair of scissors and motioned them in the air above his head.

"Firstly, you girls are gonna cut off all your clothes, I want nothing left on you; as naked as you were when you came out of your mammas. Then…" he walked over to the cart, "you're gonna drink three

bottles of ketchup; you don't finish them all... you don't move on."
He held up a ketchup bottle for all the crowd to see, the photographers
started to move into the best positions, stepping over each other as
they get the best angle.

"Then ladies, I want you to do ten rotations of the hoop. Got
it?" he asked the girls standing behind him.

They all looked nervous as the realisation of what they had to
do kicked in.

"You all ready? You sure you girls wanna do this?" All five of
them nodded enthusiastically. "Give them some love," he called into
the crowd as he put the hoop around his waist and started to thrust his
hips, sending the hoop to spin around him.

"Three bottles of ketchup?" Lizzie asked Chrome in
astonishment, "They'll never drink that much!"

"You'll be surprised Lizzie. These girls are all pre-picked; all
the girls you see here are all his die-hard fans, they all stalk him on
social media, asking to spend the night with him, some even go to his
mum's house, hoping to get just a glimpse of him. These aren't just
regular fans, these are the girls that would do anything to even stand on
the same stage as him; to them, they've already won. Anything else is
just a bonus. The pictures those photographers take, are gonna travel
all around the world. It's all marketing and promotion, he created a
product that he must now sell. It's all business."

"You bitches ready?" He screamed at the girls behind him,
"Stand behind the scissors and wait for my command."

All the girls slowly walked over to the scissors as the crowd in
front of them cheered, the closer they got to them.

"Ready?" He shouted, "Go!"

Without any hesitation, all the girls began to use the scissor to
cut away their clothes; the more they removed, the louder and rowdier
the crowd got. Fitzy walked in and around them, picking up their
clothes and throwing the scraps of fabric into the crowd.

Within thirty seconds, all the girls were fully undressed, "What
you waiting for?" Fitzy screamed at them as he picked up the remainder
of their clothes and distributed them into the crowd, "Next station!"
he barked, "Move your sweet asses," he said as he watched them scuttle
across the stage to the ketchup cart.

The girls all scrambled for straws, and began to open up their bottles.

One of the girls spluttered out a mouthful of sauce across her chest, after taking her first large strawful.

"Swallow, don't spit, you dumb bitch. Get your ass off my stage," demanded Fitzy.

The girl looked at him in horror, tears rolling down her face as the crowd all chanted, "Off, off, off." He pointed to the steps down the front of the stage.

Lizzie looked appalled as she watched the young girl who must be younger than her, walk off the stage with tears in her eyes.

"Does she get clothes?" Lizzie asked a laughing Chrome.

"No," he told her bluntly, "I wanna see pictures of her in every newspaper and morning show; standing on the underground with ketchup residue down her chest as horrified commuters stare at her, as she hold her head in shame."

"This is horrible," said Lizzie who stared in disbelief.

"This is how we sell records," said Chrome who went back to watching the remaining girls drinking ketchup.

Another girl threw up and was again, banished from Fitzy's presence.

"Off, off, off," the crowd chanted as she ran off; humiliated, another girl leaving in floods of tears.

The remaining three girls, all started their second ketchup bottle within a few seconds of each other; they all pulled faces of disgust as they drank through their straws as the crowd cheered louder and clapped faster.

"Lizzie, they weren't forced onto this, they had the option to pull out before they started," Chrome said to the concerned Lizzie, that stood there mouth open.

"I know," said Lizzie.

"There will always be girls who will do anything to be near their idol or to get their fifteen minutes of fame; people these days will do anything to get the attention they crave and validation from those they admire," Chrome said sincerely to her.

"Even so, it doesn't seem right."

"Can you think of anyone who wouldn't be up on that stage if it were their idol, or if they thought they were in with a chance of sleeping with him, or if they thought this would make them famous?"

Lizzie couldn't help but think of her sister; if this was taking place in New York and they didn't know Fitzy or Chrome, she could imagine Jane standing naked on the stage, drinking ketchup through a straw while the crowd cheered her on .

Two of the girls were now starting their third bottle, both looked like they would throw up at any moment, the third girl kept stopping to hold her stomach and take deep breaths. They all seemed oblivious to the fact that they were all naked.

"If you don't finish that bottle in five seconds, you're gonna need to fuck off my stage," Fitzy told the girl who really looked like she would throw up.

As soon as Fitzy gave his threat, she showered the photographers below her with red vomit; those that weren't caught in the sick, started to take their colleague's pictures.

"Aww," said Lizzie, who couldn't help but laugh, Chrome smirked when he noticed her inability to keep a straight face.

"Don't feel sorry for them, they're all going to make a lot of money off their pictures today."

"Off, off, off," again, the crowd chanted as the third girl finished throwing up; before exiting down the steps, she threw her bottle onto the floor, causing it to smash across the stage.

She made her way back into the crowd, first trying to avoid the pieces of broken glass.

"We're down to our final two," said an excited Fitzy, as he stood behind the girls, not wanting to get caught in vomit himself.

They both finished their final ketchup bottle at the same time, they slammed them down and hand in hand, made their way to the final obstacle, the hulu-hoop; both manoeuvring themselves through the broken glass.

"The final test," said Fitzy as he handed them both a hoop and instructed the girls as they placed them around their waists.

They both started at the same time, but quickly found spinning the hoops relatively difficult with the amount of ketchup they had consumed.

"Five, six…" The crowd chanted as the girls spun in unison.

One of the girls threw up on 'Eight', all over her competition. The girl full of puke managed to finish her ten then proceeded to slap the other girl before pumping her fist in mid-air.

"We have our winner," said Fitzy who took the hand of the puke soaked girl, trying not to get vomit on his clothes.

He turned his attention to the girl that came in second, "What do we say to her, guys?" He called into the crowd.

The crowd again, chanted, "Off, off, off" as she made her way off the stage.

A stage hand entered the stage with bottles of water and a towel.

Fitzy opened two bottles and started to tip them over the girls head and body. He then took hold of the towel and faced the girl, "May I?" he asked her. She nodded her head and grinned as he patted her body dry.

"What's your name?" Fitzy asked her when he finished drying her off.

"Amanda," she said timidly and slowly into the microphone.

"Well Amanda, you're our winner. How do you feel?" Fityz asked.

"Sick," she replied as she stood beaming. A stage hand carried the picture over to her.

"This is for you," Fitzy told her.

"Can you mail it to me?" she asked.

"Sure," He said as he sat on a chair that was brought out for him to sit on.

He sat down and patted his lap for her to sit down.

"This song Amanda, is for you," He said as a slow melodic tune started to play as the crowd went silent.

"This song always makes me cry," said Chrome to Lizzie as he started to walk off. "You see that man over there," Chrome waved at a security guy by the stage entrance, "Come find him after Fitzy has performed this song."

The security guy waved back and Chrome pointed towards Lizzie and the backstage entrance, the guy put up his thumb in acknowledgement.

"I'll see you later," he said and was gone, leaving Lizzie staring up to the stage as Fitzy was actually singing, beautifully, Lizzie thought.

She listened intensely, along with the rest of the crowd as he spilled his guts about his lost love, all while staring into the eyes of the girl on his lap.

When the song was over, the crowd stayed silent for a moment before erupting into a roaring cheer and applause.

"Thank you," said Fitzy to the crowd, as he gave Amanda a kiss on the cheek.

He motioned for Amanda to get up; they stood next to each other, looking into the crowd.

"I can't let her go home like this, can I ladies and gentlemen?"

A mixture of "Yes," and "No," bounced through the crowd.

"No," said Fitzy, as he took off his left shoe, then right; before passing it to Amanda.

Lizzie watched as Fitzy slowly, item by item undressed down to his underwear and gave Amanda the clothes off his back.

The girls in the crowd made more and more noise with each garment he removed.

"Give Amanda a round of applause please," Fitzy instructed the crowd as she dressed herself in his clothes.

Fitzy pointed her off towards the side of the stage and he gave the crowd a bow.

"Man without Fault, is out today people. Tell your friends. Thank you,"

With that, Fitzy followed Amanda off the stage.

The LED screens burst into life and started to play highlights of the launch event.

Lizzie felt moved, not just by the song that brought tears to her eye, but by him stripping off and giving the poor girl his clothes.

She took one last sip of water, a deep breath and made her way to the security guard who ushered her up to the back stage area.

"Follow me," he instructed her.

He walked her past excited record executives in suites, who were ecstatic by the launch, and took her to a door with Fitzy's name on it. He gave it a knock and walked away.

Lizzie looked in amazement as she stood there, not knowing what to expect.

"I said, I didn't want to be disturbed," said Fitzy's voice from behind the door.

"You should answer it," Lizzie heard Chrome say to him.

After what sounded like huffs, the door opened.

Fitzy, wearing nothing but a towel, was holding a glass of water and looked down at Lizzie; his body was full of sweat which gave him the appearance of a glowing adonis.

"Lizzie!" said Fitzy, in astonishment. "What are you doing here? Come in, have a sit down," he told her, moving out of the way to let her pass.

"Surprise!" said Chrome as Fitzy shut the door after them.

Fitzy started to make room on the couch when Chrome stood up.

"I'm going," said Chrome as he made his way towards the door, "Have my seat. I have interviews for the rest of the day."

Lizzie looked at Fitzy, "I'm not keeping you? Do you have many more interviews to do?"

"No," he told her, "I've done all the press I need to do for this album, well, in this country."

"Onto the next stage aye," said Chrome as he opened the door to let himself out.

"You know it," said Fitzy, winking at Chrome. "Sit, please," he instructed her.

"That was incredible," said Lizzie as she sat down, trying not to look at Fitzy as he put on another white t-shirt. She tried not to look at his body, but found looking away difficult.

"Thank you," said Fitzy, who kept taking sips of water. "I had no idea you were in the crowd."

"Chrome invited me," she told him.

"I'm glad he did."

An awkward silence filled the air; Lizzie took to looking out the window, staring at a pod as it slowly passed while Fitzy finished getting changed.

"You ever been?" Fitzy asked Lizzie when he noticed her looking out the window.

"No," she said, "But, I've always wanted to."

"Let's go!" he announced, bouncing out of the chair he was seated on to tie his shoe laces.

"Now?" Lizzie asked.

"Right now," Fitzy held out his hand to help Lizzie out of her seat. "Percey!" Fitzy screamed at the top of his lungs.

Within three seconds, a geeky, curly haired man with glasses burst through the door.

"Yes, Your Fitzyness ?" he said in a deadpan manner.

"We wanna go on the Eye, get us a pod," Fitzy barked at the unflinching man, who turned around at once and closed the door after himself.

"Your Fitzyness?" Lizzie asked, confused.

"Percy lived two doors down from me growing up. He lost a bet when we were seven, and I've been, Your Fitzyness, ever since."

Lizzie let out a laugh, "that's cute," she said to him.

The door opened once more, and Percy returned.

"All ready when you are, Sir," Percy said with a straight face and without breaking eye contact with Fitzy.

"Shut the door," Fitzy barked at him.

Without breaking eye contact, Percy kicked the door shut.

Fitzy bust out into hysterics, "Gets me every time. Percy Boy, this is Lizzie Bennet. Drop the face, she's cool. She's the girl I was telling you about from New York."

Percy's face seemed to loosen instantly and when he spoke, his voice sounded completely different, "This is Lizzie, nice to meet you," he said in a really street voice.

"What you think of the launch?" Fitzy asked him.

"It was good, I'd have included the dildo swallowing section to the tasks," he said to Fitzy in a state of giggles. Lizzie turned to him then back to Fitzy.

"Like sward swallowing but…"

Lizzie cut him off. "…But with dildos, I get it," she said snappily.

"If you think what you saw was bad, it coulda been a whole lot worse. You don't even want to know the twelve other options I had written out and tested." Fitzy told her.

"Tested?" Lizzie asked.

"We test every audience participation stunt extensively" said Percy, butting in before Fitzy was able to answer. "It may look like an improvised mess, but we have doctors in the audience and at the side of the stage."

"Let's jump in the pod," said an excited Fitzy, I can't wait for you to see London from the top of the eye.

"Okay," said Lizzie, excited at the prospect of a new experience.

Fitzy's dressing room was less than fifty steps away from the pod's entrance; six security guards walked around Lizzie and Fitzy, encasing them in a secure, hiviz bubble as they got close to the public, who screamed elatedly when they realised why they were told they couldn't have the next pod.

Lizzie found the excitement that surrounded Fitzy overwhelming; she didn't know how Fitzy put up with it. She watched as he hailed to his fans, throwing copies of his CD at them, after taking a stack from his dressing room.

"Why are you giving away so many copies of your CD?" Lizzie asked as the Eye staff closed the door after them, locking them alone into the pod.

"Every one of those people who gets their hands on a free copy, are gonna use Facebook and Twitter and Instagram and tell all of their friends about it. Each CD is worth, I don't know, two hundred impressions say, if I'm using a low ball figure. They cost basically nothing to produce, it's a cheap way for me to buy ad space and target the right people." Fitzy said without taking a breath.

"Chrome said you studied marketing," Lizzie said, impressed at how well he could articulate himself.

"I'm not just a hat rack," he said, feeling his head, realising he's not wearing a hat.

He made Lizzie smile and she let out a slight giggle. She took off her jacket and placed it with her bag on the bench in the middle of the pod, starting to look out the windows as they slowly lifted through the air.

Lizzie held onto the rail the higher they got, letting out sporadic "Wows" and "Amazing," smiling the entire time. Fitzy stood to her side, taking in the view, of her as she beamed from ear to ear.

"That's Big Ben, Westminster Abbey, The Royal Albert hall," he began listing off all of the landmarks, taking her hand as he pointed them out to her. He walked her around the pod, "There's Harrods, Buckingham Palace, London Zoo, Horse guards parade," with each place he pointed out to her, her arm limpened and he held It tighter, stepping in as close as he could get.

"There's Trafalgar Square," he continued, "The British museum, The Savoy, St Pauls Cathedral, The Gerkin, The Tower of London. And If you turn around," he stepped back and spun her around.

"And there's me," he said, staring into her eyes; both of them unblinking and not moving.

He leaned in and kissed her on the lips, she stood there and kissed him back.

They leant out of their long embrace, still staring at each other, "Not a bad view at all," said Lizzie with a smile across her face.

Unknowingly, a paparazzo had snapped Lizzie and Fitzy while they were caught in a moment of passion. Using a long lens, the photographer from across the street, packed his camera back in his backpack, mounted his motorbike and sped off back to Fleet Street.

The first person in either Fitzy or Lizzie's circles to see the picture was Tabatha, who later that evening received a text message with a link to the images.

"That fucking cunt!" she screamed and threw her mobile at the photographer who was in the middle of taking her topless pictures for a magazine.

"Who does she think she is?" She asks her friend who passed her, her mobile phone. "Think she can steal him away from me," None of Tabatha's friends wanted to remind her that their relationship ended nearly two years ago.

Chapter Twelve

Benjy paced up and down a corridor at the Everfield, waiting for Charlie to finish changing in the staff dressing room. He hadn't seen or spoken to her in nearly a week; she ignored all of his calls and texts.

"This isn't a good idea," advised Franky, who stood leaning against the wall, flicking through various profiles on his dating app.

When she finally came out, accompanied by Kitty, who now had bright pink hair, Charlie froze for a split second when she spotted Benjy waiting for her.

"Not now," said Kitty who took hold of Charlie's hand, dragging her down the corridor.

"Then when?" said Benjy as he followed them, "I thought you liked me," he said in a defeated tone.

"I do like you, that's the problem," said Charlie who stopped to face him. "I can't be seen talking to you Benjy; you don't understand."

"No, I don't. I don't understand why we're not even allowed to talk to each other. We've not had sex; all we've done is share a kiss."

The thought of having sex with him, made Charlie go red. "It doesn't matter," she told him, taking hold of his hand. "Savour that kiss, Benjy Costa, that's the last kiss I'm able to give you. I'm sorry," she ran off upset, followed by Kitty who shrugged at him as she ran backwards.

"You know, there's an app called Tinder, I've never used it, but…" Franky said to an equally upset Benjy.

"..No Franky, I'm not downloading any app," said an emotional Benjy.

"I've got to go," said Franky, who suddenly and ran off without warning.

"Follow me, please," said a Welsh voice from behind Benjy.

He spun around to see Ms Powell standing behind him, looking down at him and carrying a bottle of Scotch.

"I need you to follow me, Mr. Costa," she said without blinking. She turned around and proceeded to walk down the hallway at a pace, without waiting for Benjy to keep up.

"Where are we going?" he asked her, when he managed to catch up.

"Please, keep walking," she snapped.

After walking for a few minutes, they made their way to her office door.

"After you," she told him after unlocking the door.

'Her assistant must be home, it was nearly eight in the evening,' he thought.

"Strip," she told him as soon as the door was shut and locked behind her.

"What?" he asked.

"No, no," she said, waving her long thin finger at him.

He stood there, dumbfounded.

"If you want to keep your job, you're going to start taking off your clothes," she instructed him as she set the whiskey bottle down on her assistant's desk in the windowless room.

Benjy thought about how much he needed his job and took of his coat, setting it down on the couch behind him.

When Ms. Powell was satisfied that he was following her instructions, she opened the door of her office and walked in. "Keep going, don't stop," she called at him from the next room.

Benjy proceeded to take off his clothes, item by item; until he got down to his underwear.

He took a deep breath and put his thumbs in either side of his hip and started to slowly slide them down.

"Stop, stop," she barked from behind him, "I don't want to see any of that!"

Benjy pulled his shorts back up around his waist and turned

around. In the doorway, Ms. Powell was standing there, holding a smart three-piece suit.

"This looks about your size," she told him, looking him up and down. "It's Armani," she said as she handed it to him. "Try it on."

It took him a moment to realise she was handing him a suit. "Well, take it," she told him. "It's certainly not my size," she said as she gestured him to take it from her.

Benjy was extremely confused, but glad he wasn't being forced to be wholly naked in front of her.

"Show me your work schedule," she instructed him as he took the suit from her.

Benjy placed the suit flat on the couch and rummaged through his jacket pocket, taking out a folded and crumpled piece of paper, which Ms. Powell snatched out of his hand.

She took a pen from her assistant's desk and began to cross out a number of shifts.

"Never mind what I'm doing," she told him. "Try your suit on," she continued to cross out his shifts.

"Careful, careful," she told him as he began to get dressed, "If I see one button missing, I'm taking it out of your pay packet," she warned him.

Once he was dressed, she handed him back his schedule. All of his shifts, apart from one were crossed out; he stared at it and looked at her.

"You will no longer be working with young Charlie," she instructed him.

He looked back at his schedule, "Some of these you've crossed out aren't even with her," he pleaded with her. He couldn't afford to lose so many shifts.

"I don't even want you two working in the same department," she told him.

Benjy didn't know what to say to her; what could be said to change her mind?

"I'm putting you elsewhere," she told him. "Your first duty is to deliver this to Mr. Bennet's office," she said as she handed him the bottle of whiskey; she also handed him a keycard. "Don't lose this," she warned him as he struggled to accept both.

"Off you go," she said as he looked back at his belongings,

"Collect them later," she told him as she opened the door for him, setting him on his way.

***

Mr. Bennet knew that he couldn't keep ignoring Collin; all day, he had inundated his and Charlotte's phones, relentlessly calling, trying to arrange an appointment.

Mr. Bennet finally answered his call while having his evening drink at the Pemberly; he let Collin do all the talking, which resulted in him inviting himself over to the hotel.

"Busy day, Dodger?" said the annoying voice of Collin, a voice that made Mr. Bennet's skin crawl.

"You have no idea," Mr. Bennet said, without looking back; pulling a face at the name Collin called him.

"Any chance of a drink?" he demanded of Mr. Bennet, before he sat down.

Mr. Bennet looked around the Pemberly in search of Franky, who he spotted on his phone behind the bar.

"Franky," Mr. Bennet called out to no avail. "For God's sake," he muttered under his breath.

"Staffing issues?" Collin joked as Mr. Bennet failed to get Franky's attention.

"Franky!" Mr. Bennet called louder. Franky this time looked up from his screen and made a half-hearted attempt to look around the bar, before returning his gaze to his phone once more.

"Idiotic faggot," Mr. Bennet muttered as he lifted up his glass and hurtled it through the air, sending it in Franky's direction, hitting the mirror behind the bar, just inches away from his head.

Franky dropped his phone and let out a scream of fright.

"Do your fucking job," Mr. Bennet shouted out, as other guests in the Pemberly and those in the entrance hall, looked around for the cause of the commotion. "Let's move this to my office," Mr. Bennet told Collin as he slowly got out of his chair; giving Collin no chance but to agree and follow him.

"Clean up this fucking mess," Mr. Bennet demanded of Franky as he walked by, without stopping.

Mr. Bennet and Collin walked out of the Pemberly and across

the hotel's lobby, past workmen coming and going, in and out of the Ballroom. As Mr. Bennet and Collin stepped into the elevator, Mr. Bennet reached into his pocket and took out a small pill bottle, uncapping the top and emptied five pills into the palm of his hand.

"Indigestion," Mr. Bennet told Collin, who stared at what he was doing.

"Of course," said Collin who watched him swallow his handful of pills.

The lift doors burst open and Collin followed Mr. Bennet, who marched at speed, down the corridor towards his office.

Charlotte was seated on the sofa in his office, when Mr. Bennet walked in.

"I need the room," Mr. Bennet snapped at her.

She packed up her notepad and swiftly exited, thinking what item she could take for being spoken to in such a way. There was a pair of pearl earrings he had given his wife, on their anniversary last year; she would take those she thought, as she shut the door with force, behind her.

Mr. Bennet walked around his desk and sat down in his large leather chair with a thud, almost buckling the pistol that allowed the chair to change height.

"So," Mr. Bennet said as he sat back, surveying Collin who stood before him, "Take a seat,"

"I'll stand," Collin told him, looking down at him, a smile appearing across his face.

"What is it?" Mr. Bennet asked him, "Spit it out."

Collin took a moment before saying anything, looking down at Mr. Bennet then around his office.

"It's a beautiful office," Collin said, finally breaking the cold silence in the room.

"Out with it," Mr. Bennet spat at him, getting more and more impatient.

"It's over Art, you're done," Collin said slowly and deliberately.

"What are you talking about?" Mr. Bennet demanded of him.

"This office, this hotel, your life," Collin said in a hushed tone as he slowly walked around the room, looking at the pictures that covered the office walls.

"I'm calling in your debt," Collin said from across the room, barley loud enough for Mr. Bennet to hear.

"You're what?" he demanded of him.

"Calling in your debt," Collin said, this time louder and clearer, like he were speaking to an infant. "It's clear that selling off suites and apartments here is your feeble attempt to raise capital, but it's not going to be enough."

Mr. Bennet was looking at his movements intensely as he sat there, thinking in silence.

"There is two months left," Mr. Bennet told him in a hushed tone.

"What's two months?" Collin told him, walking towards him, "It's over. You stupidly used your hotel as collateral. This is going to be my bondage room, I think," Collin joked as he looked around the room.

There was a knock on the door. Benjy was standing on the other side, holding a bottle of whiskey to deliver to Mr. Bennet.

"Not now," Mr. Bennet screamed at the door, not caring who was standing on the other side.

Benjy could just about make out what Mr. Bennet shouted in his direction; as he turned around, he was confronted by Mrs. Bennet who stood before him.

'Hello," he said to her, not hearing her walk up behind him.

"Is that for my husband?" she asked, taking in deep breaths, holding her stomach.

"Yes," said Benjy, taking a step back, worried that Mrs. Bennet may vomit over him at any moment.

"I'll take it," she told him, holding out her hand to receive the bottle.

Benjy handed her the bottle and hurried back down the corridor; he could hear Mr. Bennet's office door open from behind him, and muffled shouting from behind the door.

"Oh, it's you," Mr. Bennet said when he realised it was his wife who came in through the door.

"Some boy left this for you," she told him, waiving the bottle in the air, as Mr. Bennet got up to greet his wife.

"Hello, Collin dear," Mrs. Bennet said when she realised her husband wasn't alone.

Mr. Bennet kissed his wife and took the bottle from her.

"Collin was just leaving," Mr. Bennet told his wife as he

forcefully placed the bottle on his desk.

"Oh, really," she said glumly as she held on to her stomach; she had no colour in her face and did her best to stand up straight.

"Are you okay dear?" Mr. Bennet asked his wife, walking over to her side and put his arm around her.

"Yes, yes. I'm fine," releasing herself from him, "I ate some bad chowder."

"Collin, we'll speak soon," Mr. Bennet called over the room, prompting him to leave.

"How about tomorrow?" Mrs. Bennet sparked up, "Jane and Lizzie return tomorrow, from London. We're having a little gathering in the ballroom."

"We are?" said Mr. Bennet, the first he'd heard of these plans.

"I will be around," said Collin. "I'm actually thinking of acquiring an apartment or two that your husband is offloading."

Mrs. Bennet didn't quite know how to respond; she had a soft spot for Collin; dating back years, when he informed her of the affair her husband was having with his mother. So, she wouldn't mind Collin owning part of the Everfield; on the other hand, she loathed the large for sale sign that hung over her home.

"Excellent," said Mrs. Bennet, grinning through the pain.

"Your darling husband, is letting me stay here for free, to see what I think of the Everfield way of life," he told her, shooting Mr. Bennet a wink when she wasn't looking. "I'll get one of my assistants to ring, to arrange delivery of the keys," he told Mr. Bennet as he slowly made his way to the door.

Mr. Bennet's neck and face turned red with rage, Collin left his office before he had a chance to say anything.

"I'm going to be sick," Mrs. Bennet told her husband as she ran off to his adjoining bathroom. She almost made the toilet before covering the floor with vomit, "Call a maid," Mrs. Bennet called out to her husband who was sat back at his desk; emptying the contents of his pill bottle, washing it down with a swig of the Whiskey on his desk.

Chapter Thirteen

"Where are all the staff?" asked Benjy as he took a case of Champagne from Franky, who passed it over the bar in the Ballroom; he looked around at how few of them there were.

"A Lady Gaga concert," Franky sneered through his teeth. He too had tickets, but had to give them up to work this impromptu homecoming party.

Franky looked up at the clock; the party is due to start in thirty minutes; already, people are waiting outside the doors to come in.

"Hurry up," Franky shouted out at a girl who was carrying a box of glasses, he mimicked pointing at his watch.

Franky and Benjy placed the bottles into the blast chiller, while the three other members of the bar restocked the bar and polished glasses.

"Sorry I'm late," Charlie said to Franky, ignoring Benjy and throwing her jacket under the cash register. She took an apron that Franky held out on his finger then ran off to dry the drink trays.

"What's she doing here?" Benjy asked him, "We're not allowed to work together."

"I was desperate," he told him, "There was no one else I could call. Don't think of this as some kind of reunion, she's not going to speak with you," Franky warned Benjy.

The final thirty minutes passed with the speed; the DJ started to play music dead on eight o'clock, irrelevant as to whether the bar staff where ready or not. Security opened the door and began to let the guests in.

Charlie and another girl stood at the door, each holding a tray of champagne glasses for the guests' arrival.

"I'm going to say something," Benjy told Franky in a hushed whisper, from the side of his mouth as he poured a whiskey sour.

"Just leave it. Her mom's worked here all her life; she got you moved, you're not gonna win this one. Try your luck with someone else," Franky bluntly told him.

"Listen to your queer friend," said an old woman at the bar, who was listening to their conversation intently as she fed the dog she held, peanuts from a bowl on the bar.

"I really like her," Benjy told her .

"I really liked my third husband," she told him.

"But?" Benjy prompted her to continue.

"He had eyes for someone else. Life isn't fair young man, your generation needs to learn that; happy ever afters only exist in the story books. Sometimes it works out, most of the time, it doesn't."

"I'm not being given the chance to get to know her," he told her as she placed her finger in her glass to give her dog a drip on his tongue.

"I wasn't given the chance to know my parents," she said, cradling her dog in her arm as she walked off, with her drink.

"Auschwitz," Franky whispered when she was far enough away, as to not over hear him.

Mr and Mrs. Bennet arrived to the hastily organised small gathering, followed by Max who stood awkwardly in his suit.

"Stand up straight," Mrs. Bennet snapped at him as she looked over her shoulder to make sure he had kept up with them.

"Thank you my dear," Mr. Bennet said to Charlie as he passed his wife and son a glass of champagne from her tray; he stood back as they continued into the ballroom.

"You see my son," he said to Charlie and the girl standing on the other side of the entrance door, "that's his last glass," he sternly warned them, before taking a glass for himself and re-joining them.

Mrs. Bennet sipped slowly from her glass, holding onto her husband's hand as they walked to a table across the dance floor. Max downed the last of his glass at the sight of them hand in hand.

"Are you okay?" Mr. Bennet asked his wife.

"Have you taken anything for it?" he took out a bottle of medication and offered it to his wife.

"No," I'll be fine," she told him, "I'll just go and take a seat."

She let go of his hand and made her way to a table and sit down; Mr. Bennet looked around the ballroom for his son, who he noticed was standing at the bar.

Benjy was just about to hand him a drink, when Mr. Bennet reached over Max's shoulder and took the glass, swallowing its contents in one go, before Max even turned around.

"Hey!" Max said to his father, after turning around and seeing who stole his drink.

"I warned you," Mr. Bennet said, prompting Max to storm off and re-join his mother at her table.

"He's cut off," Mr. Bennet told the boys behind the bar, "Franky, I shit you not, if I see him with a drink in his hand, your fired."

Mr. Bennet made his way around the ballroom, thanking guests for coming to a party he had no intention of throwing. He kept repeating lines of, "She's much better now," and "It was touch and go for a while," to those who asked how Jane was feeling. In reality, "She just had the fucking flu," was the respond he would have liked to tell people.

After circulating the room twice and consuming a fistful of pills on each rotation, he returned to his wife and son's table.

"There's no use," he stared down at Max as he reached them; forcing them to break off their intense looking conversation, "Annalise, he's not having another drink," he told his wife, without room for compromise.

"Dad, I've had one glass," Max pleaded.

"And, that's all you're going to have. You're passing your weekly drugs tests, which is great, son. Now, I don't want you to slip back into old habits. I do it because I care," Mr. Bennet sat down and moved his wife's half-drunk champagne glass closer to her and away from Max's immediate reach.

Max sat back in his seat and took out his phone, exiting from any further discussion.

Charlotte appeared out of nowhere and leaned in, next to Mr. Bennet. "The girls are back and just getting dressed," she told him;

wearing the earrings she recently took from his wife; neither he nor Mrs. Bennet noticed the large pearls that punctuated her earlobes.

"Hello, Max," Charlotte said when she realised he was sat next to her boss, "I didn't see you there, how's Los Angeles?" she asked him.

"Hot," he replied without looking up from his cell phone.

"Let me know, when they're in the elevator," Mrs. Bennet told Charlotte, prompting her to leave their table.

Mr. Bennet looked around the ballroom as more and more people continued to appear through the entrance door.

"For fuck sake, a small gathering you said," to his wife.

"We're celebrating your daughter's safe homecoming," Mrs. Bennet said as her head pounded with each word she spoke.

"She was ill in London, not fighting Extremists in the Middle-East," he snarled, "Get a grip," he snapped.

Max looked up and shot his father a disapproving look; Mr. Bennet looked right through his son when he noticed James appear, behind his shoulder.

He got up and headed straight for him.

"How's Jane?" he asked James, startling James, who couldn't remember ever speaking to Mr. Bennet.

"Yeah, she's fine, all better," he told him.

"I knew she was fine," he snapped at him, as if it had been James who was telling people she was removing from the plague.

"Mr. Bennet," James called, as he began to walk away.

"What is it?"

"Can I get an interview with you, for the show?" James asked Mr. Bennet, who looked annoyed at being called back.

He responded with a look of distaste, before continuing to walk away.

"Well, fuck you too," James said as he snatched a glass of champagne from Charlie's tray and making his way to the bathroom.

He locked the door behind him after making sure he was alone and wouldn't be disturbed.

James took off his left shoe and retrieved a small bag containing cocaine; he emptied the bags contents onto the marble surface next to the basin and turned the large pile of white powder into three fat lines which he snorted in quick succession.

"Wow," he said to himself as he felt every hair on his body stand on end. He stood looking into the mirror, as the drugs began to take effect.

"Hurry the fuck up," he heard someone shout and bang loudly on the door, "Why is this locked?"

Mrs. Bennet thumped impatiently on the door, fearing if she attempted to go to another bathroom, she may throw up on route. "Who the fuck is in here?" she demanded, as those close to her all looked away as she stared around for an answer.

She spotted her husband pouring the contents of his pill bottle down his throat, she ought to speak to him about the amount of pills he was taking, but had other things to worry about at present.

James finally unlocked the door and slowly opened it up. Mrs. Bennet knocked him flying as she rushed past him, not stopping to see if he sustained any injuries.

"Fucking oaf," she shouted back as she entered a cubical.

James could hear her vomit as he managed to let himself up and re-joined the party.

He took his camera out of his rucksack and began to record, not realising the cap was still on, and all he was capturing was the noise around him.

When Max looked up from his phone and realised his parents where no longer seated with him, he reached over and drank the remnants of his mother's drink, before looking at the neighbouring tables for any glasses left unattended.

He saw Charlie coming in his direction; she was carrying one final glass of champagne on her tray. He stood up just as she was about to pass him.

"Thank you darlin'," he said, reaching for the final glass.

"No," she told him, stepping back and moving the tray out of his reach.

"What are you doing?" he demanded of her, taking a step closer to her as she moved the tray again, out of his way; she twisted her body with the tray at shoulder height, almost behind her head.

Max continued to reach for it, grabbing Charlie's wrist to try and retrieve the drink he desired

Benjy, who had been keeping an eye on Charlie all evening; spending more time looking for her through the crowd than he had fixing drinks, happened to look over at her and saw Max attached to her wrist, seeing she was in distress and pain.

He lifted himself over the bar, and began to run to her defence. He sent Max and the tray flying as he tackled him to the ground.

Mr. Bennet, who heard Charlie's nearby yelp of pain; also came to her aid, more to diffuse the situation. He held out his hand for Benjy and let his son get back on his own two feet. "Sorry about that," Mr. Bennet said to Charlie, he saw her holding onto her wrist. He reached into his pocket and threw the half a dozen hundred dollar bills he had, onto her tray. "Why don't you shoot off home, we'll pay you for the rest of the night," he reassured her; tears were running down her face.

Mr. Bennet grabbed hold of his son's arm and dragged him off the dance floor, thankfully not many people saw what had happened.

"What are you playing at?" he demanded of Max, who shrugged his shoulders. "I know you weren't born retarded, I made sure before we took you home."

"Dad, chill, I just wanted another glass."

When they reached their table, Mr. Bennet pushed his son into his chair.

"Where's your mother?" he demanded, his face going red, "Sit here until she gets back."

Charlotte came to Mr. Bennet's side, "Lizzie and Jane are three minutes away," she instructed him; before she was able to finish what she was saying, she found her boss's hands on her, forcing her into the seat next to Max.

"Watch him," he sneered at her, "He's not to have anything else to drink."

Without waiting for her to acknowledge him, he walked off, in search of his wife.

Charlie let Benjy walk her back to the bar, saying nothing in the twenty steps it took.

"Are you okay?" Franky asked when they returned.

"Yeah, I'm fine," she said as she continued to hold onto her wrist.

"Does it hurt?"

"What do you think?" she said to him bluntly.

She uncovered her wrist and the three of them looked down at how red her skin was.

"I'm going home," she told them as she put the money Mr.

Bennet had given her, into her pocket.

"Are you still here?" Mr. Bennet said to her as he walked past them, still looking for his wife, "Tell Michael you can use my car, a driver will take you home." Without stopping, he continued to circle the ballroom.

***

"This reminds me of a poor man's Ritz," said Tabatha as she rode down in the elevator with Chrome, Fitzy and Collin.

"I like it," said Fitzy, who once again, was wearing a white t-shirt with an offensive slogan across his chest.

"It needs a lot of work," Collin told them as he looked at the gold detail inside their moving elevator. Tabatha smiled at him as he continued to scrutinise every inch.

"Jane's looking a lot better, isn't she? The moment we landed, she seemed to regain her complexion," Chrome tried to make conversation.

"Lizzie, was quiet during the flight," Tabatha said, "What's up with her?" She asked the group, looking at Fitzy in particular.

"I knew something was up. You saw the pictures, then?" Chrome asked her sister.

"What pictures?" Tabatha lied.

"Of Fitzy kissing Lizzie," Chrome told her, knowing full well she had seen them.

"You kissed Lizzie?" asked Collin, who seemed to awaken from sleeping when he heard Lizzie's name.

"At my album launch; It was nothing, we've not even spoken since," said Fitzy, as he diverted his eyes around the elevator.

"We could one day be related," joked Chrome, "Me and Jane, you and Lizzie," he nudged Fitzy in the ribs to punctuate his point.

"We were once engaged," Tabatha said condescendingly to her brother as she pointed to herself and Fitzy. She avoided looking at Fitzy; deep down she was still bitter that he broke off their relationship.

The awkward silence was broken with the ringing of a cell phone; all four of the elevator's occupants began to pat their bodies in search of the buzzing cellphone's owner.

"It's mine," called out Collin, prompting them to stop searching their pockets and bag, as the elevator doors opened up.

Everyone entered the lobby, except Fitzy who remained inside.

"I'll just be a sec," he told them as Chrome and Tabatha stared in at him, Collin had vanished into the crowd that littered the lobby. "I've forgotten my phone," he informed them and pressed the button for his floor. The doors began to slowly close, separating them.

"Don't be long," said Tabatha just in time, before the door shut.

***

As the Bentley driving Charlie home pulled up outside her house, she could see her mother was still up; the living room light was still on.

"Thank you," she said to the driver, who opened her door to let her out.

She waited for his car to drive away before opening the rusty gate and walking up the cracked garden path.

She reached into her pocket to retrieve her key; just as she was about to slide it into the lock, the door swung open, revealing the silhouette of her mother standing before her.

"Were have you been?" she demanded, before letting Charlie take a step into the house.

"I had work," said Charlie as she tried to slide past, her mother blocking her from entering, clearly she wanted to hash things out before letting her in.

"Work? Or seeing that boy? You finished work nearly three hours ago!" her voice raised and arms folded; her Columbian accent billowed down the street, Charlie could hear the voices of children, who she assumed were laughing at her expense.

"Get your ass in the house," her mother told her, barely making room for her to get past.

"I thought you got yourself kidnapped or raped," she yelled up at Charlie who made her way up the stairs, "damn this girl," she said under her breath, as she bolted and chained the front door.

Chapter Fourteen

Jane headed straight for the bar on entering the ballroom; doing three shots of half black Sambuca and Tequila rose, before re-joining Lizzie with a vodka red bull.

Lizzie had found her brother and father at their table when Jane joined them.

"How are you?" Mr. Bennet asked Jane as she sat down next to her brother.

"Fine," she told him, raising her glass to prove so, "Like nothing ever happened,"

She put her arm around Max, "You're a sight for sore eyes," she told him as he hugged her back.

"Look, my three babies, all together," said Mrs. Bennet's drawn out voice as she returned to the table. She took her cell out of her purse and snapped a photo of them.

"You should put that on Instagram," Jane said to her as she sipped her drink; Max was smelling the vodka, but conscious both his parents were looking down at him.

"Where have you been?" Mr. Bennet demanded of his wife, as he leaned in to kiss her cheek.

"Throwing up, you arse," she said, kissing his other cheek, as not to let her children hear.

"Girls, you enjoy London?" Mrs. Bennet asked, turning her attention to her children.

"All I basically saw was Heathrow," said an annoyed Jane, "Lizzie got to see some sights tho'," Lizzie started to go red when Jane winked at her.

"Good, dear, good," said a distracted Mrs. Bennet who spotted Collin put his cell phone away and walk in their direction.

"Collin, over here," Mrs. Bennet called over to him.

"What are you doing?" Mr. Bennet asked his wife.

He leaned in and gave her a kiss on both cheeks.

"Do you remember my kids?" she asked him.

"Of course, Maxaimilan," he said, reaching in and shaking Max's hand. "Jane," he kissed her on the hand, "and Lizzie." He stood before her for a moment, Lizzie expected some kind of gesture but it didn't come.

"Forgive me," he finally said to her, "You look stunning, but there's something not quite right with your outfit," he said as Lizzie's face dropped and her entire family stared at him for an explanation.

"Let me see your outfit," he demanded of her. He reached out his hand which she reluctantly took and gently pulled her forward. She stood a few feet away from her family and in the open corner of the dance floor, still attached to Collins hand.

"Trust me," Collin whispered to her as he raised their hands above her hand and slowly started to spin her, getting faster and faster.

As she spun, she started to feel her dress get warmer. Black smoke began to seep from under her second hand, floral dress. She spun faster and faster as the smoke got thicker and blacker; it was beginning to attract the attention of everyone in the ballroom.

Collin kept staring at her, unblinking and concentrating on her fully. He closed his eyes and the smoke covered Lizzie fell to the ground.

Mr. Bennet began to run to her aid, but Collin kept him back.

The smoke slowly started to clear, and standing before them was Lizzie; wearing a sleek gold dress with six inch heels. Her hair was now up and had a garden of wild flowers, woven through.

"Open your eyes," Collin instructed to her as she stood before everyone with her eyes and mouth closed.

Lizzie slowly opened her eyes and found the entire room staring at her; she looked down at her dress. Collin reached in and kissed her, she stood there without pulling away and kissed him back. Over her shoulder she could see Fitzy standing alone in the ballroom entrance, like everyone else, watching what was happening. In his hand, he was holding a bouquet of flowers which he dropped as they made eye-contact; he turned around and left the party without fully entering.

"What happened?" she asked as she took a step back looking back at Jane, who's face dropped; she too had seen Fitzy in the door way.

"Magic," Collin told her before taking a bow. The entire room burst into applause, patting him on the back as he made his way to the bar.

Lizzie returned to her family who all stared at her with their mouths open.

"How did he do that?" Jane asked as she looked around for James, hoping he captured it and wishing it was her.

"I don't know," said Lizzie who was still grinning from ear to ear, but still couldn't get over the way Fitzy looked at her.

"You were beautiful before," said Mr. Bennet to his daughter.

"How do I look now?" she asked him, uninterested in his answer.

"Nothing has changed, excuse me," he told her before rushing off.

"Is he okay?" Lizzie asked Mrs. Bennet.

"You know your father, he's probably worrying what the smoke is doing to the extractor fans," she sneered.

Tabatha and Chrome made their way to the Bennets.

"That was quite a sight," said Tabatha as she stood there with two glasses of champagne, sipping from both in turn; her arms would have been folded if her hands were free.

"Who wants a drink?" Lizzie asked, looking back at her siblings.

Jane and Max both stood up and walked to their sister's side.

"I'll be back in a second," Jane told Chrome; they kissed before she left.

Chrome and Tabatha took a seat next to Mrs. Bennet.

"You must be Chrome," she told him, looking him up and down.

"Yip," he put out his hand to shake, which she blankly stared at.

"You're much darker than I imagined you'd be," she told him.

Tabatha stared at her in disbelief, mouth opened and about to say something when Chrome began to laugh.

"Maybe it's the dark room," he told her.

"Maybe," she said, reaching back for her glass, "Max!" she muttered when she discovered it was empty.

"Your daughter is really talented, Mrs. Bennet," he told her trying to fill the silence as she looked down at her empty glass. "I can't wait to make some great music with her, one day," he said with a smile across his face.

"Maybe you could make more than music," she said with a smirk.

"I don't follow," he said, looking puzzled.

"I've always wanted a grandchild," she told him, playing on her years of making people feel uncomfortable. "Now are her good egg years, you need to poach them before they're scrambled. Saying that, my river is yet to run dry."

Tabatha began to laugh when she heard Chrome give a nervous laugh and realised the look of terror on her brother's face.

"Jane must be a special girl," said Tabatha as she shifted her body to face Mrs. Bennet.

"She is," Mrs. Bennet told her.

"This is the longest I've seen this one…" she nudged her brother, making sure he was included in the conversation and hearing every word, "…sticking to the same girl," she continued, "It must be getting serious!"

"I think it is," Mrs. Bennet agreed with her, "Jane really seems to like you, Mr… Chrome."

The three of them began to search the room, from their seats for Jane, who they spotted speaking to a group of well-dressed men who all wanted to speak with her. She played up to the attention and laughed along with them.

"She's very popular," said Tabatha who handed one of her glasses to Mrs. Bennet.

"Thanks," she said, "She is, always has been; takes after me in that sense," as she looked out for her other two children.

Lizzie and Max were on their way back from the bar; Lizzie was allowing Max to take sips of her drink, unsubtly. Mrs. Bennet hoped her husband wasn't looking in their direction; instead he was lingering over her shoulder.

"Dear, would you give me a hand with something?" he asked his wife who jumped when she heard his booming voice from behind her.

"Excuse me," said Mrs. Bennet, who took her husband's hand and walked away from their table.

Lizzie was stopped by Collin on her way back to her table; Max left them alone when he got Lizzie's drink out of her hand. They began to walk together, ending up at the ballroom's entrance where Fitzy's flowers still stood on the floor.

Collin picked them up, and began to read the attached card.

"They're for you," he told her as he handed them over.

She knew who they were from without even opening the card, "they're from Fitzy," she said as she put the card back in the envelope.

Collin walked her over to The Pemberly. "Much quieter here," she told him as she pulled back a stool at the bar for her.

She put the bouquet on the bar next to her.

"They look expensive," he told her as he took a better look at the flowers. "Two chardonnays," he instructed the barman.

"He's not exactly a poor man," she told him.

"No, he's certainly not a poor man," Collin sneered.

Lizzie turned to look at him, "What's with the tone?"

"He didn't exactly make his money, the old fashion way."

"He's a musician; he created a product that people wanted to buy."

"That's not what I mean," he told her. She could tell he was trying to choose his words carefully.

"What, do you know about his business? His record label?" Collin asked her.

"Not much, why? He and Chrome are business partners and also make music together."

"Yes… I want to warn you Lizzie, I know you and him have been spending some time together."

"Warn me about what?" Lizzie asked him, not noticing the bar man place a glass of wine in front of her.

"He's a crook; for all I know they both are. He stole from his investors, doing dirty deals under the table to get their American operations running."

"You're lying" she told him, "Why would you say that?"

"I'm not lying," he said, taking a sip of wine.

"Prove it, you expect me to just walk up to him and say, are you a crook who stole from your investors?"

"No," he told her, "ask your father."

"My father? What's he got to do with all this?" She demanded of him, hushing her tone as to not let anyone overhear what they were talking about.

"Well, your father was stupid enough to get caught up in his lies and lost all his money," Collin said without taking a breath and looked her dead in the eyes.

"You're lying," she shouted.

The guest around her began to look over at her.

"Why is he selling off part of this hotel? Go on, ask him. Ask your father if he's broke or not," Collin got up and placed a fifty on the bar. "I'm sorry to be the one to tell you this," he said before leaving her at the bar alone.

She watched as he left the Pemberly and headed out into the cool New York night.

Lizzie stood there for a moment; trying to digest the information she had just been fed. She lifted the wine in front of her, drinking it in one and marched out of the Pemberly across the lobby and back into the Ballroom.

Lizzie looked around the room and saw her father snatch a glass out of her brother's hand. She headed straight of him, ignoring all the guests who wished to speak with her.

"Dad, can I have a word?" she asked him.

"Did you give this to your brother?" he asked, holding up a glass.

"What?" she said, trying to concentrate on what he was saying.

"A drink, did you give your brother a drink. I knew letting you have one would be a bad idea," He said to Max.

"Dad, I need to speak with you," she demanded.

"Out of my sight," he scolded his son, who shot away immediately, "Lizzie, is everything okay?" She looked upset.

"Not here," she said as she took her father's hand and let him through the ballroom and into the kitchens.

She turned on the light and they ended up in the same spot in the kitchen that her mother and brother stood during the last time the Bennets used the ballroom.

"Lizzie, what's the matter?" he demanded of her, getting annoyed as the anticipation built.

"Are we broke?" she blurted out, she can't believe what she's saying.

'Where did you hear that?" he demanded of her.

"Dad? Is it true?"

"No, don't be silly," he told her.

"You're lying," she said to him, "I always know when you are."

Mr. Bennet stood there speechless, unable to look at his daughter.

"Does mom know?" she asked.

"No," he demanded, "And she can't find out. You can't say anything to her. Promise me, Lizzie." He pleaded with her. "I'm fixing it."

The kitchen door bust open and in flew Max, pulling his mother by the hand and holding a bottle of Tequila in the other.

"Not tonight, I'm not feeling well." Mrs. Bennet could be heard saying, as their voices echoed around the kitchen.

Mr. Bennet and Lizzie stepped out from the shadows and presented themselves to them.

"What the fuck is going on?" Mr. Bennet demanded of his wife and son, who stood frozen.

Mrs. Bennet looked at Lizzie, who looked upset, to her son and husband.

"Tequila," she murmured.

"What?" he demanded.

"Tequila," she repeated, pointing to the bottle in Max's other hand; they broke off their hand holding when they realised they weren't alone.

"Are you crazy?" Mr. Bennet asked his wife.

She didn't know what to say, no words seemed to form when she tried to explain their actions.

"You two, go back to the ballroom," Mr. Bennet demanded of his children. Max didn't need asking twice and shot back through the door he entered. "You too, Lizzie. We'll talk tomorrow," he told her, giving her a kiss on the cheek. She slowly walked her way out of the kitchen and left her parents alone.

Mr. Bennet took a step towards his wife and slapped her across the cheek. The sound echoed throughout the entire kitchen.

"Are you trying to ruin everything?" he asked her, "The last thing I need is for him to fall off the waggon."

Mr. Bennet reached into his pocket and retrieved his white pill bottle, taking out the remaining two which he swallowed while staring at his wife; a red mark slowly appeared across her face.

"Get back to the suite," he demanded of her. She stood still, arms folded. "I'll tell the kids you're not feeling well."

He moved out of her way to let her pass. She took a step forward and stopped infront of him; turning to face him, she stood looking into his face for a moment.

Without any hesitation, she spat at him, covering his face before ending her night.

He waited for her to leave before taking out his handkerchief and wiping his face dry.

Chapter Fifteen

It was past eleven and Charlie was still laying in bed; the smell of cooked bacon wafted through the house and became her motivation to get out of bed .

When she finally retreated from her comfy sanctuary, she noticed a dark purple bruise on her wrist; it no longer hurt but looked a lot worse than it was.

"Oh crap," she said as she frantically looked for a shirt long enough to cover it.

"Charlie, get your butt downstairs," she heard her mother call up to her.

"I'm coming," she yelled, as she continued to search for something to wear.

As a last resort, she grabbed a long sleeved sweater that hung off her closet door and hastily put it on as she clambered down the narrow, poorly lit stairs.

"What time do you call this?" her mother exclaimed as Charlie entered the kitchen and took her seat at the table.

"I heard that that boy was working last night too," her mother said as she turned around with a bacon sandwich on a plate for her, placing it down on the table in front of her.

"I didn't know he'd be there," said Charlie as she bit into her late breakfast. Pools of sweat began to pool around her temple. The kitchen was stifling and she was wearing a thick woollen sweater.

"Unlikely story," said her mother, unconvinced in her story, as she sat down in the seat opposite her, cradling a cup of coffee in a chipped, Everfield Hotel mug.

"I was called in last minute, Franky asked me to help out," pleaded Charlie, wishing her mother would believe.

"I'm gonna have words with that queer boy," she said as she began to study Charlie and noticed how red in the face she was beginning to look. "What you wearing a sweater in the house for? It's not winter."

"I'm cold," said Charlie as she took another bite of her sandwich.

"Take it off," she instructed Charlie.

"I will when I shower," said Charlie who tried to say it as calmly as she could, not wanting it to be a big deal.

"I'm not having you pass out in front of me, take off the damn sweater."

Charlie put down her sandwich and looked up at her mother, staring off with her.

"I'm not gonna ask you a third time."

Charlie wiped her hands on a napkin and began to pull off her sweater.

Her mother gasped, spilled her coffee all over the table when she noticed her wrist.

"I knew something wasn't right," she bellowed at the top of her lungs.

"It was that boy, wasn't it? Wouldn't he take no for an answer?" She grabbed Charlie's wrist from across the table for a closer inspection.

"Wait 'till I get my hands on him, I'm gonna hack off his testicles with this butter knife," she said picking the knife off the kitchen table and stabbing the butter repeatedly.

Charlie began to cry, she found herself unable to communicate with her mother, no matter how hard she tried, words simply refused to leave her mouth.

Her mother picked up her wall phone, almost yanking the cord out of the receiver and began thumping the numbers with her stubby fingers.

"I'm gonna get him fired," she yelled, still dialling the phone. "The next call I'm making is to the police."

"It wasn't him, he had nothing to do with it," Charlie managed to blurt out through bouts of tears. Charlie could hear the phone ringing as her mother stood before her, hand on hip, phone inches away from her ear, waiting for the call to be answered.

The phone continued to ring as Charlie stood up in front of her mother, tears rolling down her face.

***

Chrome woke up to three missed calls and half a dozen texts from Jane; he left his phone on the bedside table as he showered and packed an overnight bag.

As he began to dial a cab, again Jane started to ring him. He threw his phone down onto the bed and left his room. After the party last night, he stayed in Collin's suite, as did Tabatha and Fitzy. He threw his small bag over his shoulder and shut the door behind him, as to not wake anyone up.

He made his way through the Everfield's hallways and down the stairs, to reduce his chances of bumping into anyone.

As he lay in bed last night, he began to think about himself and Jane; things had been moving fast, too fast for his liking. Although he didn't treat women unkindly, he was a one night stand kind of guy; the last time he had a serious girlfriend, he was seventeen. He had spent the last ten years, concentrating purely on his music and business, and didn't really see the point in changing any of it; he had become successful in things being the way they were.

He made his way into the service hallway, hoping no member of staff would ask what he was doing being in a restricted area. Most of the staff knew his association with the family and averted their eyes when they saw him walking towards them.

He stepped into the deliveries entrance and as he turned the corner onto the side street, he felt what felt like a punch to the chest. He looked down and saw Lizzie standing before him, in her running gear; she had been listening to music and bumped into him.

"Sorry," she said instinctively, before looking up at who she ran into.

"Lizzie," he said looking down at her, "sorry he said," knowing it was her fault for running blindly around a corner.

"Are you leaving?" she asked.

He started to wave for a taxi, with his back to the wall and Lizzie standing in front of him.

"For a day or two, yeah," he said as a taxi swerved across the road and pulled up beside them. "Just L.A for a few days," he said to her as he took his bag off his shoulder and slid past her towards the waiting car. "I have a DJ set," he told her, not really interested in talking to her.

"The Oprah gig?" She asked.

"Yeah," impressed she remembered them talking about it.

"Ohh, okay," she said, moving out of his way to let him enter his car, "See you soon," she said to him as he shut the door.

"See you soon," he told her through the open window. The car drove off leaving her panting from her run and the whirlwind encounter with Chrome.

Lizzie began to jog on the spot, plugged her headphones back in her ear and continued into the service entrance. She jogged through the hotel and up to her room, this time making sure to slow down whenever she ran around corners.

Lizzie prided herself on being a good judge of people and unable to make rash decisions; recently she had failed at both, she thought to herself as she began to get unchanged out of her running attire. She stepped into the shower and thought of nothing else but Fitzy, and how she could begin to fall for him; he had ruined her father and gotten his claws into her.

When she got out of the shower, she looked at her childhood clown clock on her bedside table; as a young girl she had been obsessed with clowns and insisted on having a circus filled room, until she watched a PBS documentary about animal cruelty and refused to sleep in there. She kept the clock, reasoning that they had nothing to do with rearing the animals.

She was late; she was due to meet her mother, sister and brother for breakfast ten minutes ago. She quickly found something to wear, and put on a beanie rather than attempt to tame her hair and fled her room, again running around the corners without looking.

Jane was the first to arrive; she sat alone on a table in the middle of the ballroom, texting away ferociously.

"Sorry, I'm late," Lizzie panted as she sat down next to her sister, who was now attempting to call someone.

"Bastard," Jane shouted, slamming her phone down on the table and cracking the screen.

"Who?" asked Lizzie as she poured herself a glass of orange juice from the jug in front of her.

"Chrome, he's ignoring my calls and texts," Jane said with her head in her hand. "I even went up to Collin's suite, but no-one answered."

"Maybe he's still flying," said Lizzie as she buttered a piece of toast.

"Flying where?" she asked, staring at her sister in disbelief.

"L.A," said Lizzie, biting into her well-buttered toast.

"Why would he be going to L.A?" Jane asked, thinking to herself, "that complete jockstrap," she said loudly as their mother and Max entered together.

Mrs. Bennet was wearing a huge pair of extremely dark sunglasses, covering the majority of her face.

"He went to that DJ gig," she said to herself, "Why would he go without telling me?" She asked herself rhetorically; thankfully, as no-one was paying attention to her.

Lizzie's phone began to buzz excitedly; Jane thinking it was hers, picked up her phone, but again threw it across the ballroom when she realised it was cracked.

"Mom, I need a new phone," Jane whined.

"Then go get one," she snapped, without looking at her daughter, instead taking slow sips from her water.

"Is that Fitzy?" asked Jane, "Ask him to ask Chrome to call me."

"It's not him, it's Collin," she told her, "He's been texting me all morning," she said, reading the message and putting her phone down without responding.

"I'm not surprised he keeps messaging you after last night," said Jane, a smile creeping across her face for a moment, before she realised she was upset. "What was up with the kiss? I thought you liked Fitzy. I'd have kissed Collin after the magic trick he did. What about you mom?"

Mrs. Bennet realised she was being spoken to and looked up at Jane, "What about me?" she asked coldly.

"Would you have kissed Collin? If he did that trick on you?"

Jane asked her mother.

Mrs. Bennet took a moment to answer, pruning her lips together as she began to speak slowly, "He must be half my age, you idiot girl," said Mrs. Bennet, finishing off the conversation.

Jane sulked to herself at being spoken to in that way.

Max sat back and looked around the table; everyone seemed distracted and miserable to be there. "Well, this is fun," he said loudly to his sisters and mother.

"Has anyone seen dad this morning?" Lizzie asked the group. No one gave her an answer. "Mom?" Lizzie asked.

"He was gone before I got up this morning, Lizzie."

"Okay," she said like a teenager scorned.

"Mind your tone, all of you," Mrs. Bennet told her children, pointing at them with her long, thin finger.

""It's a bit funereally like, what's the matter with everyone," he asked as he bit into a croissant. "Isn't this weekend meant to be Jane's homecoming? I'll ignore the fact I never got one," he sniggered to himself, "But I'll let that slide. But seriously, lighten up people."

The three of them averted their attention away from him as he looked at them all in turn. Jane ran across the ballroom to retrieve her phone when she heard a noise, which turned out to come from Lizzie's phone; this seemed to annoy her even more.

"Maybe we should all get away for a few days? Go up to the lake house?" he told the group, "Away from any cell reception," he suggested as he looked at Lizzie trying to ignore her messages and Jane trying to squint to see if she could read any responses through the broken glass of her phone screen.

"We should ask dad, if he wants to come too," Jane suggested.

"No," said Lizzie and Mrs. Bennet almost in unison; they both gave each other a look.

"Okay, okay," said Jane, "It was just a suggestion."

Mrs. Bennet reached into her purse and began to reach for her phone; when she had it in her hand, she began to type ferociously.

"We leave in ninety minutes," she told the group.

She placed her phone in her bag, swung it onto her shoulder, got up from the table and left without saying another word.

"I guess we're all going away then," Max said excitedly.

"Where are we going?" said James, who came out of the kitchen eating from a tub of ice-cream.

"You, aren't going anywhere," said Lizzie who got up out of her chair.

James walked over to the table and sat down next to Jane, staring at her, hoping she'd put Lizzie in her place.

"She's right," Jane said, feeling Lizzie glaring at her, "Take a few days off, we'll be away for three days max," she told him.

"What am I supposed to do?" he asked her pathetically.

"I don't care," she told him as she forcefully unzipped her purse and threw her broken phone inside; she left her bag on the table as she walked over the bar to get a bottle of water out of the fridge.

"You need to pay for that," Lizzie reminded Jane.

"When have we ever had to pay for anything around here?" she muttered to her sister as she filled her arm with prepackaged cookies and bags of nuts.

As Jane and Lizzie were arguing over whether they should have to pay for what they use, Max was on his phone and James began to look into Jane's bag. There was nothing of significance in there, except for her keycard that he took and slid into his pocket when he was sure no-one was looking.

Jane returned to the table and emptied the contents of her arms into her purse, "We have the flight, and I doubt there's any food at the house."

James stood up once Jane returned and began to walk towards the ballroom's main doors, "See you all then," he said, rushing off.

"He quickly changed his tune," said Lizzie; after a second, she could care less about him.

***

The Bennets had Buster drive them to Teterboro private airport; they waited in the small departure lounge for them to be given the all clear to board their Jet.

"We should drive," said Lizzie who turned her phone on silent; the constant buzzing was starting to annoy her.

"Nonsense, we're here now; why drive when you have a jet?" asked Mrs. Bennet, who was still wearing the dark glasses to cover up her black eye.

"It's cheaper," said Lizzie. Although she couldn't see her mother's eyes, she sensed that she was currently rolling them at her.

"The Annalise is now ready to begin boarding," a voice said over the tannoy.

"Let's take a selfie," Jane suggested; she began to dig through her purse and when she looked at her phone's screen, she screamed in frustration. "Fuck. Mom, we'll use your phone." Jane held out her hand to receive Mrs. Bennet's phone, who handed it over reluctantly.

The four of them stood together for the snap, Max the only one smiling for the picture.

"Done?" Mrs. Bennet asks Jane, holding her hand to receive her phone back.

Mrs. Bennet took a moment to look at the picture; she likes the way she looks in it. Having just downloaded Instagram, she posts the picture, even hash-tagging vacation, private jet, family and lake house.

They all exit the departure lounge and walk the short distance to their awaiting jet. One at a time, they climb the few steep steps, nodding to the pilot as they enter.

Once on board, the four of them spread themselves out; no-one sat next to anyone.

"We're about five minutes from take-off, said the pilot as he walked through to his seat.

Lizzie's phone again began to buzz, which again sent Jane into a flurry of excitment

"Maybe this is why you've been single for so long," Lizzie said cynically under her breath.

"What?" said Jane who only half heard Lizzie mutter something.

"Nothing," said Lizzie, who looked at her phone.

Collin hadn't messaged her, but Mary; a college friend of hers. She was surprised she was being messaged, and opened it immediately; thinking something was wrong.

'Smile, you're on holiday,' the message read. Lizzie looked around and out the plane's window.

'Where are you?' Lizzie replied back.

'On my parent's farm, I still get Instagram in cow country, I had no idea you had a lake house!'

Lizzie looked at her mother who was using her phones forward facing camera to check out her hair. "Mom, what did you do with that picture you took?" Lizzie called down to her.

Mrs. Bennet, shocked at being shouted at by Lizzie, slowly turned her head to face her.

"I posted it, on the Instagram," she told Lizzie.

"It's just Instagram," Jane snarled, "No, the."

"Delete it," Lizzie demanded.

"Why?" her mother asked.

"We don't need to show the world how wealthy we are, just get rid of it," Lizzie demanded.

Mrs. Bennet didn't like how she was being spoken to. Reluctantly, she removed the picture.

"It's gone," Mrs. Bennet called up the plane.

"Christ, what's crawled up your arse," Jane asked Lizzie, "See a documentary last night about saving or how money is bad for you?" Jane sneered.

"We're all ready to take off," the pilot announced through the plane.

***

Moments before Mrs. Bennet deleted the picture, Tabatha was looking through the alias Instagram account she had set up to spy on the Bennet's. "No need to show off," she said out loud as she sat, afternoon drinking with Fitzy at the Pemberly.

"Who's showing off?" Fitzy asked, he looked miserable, like he'd recently been crying.

"Just some sketty bitch," said Tabatha who reached and put her arm around him. "No one important," she said to herself.

Chapter Sixteen

Mr. Bennet sat at his desk, playing with his recently emptied pill bottles' contents with his pen, moving them a few inches to the left, then again to the right; once he was bored of that, he began to flick them between a paperweight and his glass of water. Every time he scored, he swallowed the pill until all six were gone.

The door opened after a short knock, Charlotte entered, carrying a pile of documents, which she dumped on his desk. "Your wife's plane just lifted off," she told him as she refilled his water glass from the small office bar in the corner of the room.

"When are they back?" he asked, as he began to riffle through the paperwork she brought him.

Before she managed to answer, there was another knock at the door.

"Three days," she said, "Come in," Charlotte shouted.

Benjy slowly opened the door and peered in, Charlotte and Mr. Bennet stared at him as he started to take small steps towards them.

In his hand was another bottle of Whiskey, he was told to deliver to Mr. Bennet's office.

"You've worked the Bar right? You were at the party last night when…" Mr. Bennet asked Benjy as he got closer to him.

"Yes," Benjy said, standing directly in front of his desk, he attempted to hand the bottle over the desk.

Mr. Bennet pointed to his corner bar.

"Thank you, Charlotte," Mr. Bennet told his assistant, his way of telling her to fuck off.

"Make me an old fashioned," Mr. Bennet called over when Benjy reached the bar.

Charlotte left, looking at her watch; she knew while his wife was away, he'd be on a constant bender.

Benjy tried to quickly familiarise himself with the new bar and tried to remember what went in the cocktail.

"Hurry it up," Mr. Bennet demanded as he threw the entire pile of papers that Charlotte had just been delivered, into his waste bin.

Benjy began to make the drink, remembering the recipe when being shouted at. When he started to search for sugar cubes, the door burst open; Miss Tyson, Charlie's mother came running across the office, dragging Charlie along like a rag-doll, followed by Charlotte.

"He's not available, I told you!" Charlotte shouted after her.

Charlie and her mother reached Mr. Bennet's desk; Charlie's mother threw the money he had given her daughter last night at him.

"I'm going to call security," Charlotte screeched, taking out her cell phone.

"Wait," said Mr. Bennet to Charlotte as he looked back and forth between the two women standing before him.

"Don't you change my sheets?" Mr. Bennet asked Charlie's mother.

"My job has nothing to do with why I'm here," she bellowed at him, "Your son hurt my daughter," she shouted, pushing Charlie forward.

"Boy, my drink," Mr. Bennet called over to Benjy, who really didn't want to be caught in the middle of anything,.

He slowly made his way across the office, the drink shaking in his hand as he walked towards them.

"You," Charlie's mother called at him, when she saw him walking towards them.

"You know each other?" said Mr. Bennet after he got his drink in his hand. "You have this young man to thank for your daughter not having a broken wrist." Mr. Bennet's pills were starting to take affect and felt his body begin to lighten.

"What?" Charlie's mother demanded, looking from Charlie, Benjy and Mr. Bennet.

"Max never would have hurt your daughter, he just has a bit of a temper; if you meet his mother, you'd understand," Mr. Bennet said, trying to make a joke.

"What's he got to do with it? You said he wasn't involved," she said to Charlie.

"He leaped over the bar and ran to your daughter, tackling my son to the ground. It was all very exciting." Mr. Bennet told her.

"Where's your son?" Charlie's mother demanded.

"Out of the city, out of state," he told her.

"Next time I see him walking around the hotel, he can expect more than a bruised wrist from me," she proclaimed.

Mr. Bennet gave Charlotte a look, to get his office cleared out.

"You have a conference call in two minutes," Charlotte told her boss as she looked down at her watch.

Charlotte put her arms around Charlie and her mother, who pushed her away with her shoulder, "You don't touch me," she told her as she started to make her way to the door.

When Charlie and her mother got to the door, she turned around and saw Benjy staring at Charlie from next to Mr. Bennet's desk.

"Wait here," she told her daughter. She walked towards Benjy at speed, causing him to gulp the air in his mouth.

"You like my daughter?" she asked him.

"Yes."

"You going to hurt her?"

"No," he sincerely told her, unsure where this was going.

"Dinner, tonight. My house, where I can keep an eye on you."

Benjy's face began to light up; he looked over at Charlie who couldn't believe what her mother was saying

"Dress nicely," she warned him, "none of your hip-hop clothes," she warned him.

"Yes, yes of course," he told her.

She nodded, turned around and marched back to her daughter who threw her arms around her.

Charlotte eventually managed to close the door after them. "You do have that call, Mr. Bennet," she told him.

"Cancel it," he told her, "Cancel everything," he demanded. "Another drink," he said to Benjy, waiving his empty glass in the air for refilling.

"I need to get out of the hotel," Mr. Bennet told Charlotte as Benjy made him another drink.

***

Mrs. Bennet and her children all clinked their Champagne glasses together, as their plane glided through the air.

"To a fun weekend," Max proclaimed as they all sipped their drink.

***

"Well, this is fun," James said to himself as he sat alone at the Pemberly; taking advantage of the free drinks he's been afforded since living here, also rent free. As he was about to start on his third beer, he noticed Mr. Bennet almost running across the lobby, by himself.

Mr. Bennent exited the hotel and got into his Bentley that waited for him at the bottom of the hotel steps.

James quickly finished the beer, making it disappear within seconds of starting it. He left the Pemberly, slowly walked across the lobby, and edged towards the elevator that he had seen Mr. Bennet exit from; only a minute or so ago.

He looked around at the concierge desk; Michael was busy speaking with on old woman, while her dog began to run around her legs, tangling his lead around her legs.

James took the keycard he had taken from Jane's bag and slowly inserted it into the slot, he was relieved and let out a long breath when the yellow light around the call button lit up and the doors began to part. He quickly stepped in as the doors slid shut behind him immediately. The elevator only stopped at one floor, he pressed the button to go up and looked around the large elevator as he waited to reach the Bennets' private floor. He stepped into the long hallway that housed the Bennet children's room, Mr and Mrs. Bennet's suite and Mr. Bennet's office. James had visited this floor a few times, to film interviews in Jane's room. When he got out, he took a look up and down the hallway, it was empty. Slowly, he began to make his way towards Jane's room; when he was stood outside, he gave it a short sharp knock. James waited for a few moments, as he expected, there was no reply. He slid the keycard into the lock and slowly lifted down the handle, the door creaked open. He took one last look around, even up above him, where a security camera was pointed at Jane's bedroom door; he looked directly into it before entering and leaving the door slightly ajar.

Luckily for James, at that moment, Charlotte was in the camera control room; bouncing up and down on the lap of Alex, the hotel's head of security. They were busy concentrating on each other, leaving the hotel blind from above.

James began to slowly walk around Jane's room, taking it all in. The room smelt of lavender and was mildly untidy. He walked over to her vanity table and began to flick through a small pile of photographs; a mixture of childhood snaps, drunken nights out and one of her in just her panties, taken on her bed only a few feet away. James started at the picture for a moment. He turned around and threw the picture down on the bed behind him. He continued to look around the room and stumbled upon her laundry hamper, he started to rummage through it until he came across a pair of black lace underwear. He lifted them to his nose, inhaling them deeply. His trousers began to bulge as his sinuses filled with Jane's scent. He threw the panties back, landing it upon the photograph on the bed.

He walked back to the bed, readjusting his throbbing member as he walked, before sitting on the edge of the bed; he unfastened the button of his pants and slid them down to his knees. He massaged himself through his underwear as he slowly sat down.

When he made contact with the bed, a crunch filled his eardrums. Shocked by the sound, he moved and again, a crunch followed with every movement he made. He shot up and pulled back the bed covers.

He took a few steps back when he discovered what the duvet was concealing. "What the fuck?" he said to himself, as he moved in for a closer look.

Under the covers, covering the entire edge of the bed was bags and bags of white powder; huge clear bags that glistened under the florescent lighting above.

"What's this girl into?" he asked himself as he surveyed the bags, lifting them up, trying to judge their weight. There was way too much for one person, he told himself.

He unzipped one of the bags and ran his fingers through the powder, pinching a pile and letting it run over his skin.

James picked up the panties and photograph that slid onto the floor, shoving them into his coat pocket for later. He went back to the powder and rubbed a small amount into his gums. He began to jump up and down excitedly when he realised the powder was pure coke. He pulled up his trousers and re-buckled them. Still jumping excitedly, he pulled back Jane's bed covers and left the room, trying to walk normally.

Chapter Seventeen

Mr. Bennet sat back and drank his drink, while a girl, younger than all of his children gyrated topless in front of him. He moved his shoulders in tune to the music without taking his eyes off the breasts that danced before him. His phone, on the table in front of him, began to vibrate; the sound lost under the heavy thumping of the music.

***

"I've just text' dad," Lizzie told everyone as they were about to step into a limo after landing.

"I'm sure he'll be fine without constant updates, Lizzie," Mrs. Bennet snapped at her daughter as she slid into the car, still wearing the huge sunglasses in the overcast weather.

As they drove through the countryside, their phone signals became weaker with every mile they drove. Jane had managed to get Michael to send someone out to the Apple Store in Times Square, while she packed for her trip away.

"Fucking cunt," she screamed when the phone cut off as she attempted to call Chrome; it rang for a short moment before she totally lost signal. "What's the point of having a house out here, if there's not reception?" Jane demanded of her mother as the car drove through a set of high cast iron gates, into a large gated community .

The group of houses sat in the middle of two large mountains with a large lake at the rear. As they slowly drove past the houses, they seemed to get larger and grander the further they drove; the final house, which sat directly on the lake, was more exuberant than the rest and belonged to the Bennets.

"I have one bar," Max told them as the car pulled up outside the front door, "Oh wait," he told them, "never mind," as his phone lost reception.

Mrs. Bennet unlocked their house, her children followed her as she snaked her way into the kitchen, the first point of call was to the wine cellar that adjoined the kitchen. She began to search the rows of wine, like she was in a library looking for a particular book; pointing to bottles which Max and Lizzie, between them, took off the shelves.

Jane waited in the kitchen and was already bored; she flipped impatiently through the television channels until her mother and siblings returned.

"Look what we have!" Max called out as they climbed the stairs into the kitchen, holding the bottles he held in his arm, above his head.

The driver stood in the doorway when he was done with bringing in their luggage. Mrs. Bennet looked in the cupboards and handed him a can of soup as a tip; knowing he wouldn't get any cash, he muttered as he left, slamming the door behind him.

"Let's get these chilling," Max suggested when they were all together.

"I brought a red for us to drink while we wait," said Mrs. Bennet as she looked through the kitchen draws for a bottle opener. "Glasses," Mrs. Bennet shouted, pointing between Jane and the cupboard.

Jane jumped down off the stool and retrieved the glasses her mother demanded.

From a height, Mrs. Bennet began to pour them all a glass.

"Just a small one for me," Lizzie instructed her mother.

Mrs. Bennet ceased pouring the wine and turned to her daughter, the kitchen was silent and Jane and Max listened intensely to what she was about to say.

"For God's sake Lizzie, we're on vacation, we're here to have a nice time and enjoy ourselves. For once in your life, take that stick out of your arse and drink the fucking wine," Mrs. Bennet told her, then resumed to pouring the wine like nothing had been said; she made sure to give Lizzie the glass that was filled to the brim.

"Thank you," said Lizzie when she received her glass.

"Family time," said Max as they prepared to clink glasses.

"And Dad," said Jane, "Shame he works so much."

"A shame," said Mrs. Bennet as everyone began to drink.

The second the wine touched her lips, her whole body started to ache, she forced the wine down, ignoring the temptation to stop drinking and throw up.

***

Mr. Bennet threw up all over the poor young girl that danced in front of him, causing her to let out a scream that brought every security guard in the strip club to his table.

"It's probably best we get you home, Mr. Bennet," one of the security guards told him as he helped the young girl off him.

Mr. Bennet was helped up by two men who walked him across the club and out to the sunny and very busy New York street, where is car was parked, waiting to take him back to the Everfield. Vomit rubbed off his clothes and smeared the interior of his Bently; it wasn't the first time Mr. Bennet had coated the inside of this car with his body fluids.

He sat back in his seat, watching the streets glide by him as he held his drunken head back. He reached into his pocket and took out his pill bottle, giving it a shake to try and guess the amount he had left; based on the shallow rattle it gave, there wasn't many. He swallowed the few remaining pills and fell into a sleepy state, only awaking when his driver shook his shoulder when they arrived back at his hotel. Mr. Bennet got his groggy body out of the car and slowly climbed the front steps of his hotel, taking no notice of the small crowd of people that stopped to stare at the vomit soaked man who staggered past them.

He managed to reach the far end of the lobby by himself; refusing help from everyone who came to his aid as he staggered comically; Michael and Mr. Hilbert, stood back and let him be, as he opened the elevator door after multiple attempts of inserting his keycard. Mr. Bennet reached his family's floor and used the wall to guide his way down the hallway to his office; he went straight for his desk and began to rummage through the draws, searching for another full bottle. His search was unfruitful; instead turned his attention to the adjoining bathroom where he walked over to the mirror and opened the cabinet above. Lines of pills, bottles, creams and lotions lined its shelves, he ransacked through the shelf of medication, discarding aspirin and flu medication. When he found what he was looking for, he opened the pill bottle with all his force; sending a stream of yellow and white medication over his shoulder and onto the floor. He attempted to catch them, instead slipping on the zebra skin fur rug, a trophy of a hunting trip to Zimbabwe.

He flew through the air; his weight propelling him towards the edge of the toilet basin.

His vision cleared immediately for a split second when he felt his head thump against the toilet. The rest of his body hit the cold, hard bathroom floor, sending a hollow, booming sound that echoing around the tiled walls.

Finally, his head came into contact with the floor and his eyes closed, blood began to pool around him as he lay there, motionless.

Silence filled the air as the blood seeped into the Zebra rug.

***

Mrs. Bennet tapped the remaining few drops of red wine from the bottle into her glass; raised it to her eye level, inspecting the inch or so of wine her glass held.

"You'd see it a whole lot better if you took off your shades," Max told her as he filled his mouth with chips and dip.

Light music played in the background, replacing the noise of conversation that should fill a family gathering.

"I'm going to head out," Mrs. Bennet told everyone, as she finished off her wine. The wine that was chilling wasn't quite ready and she needed something to mask the nausea feeling that continued to take over her. She had become masterful of hiding any issues she had, even when she felt ill.

"Let's all go out," Lizzie suggested; bolting up out of her seat and putting on her jacket.

"Sure," said Jane as she finished off the last of her glass.

Through their walk, Jane was glued to her phone as she tried to get hold of Chrome; she became more annoyed with every failed attempt to call him, when they got a short burst of reception.

"Maybe, he's no longer into you," Max shouted to her, from the rear. Jane raised her arm to quiet him as she listened intensely to every ring that went unanswered.

"It's your fault," Jane turned to Lizzie, prompting her sister to stop looking at the mountain views.

"What's my fault?" Lizzie asked.

"Chrome, ignoring all my calls."

"Can I ask how you came to this?" Lizzie asked, she noticed her mother and brother had continued walking, leaving them to walk at an almighty slow pace.

"If you only kept your tongue in your own fucking mouth, instead of swapping saliva with anyone who shows you the slighted bit of interest," Jane began screaming at Lizzie.

"It was just a kiss, and has absolutely nothing to do with you. For once, I wish you'd stop being so narrow-minded and think that the entire world resolves around you, because it doesn't. You really have no idea what's happening around you, do you?" Lizzie barked at her sister without taking a breath, stunning Jane into silence. Lizzie sped up to catch up with her mother and brother, leaving Jane to meander behind.

The four of them walked the short distance to the local town, the fresh air removed the effect the wine was starting to have on the children, but made Mrs. Bennet's desire to throw up, even stronger.

"Let's all split up," Mrs. Bennet suggested when they reached the small main street, occupied by mostly independent stores; she looked up and down for a drug store.

"Mom, I'll come with you," Jane called to her, when she finally reached the rest of the group.

"I guess, that leaves me and you, sis," Max said to Lizzie, poking her playfully in the side.

"That's not what I had in mind," Mrs. Bennet told her children.

"Come along mother," Jane called back after overtaking them, "I need some vodka," she muttered to herself.

Mrs. Bennet followed Jane into the market, leaving Max and Lizzie outside.

Lizzie looked up and down the street, her eyes latching onto a bakery across the road; the smell of fresh bread seemed to lift her to its front door.

"Everything okay between you and Jane?" Max asked as they

entered the small, dark yeasty smelling shop.

"It will be," she replied as she started to browse all the breads and pastries on display. She began to throw a dozen croissants into a box, "breakfast," she told him as she handed him the box to carry. "What's up with mom?" Lizzie asked as she handed over her credit card to pay.

"What do you mean?" Max asked, not sure what she was talking about.

"She's acting weird, has done since I got back from London."

"I've not noticed anything," he told her as he put the box of croissants into his backpack.

"Thank you," Lizzie called to the shop assistant as they left. They re-entered the main shopping street and sat on a bench in the square, waiting for their sister and mother to reappear.

Jane spent the entire time in the market, flipping through the magazines, criticising the weight and popularity of the girls on the covers.

Mrs. Bennet left Jane to critique the girls she saw as unworthy of gracing the magazine and searched the pharmaceutical isle for nausea medication, reading the back of the most expensive option. As she was about to fling it into her cart, her eyes caught upon the pregnancy test in front of her. She stopped, put the nausea medication back and picked up the pregnancy stick.

"Why can't we be like the Kardashians?" Jane demanded from behind Mrs. Bennet.

Mrs. Bennet threw the pregnancy kit into the cart, covering it with Kale and turned around to face her daughter.

"What?" Mrs. Bennet asked as Jane stood before her, holding up a copy of Vogue with the Kardashians on the cover.

"The Kardashians, why can't we be more like them?" Jane demanded as she threw the magazine into the cart.

Mrs. Bennet looked where the magazine landed, making sure it didn't move any of the cart's contents.

"They have a reality show?" Mrs. Bennet said, uninterested in Jane's conversation.

"I have a reality show," said Jane as she started trying on a lipstick, from the shelf infront of her.

"You, do not have a reality show," Mrs. Bennet spat at Jane as she started to manoeuvre around her daughter.

"Yes I do," Jane said confidently.

"What you have, my dear, is a sad, fat, middle aged man following you around with a camera. Go find your sister and brother and I'll bring the groceries," She told Jane.

"Fine," Jane told her mother and stormed off.

Mrs. Bennet pushed the cart to an open checkout and started to place her items on the moving belt. When the young girl, scanning the groceries got to the pregnancy test, she stopped and looked up at Mrs. Bennet. Mrs. Bennet looked around and nodded over at an annoyed looking Jane, who pouted into the mirror of a revolving stand, trying on pairs of sunglasses.

When the groceries were all scanned and packed, before leaving the store, Mrs. Bennet rummaged through the bags to find the test, concealing it in her bra.

Chapter Eighteen

"Okay, I'm off," Benjy informed Franky as he began to log himself out of the cash register, "Thanks for letting me get off early."

"Wait, wait," said Franky who was still serving and making three cocktails, "You can't leave, I have a full house and a line six people long. You need to stay another hour."

"I can't," said Benjy who looked around the bar, "You'll be fine, I really have to go, you'll be fine," he tried to reason with Franky, winking at him. He took off his apron and began to roll it up.

"Benjy, you can't go," he told him as he threw cocktail shakers up into the air.

"But Charlie..." Benjy tried to explain.

"Dude, I know but we're slammed. You leave and you're fired." Franky said to him sternly.

"You can't fire me," said Benjy confidently.

"Not from the Everfield, but I can make sure that you never make another drink in the hotel again. Now, put your apron back on and make me two Manhattans' and a Cosmo."

Three men who stood at the bar with their money in their hands, stared back and forth between Franky and Benjy.

"Let me make a call first," pleaded Benjy who didn't want to ruin his chances with Charlie.

"You have twenty seconds," said Franky as he began to tray up the drinks he'd just made.

"Okay," said a defeated Benjy. He reached into his pocket and took out his phone; the screen was completely dead and wouldn't switch on. "Shit," he shouted.

"Watch your language," said Franky after returning to the bar with his empty tray, "You get hold of her?"

"No, my phone's dead. Can I borrow your charger?" Benjy asked in a panicky voice.

"I don't have an iPhone," Said Franky who stared down at the rolled up apron in his hand.

"I need to call her," pleaded Benjy.

"And I need two Manhattans' and a Cosmo. Look, more people are coming in, I'm alone and you're staying."

"I thought we were friends," Benjy said to him.

"Benjy, we are, but this is work. Now put your phone away and put on your fucking apron."

***

Charlie's mother was taking a joint of lamb out of the oven and placed it to rest on the work top when Charlie came bouncing into the kitchen. She wore a dark blue dress and had her hair in a high ponytail.

"You look beautiful," her mother told her. "Why don't you go into my bedroom and put on some of grandma's perfume?" she suggested.

"Yeah?" said Charlie excitedly.

Her mother laughed as she watched her run out of the room, nothing felt better to her, than seeing her daughter smiling.

***

"Can I go now?" Benjy pleaded with Franky, he was five minutes late for dinner.

"Is there a line?" Franky asked.

"Yeah," Benjy said sombrely.

"Then, what do you think…" Franky told him as he passed James a double bourbon.

James sipped at his drink and tapped his phone impatiently. "Come on Carrie, where are you?" he muttered to himself.

"Uncle Jamie?" said a voice behind him; he spun around on his chair and looked the young girl up and down.

"Carrie," he said, getting off his stool and giving her a hug.

"You said there was some…" She started to speak but was cut off by her Uncle.

After breaking off their hug, James ushered them off to a recently evacuated seat in the corner of the Pemberly, away from preying ears.

"You're looking well," James lied to his niece whose face was covered in severe acne and small sores.

"You never said you were in New York," she said to him as she wiped her nose on her sleeve.

"I've not been here long. I have a question, Carrie. Are you still using?" he asked her in hushed tones.

"A little, here and there," she lied, the true extent of her current drug use was much more, "If I'm at a party or something."

"Right," James said, staring at her. The amount of cocaine upstairs was too much for him to enjoy by himself. "Let me show you, what we've got." He got up and prompted her to follow him. Carrie began racing through the Pemberly, bumping into guests as she made her way out.

"Watch it, junkie" Tabatha sneered after almost getting knocked over by Carrie. She and Fitzy slowly made their way through the Pemberly; filling James' and Carrie's table at the back.

After making their way out of the Pemberly and across the lobby, James and Carrie stood before the Bennets' private elevator.

"Look straight ahead, don't look around," James warned her as he slid Jane's keycard in, to unlock the door.

The doors separated before them and they slinked inside, James shut the door and pressed the upwards button, propelling them to the Bennets' floor. He opened up his backpack and took out his camera, beginning to film as they stepped out into the hallway.

"What are you doing?" Carrie asked.

"Working." He led her down to Jane's room and opened the door using her key.

"Whose room is this?" Carrie asked as the door swung open.

"Miss Jane Bennet's," James led her into the room, leaving the door open.

"The socialite?" Carrie asked as they stood in front of Jane's bed.

"Look what Miss Bennet is hiding under her covers," said James with a smile across his face.

James slid back the duvet to reveal what was hiding underneath.

"Oh my God," said an excited Carrie as she picked up a bag and tore it open, sending a cloud of drugs into the air above. She turned to James, "This is real? All of it?"

James nodded his head, causing the camera to bounce up and down.

"What are we waiting for, Uncle Jamie?" said an excited Carrie who cupped a handful of the white powder and dumped it on the vanity; first sliding its contents onto the floor for a clear surface.

"Pass me that card," Carrie demanded, pointing to Jane's keycard that he was still holding on to.

"Remember to share," James joked as he flicked her the card from across the room.

***

"Two stools opened up," said Fitzy as he stood up and began to walk towards the bar.

"I guess I'll follow you then," Tabatha muttered under her breath, taking hold of her wine glass and following her ex-fiancé to the bar.

"I can't believe she kissed him," moaned Fitzy as Tabatha sat down next to him.

"Well, she did," Tabatha said unsympathetically as she sipped from her glass, "You guys only kissed the once, right? You guys weren't dating, so just move on, forget about that American bitch," Tabatha said loudly, her British accent voice carried over the busy bar; causing some people to turn and look at her. "Get back to your drinks," she shouted down to a woman six stools down that was giving her an unimpressed look. The woman Tabatha shouted at, slid her glass towards Benjy; who looked miserable while making a cocktail. The young woman left her stool and walked out of the Pemberly.

Less than a minute later, her seat was filled by Collin, who swarmed in on his cell phone, winking towards Fitzy and Tabatha when he sat down. He sat further down the bar, finishing off the drink that belonged to the young woman, and occasionally shooting Fitzy smug looks while he spoke on his cell.

Fitzy hadn't seen Collin since they shared the elevator together before The Bennets' party. "There he is," Fitzy said quietly to Tabatha; who knew perfectly well, there he was, having just given him a small wave.

"What should I do?" Fitzy asked.

"What about? Lizzie or Collin down the bar?" she asked as she fluttered her eyelashes towards Collin whenever Fitzy looked away.

"How long have we known each other? Our entire lives? Trust me, forget about her, move on; there are plenty of girls out there that would give anything to be with you."

"I'm going to ring her," Fitzy announced, getting his cell phone out and began searching for her number.

Tabatha finished off her wine as Fitzy began to call Lizzie.

"She's turned her phone off," Fitzy said angrily.

"Her phone's not off," Tabatha said under her breath, not intending Fitzy to hear.

"What do you mean?" he asked her.

Tabatha didn't know how to explain that she knew where Lizzie and her family were. She was relieved when an explosion of pandemonium filled the hotel lobby and let her off answering Fitzy's question.

✳✳✳

Charlotte and Alex climaxed at the same time, beads of sweat slowly trickled down her back as she tried to catch her breath.

"Hug me," she said to Alex, who sat back in his chair, still inside Charlotte.

Alex opened his eyes and reached forward and put his arms around her, wanting her to get off and leave. He looked up at the bank of monitors behind her shoulder and his eyes diverted to the Bennets' corridor. Both Jane and Mr. Bennet's office doors were both open.

"Off, get off," Alex shouted, startling Charlotte as she slowly climbed off him.

"What's going on?" she asked as she watched him hastily put his clothes back on.

"The family's floor," he pointed at the screens, "None of them are in the hotel and maid service did there floor first thing."

"Shit," she said as she tried to put her clothes on as fast as she could, thinking that Mr. Bennet was out and wouldn't be back for hours.

"Hurry up," Alex barked, as he waited for Charlotte to zip up her wrinkled dress.

***

Blue flashing lights could be seen through the hotels main front doors from the Pemberly. The sound of sirens began to fill the hotel's lobby.

Fitzy and Tabatha turned around when they heard the doors burst open and police and paramedics fly in and swarm the hotel lobby.

They watched as Mr. Hilbert uses his keycard to allow a group of officers and paramedics into the Bennets' elevator.

"What's going on?" Collin asked Benjy, who was relieved that from the moment that the police entered the hotel, people stopped ordering drinks.

"Someone's died, someone died," Franky came screeching into the bar towards Benjy, "Aren't you glad you didn't leave?" he joked.

Benjy threw him an unimpressed look.

"Lighten up," Franky said to him.

"Isn't that the elevator that goes up to the Bennets' floor?" Collin asked Franky and Benjy as they all watched as manypeople crammed themselves into the elevator as possible.

"Shit, it is!" Franky realised, "Someone died on the Bennet's floor," Fraky said loud enough that most of the drinkers left in the Pemberly could hear; they all looked over to him for more information.

"Lizzie," said Fitzy who bolted out of his seat and ran through the lobby to the elevator.

Tabatha slowly slid off the stool and walked behind him, eventually reaching him as he was pleading with the officers to let him up.

"I know the family, is Lizzie up there?" he demanded of them, "Is she okay?"

"Get out of here," the officer warned him, as they read what was written on his t-shirt.

"Did someone die?" Fitzy pleaded with the officer for information.

"I'm not gonna tell you again," said the officer who was beginning to get annoyed by Fitzy.

"Let's get another drink," Tabatha suggested when she reached him. "We can keep an eye on things from the bar," she told him as they walked back through the lobby towards the Pemberly.

"I pray to God, nothing's happened to Lizzie," Fitzy said as they sat back in their stools.

"For fuck sakes, Fitzy. Man up, she hasn't died, calm yourself down and order another fucking drink. She's out of the city, with her family. She's perfectly fine and out of any phone signal."

"What?" said Fizty, who started at her, "How do you know all his?"

"Her mum posted a picture on Instagram of her and the three little Bennets before they flew off," she said as she waved her glass in the air, trying to get Benjy's attention.

***

"I'm going to call it a night," Mrs. Bennet declared as they all drank wine in the sitting room, sat on a sofa and beanbags.

"It's only nine o'clock," said Jane who was slurring her words.

"I'm tired," Mrs. Bennet told them as Jane started to refill her mother's glass, "No Jane!" she said to Jane, who was ignoring her plans.

"You've had, like three glasses since you got back, you have a lot of catching up to do," Jane told her.

Mrs. Bennet reluctantly took the glass from Jane and slowly took a sip while thinking of the pregnancy test upstairs.

***

When the lift doors opened up, the entire lobby and Pemberly bar craned their necks to see what was happening.

A stretcher, with a body bag left the elevator; accompanied by several police officers and paramedics; who pushed it across the lobby and into an awaiting ambulance that was parked outside the Everfield.

"Shit just got real," said Tabatha as she finished off another glass.

Chapter Nineteen

Mrs. Bennet finally managed to get free of her children and made her way upstairs and opened her bedroom, the TV was still on from when she was getting changed earlier in the day. She put it on mute as she entered the adjoining bathroom as the evening news started to play. She shut the bathroom door behind her and took the pregnancy test out from under a pile of towels.Her hand started to shake as she held it and broke the packaging open. She examined the white stick and began to feel sick as she thought about how her life would change if the test turned out to be positive. Her main concern was how her body would cope with another baby, not about bringing in another life into the world; as an older woman, she knew she wouldn't spring back to her slim physique as she did when she was younger. She threw the packaging in the small trash bin and walked over to the toilet. Sitting down, she began to pee; the sound of her urinating on the stick filled the room.

In her bedroom, the news on the TV brought up footage of a body being brought out of her hotel, next to an image of her husband.

***

"From what I'm hearing inside," said a reported who was standing outside the Everfield, as police cars pulling up and left around her, "I'm learning from sources in the hotel, that the deceased is Mr.

Arthur Bennet, the often outspoken hotelier. Police have not named him, but that's what I'm hearing from various hotel employees."

***

Mrs. Bennet finished urinating and shook it before lifting it up to examine it. "Three minutes," she said as she sat there, staring into the white stick that could change her life forever.

***

"Mr. Bennet is known to have had an issue with prescription medication, dating back years to around the time that his best friend, Collin Williams Snr. died in a skiing accident, during a joint family vacation. It's not known at this time if Mr. Bennet's addiction had any part to play in his death, this evening," the reporter was still outside the hotel, moving as far as she could towards the front entrance.

***

Mrs. Bennet took a look at the results after her three minutes were up; she spent almost as long looking at the stick, than she had waiting for its conclusion.

***

"It's not my drugs!" Carrie screamed as she was being dragged out of the hotels front doors; two officers manoeuvred her down the steps in cuffs, past the reporter who wasn't expecting her. The camera panned fast to track her as she came towards them.

"It's that Jane Bennet's," she scratched.

"What drugs?" the reporter asked, running over to Carrie, leaving the camera man to follow.

"My uncle found it all in her room, mountains of it," Carrie continued as she was being stuffed into an awaiting police car.

"More drama at the Everfield Hotel in New York," the reporter said, turning to the camera, "I'll try and find out what's happening and keep you posted," she signed off.

***

Mrs. Bennet weeped, as she sat on the toilet, still holding the positive test in her limp arm. Uncontrollable sobs poured from her as a million thoughts circulated around in her head as the television in the next room displayed a black and white picture of her husband with his birth and death dates in gold swirly writing.

***

"C'mon Franky," Benjy pleaded as he continued to make more drinks, "Can't we just shut the Pemberly down for the night?"

"Are you soft?" Franky said to him as he took payment for a round of drinks, "I can't work this alone," he told him, pointing effeminately at the crowded bar.

"What if I got you help? Someone to take over for me?" Benjy suggested.

"Good luck," said Franky, who wasn't confident in Benjy's optimism.

Benjy began to think of who could cover his shift.

"Kitty," he said out loud as he noticed her from across the lobby, packing up her flower stand. "Give me one minute," said Benjy before darting off, hurtling before a startled Kitty.

"Hey Benjy," she said when she noticed him standing before her, "Charlie said you guys are having dinner at her house tonight!" she said in a surprised tone, "How you pull that off?" she asked .

"I need a favour," said Benjy who looked panicked.

"You hear about Mr. Bennet?" she asked.

"Never mind about him, back to my favour."

"What is it?" she asked in a helpful tone.

"I need you to work the Pemberly this evening," he told her.

She burst out laughing, "You're kidding right? I've never worked behind the bar, I sell Roses and do the hotels flower arraigments, I don't know the first thing about making drinks, drinking them, yeah, but I can't do that!"

"Please," wined Benjy who noticed Franky kept looking over to them, "If you don't, I may never get a chance with Charlie again, I'm so late as it is."

Kitty looked over at how busy the Pemberly was, more people kept arriving, wanting to get a front row seat of anything else that may happen at the hotel this evening.

"Ok, ok," she said as Benjy attempted to guilt her into it, by making his eyes as wide as possible.

He put his arms around her and squeezed her hard, "Thank you!" he shouted.

Franky looked over and smiled, "Go get your girl," he said under his breath.

Kitty nervously made her way over to the Pemberly and put on Benjy's apron. "What now?" she asked Franky as Benjy fled out of the hotel, without looking back.

"We've been waiting for ten minutes," Tabatha shouted over at her.

"Take their order, I guess," said Franky who gave her a gentle push in Fitzy and Tabatha's direction.

"What can I get for you?" Kitty asked them.

"Some better customer service, for a fucking start," said Tabatha in her snooty British accent.

"I still can't get hold of her," said Fitzy, who was still trying to ring Lizzie.

"Quiet," said the man who sat in the stool next to them, as he pointed towards the television on the wall; it was playing the News, the same thing that was being broadcast in Mrs. Bennet's bedroom.

"I only came in for a conference," said the man who shushed Fitzy, "What a day to come!" he said excitedly as he returned to watching the TV.

"I've done nothing wrong," Carrie screamed as the elevator doors slid open. She was being forced through the lobby by two officers, "My uncle found it all in that Jane girl's room," she was shouting loudly; the entire congregation of the Pemberly watches as she was being escorted out of the hotel.

"At first, I didn't wanna come on this trip," the man next to Fitzy said to him, "But I'm so glad I did!"

"Shut up," Fitzy told him as they watched Carrie disappear through the hotels doors. The old doorman stood back, watching the young woman in handcuffs, glided past him.

The entire Pemberly watched in silence as they saw the young girl, who'd just walked past her, being escorted down the hotel steps.

"Draw up the paperwork," Collin could be heard saying across the bar. "The Everfield's mine, as soon as the family steps foot in the hotel, I want those documents in their hands."

Fitzy looked over at Collin who was on his phone, preparing to leave. He strained his ears to try and over hear his entire phone conversation.

"…Yes, I'm watching the news, I don't care if he's just died. If he was stupid enough to use the hotel as collateral, then more fool him," Collin threw down a few notes onto the bar and slid off his stool, "Remember, keep my name off the paperwork, I don't want them knowing I have anything to do with this…"

Fitzy jumped down from his stool as Collin began to walk past him. "What was that call about?" Fitzy demanded from Collin, who was trying to pass him.

"Nothing to do with you," said Collin as he still tried to exit the Pemberly.

"What's going on? You own the Everfield? What's it being used as collateral for?" Fitzy was confused but knew something was up.

Tabatha watched them intensely as she finished off her drink; when her glass was empty, she took out her cell and began recording them.

"This is nothing that a tambourine playing hoodwink needs to concern himself with," said Collin, who was getting increasingly annoyed at being trapped from leaving, "Now get out of my fucking way."

"There's no way you own the Everfield," Fitzy shouted; everyone in the bar, including Franky and Kitty were watching the two men.

"Actually, yes I do!" he said smugly, "And there's nothing you nor Lizzie, or any member of the Bennet family can do to stop me. I'm going to tear this dump down and put seventy floors of steel and glass. Now move. I'm not going to tell you again," he said to Fitzy coldly.

Without thinking, Fitzy struck Collin, causing a fountain of blood to spurt from his nose as he screamed in agony.

"Assault, assault," Collin shouted, intent of making as many people as aware as possible, "Somebody help," he projected in the direction of the officers guarding the elevator, "I've been attacked."

Tabatha shot off her stool and began moving around Fitzy to get a better shot of the blood pouring from Collins nose.

Fitzy stood there, in shock at what he'd just done, "I'm sorry," he apologised.

"Are you recording this?" Collin asked her, with tears and blood protruding from his face.

Tabatha said nothing, still pointing her camera in his direction.

"Officer, officer!" He continued shouting, making sure they noticed. They left their post and began to run across the lobby towards the Pemberly.

When Fitzy noticed the satisfied look across Collins face, he turned around and looked over at the running officers, heading in his direction.

"Shit," said Fitzy as he tried to make his way through the Pemberly.

"He's getting away," Collin shouted as he shook his head, deliberately letting the blood stain the front of his shirt, "He's trying to escape," Collin pointed at Fitzy who was now behind the Pemberly bar.

Franky and Kitty stood in shock as Fitzy rushed past them and tried to exit into the stock room. As he tried to run through the door, he ran flat into the chest of a Police officer.

"Ah, crap," he said to himself, when he realised there was nowhere to run. "Find Lizzie," Fitzy shouted at Tabatha who was still filming the incident.

The police officer put Fitzy's arms behind his back and started to cuff him.

"Get Lizzie back to New York," Fitzy yelled across the bar; as everyone looked at him, more and more people now had their phones out, recording him getting arrested.

The news-caster, who was broadcasting from outside the hotel, had now made her way into the lobby; she was standing outside the entrance off the Pemberly, prompting her cameraman to zoom in on Fitzy.

"I want him deported," Collin was shouting hysterically at an officer who tried to calm him down, "I want to press charges!" he screamed, like a child.

Tabatha tried to free Fitzy from the two officers that were now escorting him; in her drunken state, she believed that she would be able to free him.

"Let go, or you'll be arrested next," an officer said to her as they passed.

"Find Lizzie," Fitzy repeated, looking into her eyes before he was dragged from the Pemberly.

The TV camera followed Fitzy as he made his way through the lobby and out the front door.

"This is now the second arrest to be made at the Everfield hotel this evening," the reporter said to camera, "Currently, it's not yet known if the arrests are connected," she said with a glint in her eye as she made her way to the Pemberly and tried to find a seat in the back, to watch out for any more developments.

***

"Charlie, I'm sorry," her mother said to her, putting an arm around her, trying to make her feel better. They were both seated at the kitchen table when the doorbell burst into chimes. Charlie raced out of her seat and was half way to the front door when her mother stopped her.

"Sit back down," she demanded as she slowly got out of her seat and left Charlie alone in the kitchen. She made her way through the house and before opening the door; she pulled back the curtain and saw Benjy standing in a sweaty mess on her front door. She slowly opened the door a crack and stood before him, staring without saying a word.

"Sorry, I'm late," he said, panting; trying to get his breath back.

"Damn right, you're late," she told him, looking at her watch, "I gave you a chance, against my better judgment and you blew it!"

"But," he tried to explain, before being shut down.

"Enough," she shouted, demanding his silence, "I don't want to hear it. It's over."

"I couldn't get away from the Pemberly," he pleaded.

"No phone call? Your phone broken? If you could see how upset she is, when you didn't bother showing up. One thing I won't stand for is seeing my baby getting hurt, and that's exactly what you just did," using her index finger to punctuate her final few words with jabs to his chest.

"Mr. Bennet's dead," said a deflated Benjy.

"What you talking about?" she said, scrunching up her face, "are you high?"

"The hotel's in pandemonium, there's no order, police are everywhere, people are getting arrested."

"What you been smoking?" she demanded of him, "Why you saying this?"

"Because it's the truth," he told her, "Switch on the news, you'll see."

Benjy stood looking up at her as she made room for him to pass by.

"Boy, if you're lying, I'm gonna hit you," she told him as she made enough room for him to come into her house, "take off your shoes," she pointed to his feet, "I don't want no city dirt, messing up my carpet."

Benjy took off his shoes and lined them up with the rest.

"Show me," she said, pointing Benjy in the direction of the living room.

"Benjy!" said Charlie who was standing in the kitchen doorway; the light from behind her made her outline glow; her face lit up when she saw him appear from the kitchen door. She began to greet him and stopped when her mother appeared from behind her.

"He gonna show me something on the TV first," Charlie's mother told her as she searched behind the cushions for the remote.

"What's going on?" Charlie asked her mother.

"This boy is spinning some story, saying Mr. Bennet is dead."

"What?" said Charlie gasping "Is this true?"

"We're about to find out," her mother said as she slapped the remote into Benjy's open palm, causing a loud slapping noise to fill the quiet air that still had a slight aroma of the dinner that never was.

"Go on," Charlie's mother said, "Show me," her arms were folded as she waited for Benjy to switch on the TV.

As certain as he was, about what was going on in the Everfield, Benjy doubted himself for a split second as he powered up the television; holding his breath as he flipped through the channels until he found the right one.

"Officials are still remaining tight-lipped about the identity of the deceased," the reporter spoke to the camera, "but, more and more hotel employees are naming him as the deceased."

"Holly shit," said Charlie as she and her mother stood still with their mouths open.

"Language," Her mother said, after a long delay.

Benjy moved across the room as Charlie's mother stood frozen, staring at the TV.

"Sorry, I'm late," Benjy said to Charlie, hugging her as she watched the news over his shoulder.

"Dinner's ruined," Charlie's mother shouted from across the room, causing them to break their embrace.

Benjy looked around the room and spotted a phone charger; Charlie and her mother watched as he walked towards it and plugged in his phone.

"How about we get a pizza?" Benjy suggested, "My treat."

Chapter Twenty

Lizzie was awoken at almost six o'clock by a loud thud on the front door; she made her way out of her bed and slid open the curtain; a teenage boy rode off with a bag of newspapers slung over his shoulder.

She picked up her phone from her bedside table and went downstairs, opening the door and retrieving the rolled up newspaper that lay on the welcome mat. She closed the door as gently as she could; trying to give her family a few hours more sleep.

In the kitchen, she switched on the television and coffee machine, and lay the rolled up newspaper on the table. A commercial for dishwasher soap played as her cup slowly started to fill with steaming black coffee. When her cup was full, she switched off the TV; just as the introduction to the news started to play. She returned to her bedroom, nursing a thumping headache caused by a night of heavy drinking with her mother and siblings.

She drank her scolding coffee, almost in one go as she got herself undressed for her shower. She entered her en-suite bathroom and turned the shower faucet on; steam started to fill the bathroom as she put her towel of the rack to use after washing away the smell of stale smoke that she could smell coming from her skin. Max had bought a carton yesterday and he and Jane smoked the whole pack.

Before stepping into the powerful jet of water, she looked around and noticed the lack of shampoo; she began to search the empty cupboards in the bathroom, before applying a towel around herself.

She turned off the shower and left her bedroom, slowly making her way down the hallway and slowly opening a door.

Her mother was asleep in her bed, with an eye mask covering most of her face. Lizzie watched for a moment as she let out rhythmic hums of calm breaths.

Lizzie slowly crept through her mother's room and into the bathroom, opening and closing the door behind her, without waking her mother up. She pulled back the shower curtain and it too, contained no products. She opened up a well-stocked cabinet and began to search its contents; in it, she found what she was looking for; she took out two bottles, one for her and another she placed on the side of the bath for her mother to use.

Walking across the room, she began to peel off the plastic wrap and looked around for the bin to discard the trash she's just created. Eventually, she found it behind the door; she threw the yellow plastic away but stopped almost immediately after using the trash bin. She looked closer at a white stick that poked through a wad of toilet tissue.

Slowly, she put her hand into the bin, conscious not to touch the wrappers that would crackle if she came into contact with them. She lifted out the pregnancy test and stared at the positive red cross before her. Her naked feet sunk into the tiled floor she stood on as all sound escaped her; the birds tweeting outside and a car backing out of a neighbours drive were plunged into silence as she stared into the white stick.

Lizzie's hearing came back as the springs of her mother's bed started to compress and retract. She Lizzie slowly opened the door and peeked towards her mother's bed; she was still asleep.

Lizzie threw the pregnancy test into the sink basin, grabbed the shampoo she sought and made her way, at speed through her mother's bedroom, getting out as fast as she could. When she closed the door bend her, making no attempt to muffle the sound, her mother shot upright, removed her mask and looked around the empty room.

Mrs. Bennet stepped out of bed and slowly walked over to the open door of the lit bathroom. She peered in and noticed the trash bin in the centre of the floor, she ran over to it and threw the contents on the the floor, hastily rummaging in search of the discarded test. Becoming more and more desperate to find it the longer she looked.

She stood up and let out a howl, plunging her eyes into tears as she noticed the test laying in the bathroom sink. Still crying; Mrs. Bennet turned around, switched off the bathroom light, closed the door behind her and shed tears all over her pillow as she climbed back into her bed and wept; hoping that when her tears finally dried, the test and pregnancy would go away and things would go back to the way they were.

***

Lizzie sat upon a kitchen stool, biting her nails obsessively. The smell of shampoo and fresh coffee filled the silent dark kitchen. She nibbled on a croissant in between bouts of gnawing her unpolished nails. While eating, she unrolled the paper, without paying attention to what she was doing.

"Good morning," said Max as he flipped the light switch, temporarily blinding Lizzie as the room dazzled with newfound brightness.

Lizzie sent the elastic band from the paper, flying across the room in her brother's direction as her croissant dangled from her mouth.

"How, lady-like," Max said to her as he poured himself a cup of coffee and pointed to the crumbs spread across her chest. Lizzie dusted herself with the paper before laying it open on the breakfast bar.

"What's your boyfriend up to now?" Max asked as he kissed her sister on the cheek; a cup of coffee in one hand and pointing down to the newspaper with the other.

"What?" she asked as she looked down at the double spread dedicated to Fitzy's arrest last night.

"He's not my boyfriend," she told him coldly as she looked at the pictures of him being escorted out of the Pemberly; Tabatha could be seen in the background with her phone out.

Max leans in over her shoulder to read the article, "Look!" he points to a related article, "Unidentified male died at the Everfield," Max read out, pointing to the story for Lizzie to see for herself.

"Bloody hell," she said as she sipped on her coffee, "We've been gone less than twenty-four hours!"

"What's going on?" asked Jane as she joined them in the kitchen. "Holy shit," she said as she sipped from Max's coffee and read the article.

"Hey," he said, noticing his cup was empty.

"There's a fresh pot," she told him, pointing to the coffee machine.

"Then pour your own, you cheeky bitch," he told her, mimicking her by pointing to the coffee.

Jane buttered herself a croissant and sipped on her own coffee as she continued to move, staring at her phone, as if the harder she looked at it, the more likely she would get reception.

Just as the clocked chimed eleven thirty, the Bennet children were about to disperse when Mrs. Bennet finally joined them. She was still dressed in her night dress and stood still, as all three of her children looked up and said nothing when she entered the kitchen.

"What's going on?" she asked harshly as all three of her children continued to look at her. "I'm not in the mood," she told them, "say whatever it is you three have to say."

"Someone died at the Everfield last night," Jane said, cutting the tension in the room.

"That's it?" she asked, a sence of relief came over her as she made her way to the empty coffee pot. "You three not interested in refilling this, after drinking it all?" she snarled at her children as she played barista.

Lizzie watched her mother with great attention as she made her way through the kitchen, looking for a mug.

"What you staring at?" she interrogated Lizzie.

"Nothing, just daydreaming," said Lizzie.

"Daydreaming's for the poor," she snapped as Lizzie reread the article for the twentieth time, about Fitzy punching Collin at the Pembelry, last night.

"Isn't that, that trashy English girl?" Mrs. Bennet asked as she walked behind Lizzie and tuned the lights off.

Mrs. Bennet continued her walk around the kitchen as she waited for enough coffee to fill her cup and opened the blinds. She filled the kitchen with light and the sounds of her screams.

Tabatha was standing before her. Her hair was a tangled mess, makeup smudged and her hot pink shell-suit ripped to pieces.

"What the fuck?" Jane said, as she stood up and joined her mother at the patio doors.

"You had to be in the biggest fucking house, didn't you," she shouted through the panelled glass, "And the one furthest away!"

"What are you doing here?" asked Lizzie who was now standing with her mother and sister, Max followed soon after.

"Are you gonna let me in, or what?" Tabatha shouted at them as they stared at her.

"What do you want?" Max asked, as Mrs. Bennet unlocked the door and swung it open.

The Bennet's stood still, blocking her as she attempted to step in.

"Is that coffee?" Tabatha said, smelling into the kitchen.

Lizzie moved to let her in, determined that she would get an exploitation from her, about Fitzy's actions.

"What happened at the Everfiled last night?" Lizzie demanded as Tabatha dove for the first cup of freshly brewed coffee; inhaling it in one go. She poured herself a second cup, drinking that almost as fast.

Mrs. Bennet watched with pruned lips as she saw the pot of coffee she had just put on, quickly disappear.

"What are you doing here?" Jane asked as Tabatha finished off her second cup; she was about to pour herself a third when Mrs. Bennet put her hand over the pot to stop her.

"Answer her question," she told her as she guarded the remaining coffee for herself.

"Do you guys not watch the news?" she asked them as she let the last few drops, land on her tongue.

Lizzie thrusted the newspaper into Tabatha's hand, "Why do you think for one second, I'd be remotely interested in Fitzy getting arrested? As soon as we get back to New York, my father will throw you, Fitzy and your brother out of our hotel; and you'll never set foot in there again."

"Chrome is buying a suite, Lizzie" Jane told her.

"I don't care, I'll make sure that dad blocks the sale. We all know he can't say no to me, and this is not going to be the first time he does!"

"You can't," Tabatha told them, not confidently or her usual snooty self, but calmly with sincerity in her eyes.

"Ohh yeah," Lizzie demanded of her, "And why's that?"

"He's dead," Tabatha said uncomfortably as she watched them all staring back at her, unable to understand what she was telling them.

"What are you talking about?" Mrs. Bennet barked with one eye on the coffee pot that was again, filling up.

Tabatha reached into her back pocket and took out a folded copy of the New York Times.

"See for yourselves," she told them, as she handed Mrs. Bennet the Newspaper.

She dropped it to the ground as soon as she saw her husband's face on the cover. The three Bennet children looked down at the fallen paper as Mrs. Bennet sobbed uncontrollably.

"You need to start talking," Lizzie told Tabatha viciously, through her teeth as she watched her make herself another cup of coffee.

Mrs. Bennet let out a scream as the entire weight of everything crushed down on her; Max cradled his mother as all the Bennets tried to console each other.

Tabatha took the basket of croissants and another cup of coffee and made her way outside, sitting on the back decking as she listened to the Bennets mourning the loss of their patriarch.

"It says he had a drug problem," Mrs. Bennet read from the paper, "Why would it say that?" she asked her children.

"Because it's true, mom," Lizzie said to her, deciding that sugar coating things would be a bad idea.

"Only when he's stressed," Mrs. Bennet told her, trying to rationalise his pill popping, just to calm his nerves."

"Why didn't you say something?" Jane asked her mother.

"I didn't like to butt in," she told her children as they all stared her.

"Well, maybe if he had someone to talk to, a wife to confide in, none of this would have happened," Lizzie spat at her mother, "You have absolutely no idea what's going on in your hotel, do you?"

"And, what's that supposed to mean?" Mrs. Bennet stared down at her unflinching daughter.

Jane and Max stood back, watching Lizzie and their mother speaking to each other, in a way they had never encountered before.

Tabatha sat as close to the patio door as she could, without being seen by the Bennets; feeding in as much information as she could about their world, to recall at a later time.

"You're broke mom."

Lizzie watched at the colour poured from her mother's face.

"What are you talking about?" Mrs. Bennet asked Lizzie, in a quiet, calm tone.

"The money… It's gone."

"Where's it gone too?" Jane asked.

"That's something we all need to find out," Lizzie said as she looked at the door and caught Tabatha peering in; catching on to every word of the family's discussion.

Tabatha's usual look of self-righteousness escaped her as she witnessed a family lose everything they had.

Chapter Twenty-One

The Bennet family and Tabatha sat in silence as their plane set off. Champagne was nowhere to be seen, instead, bottles of water lay in their laps as they glided through the clouds in the direction of home.

Tabatha sat at the very back of the small aircraft looking into the windows, often seeing the reflection of the Bennets' sorrow faces, staring into the emptiness of the clear, cloudless sky. Max sat with his mother while Jane and Lizzie sat alone. Lizzie kept looking back at Tabatha, who occupied the seat behind her; opening her mouth to say something but closing it before muttering a word.

Tabatha unbuckled her belt and slid into the seat next to Lizzie. She had a shower at the lake house and managed to find an outfit belonging to Jane, that didn't repulse her.

"How are you doing?" Tabatha asked, not expecting an answer from Lizzie, who just stared back at her with her hollow eyes, void of light and warmth.

"I've lost three parents," Tabatha continued, filling the awkward gap of silence, "My birth parents and my dad, I was six when he died."

Lizzie looked into the face, of a woman she wasn't too keen on and saw the sadness in her eyes as she mentioned the passing of her own father. "I didn't spend much time with him, but the time I did, it's with me every day."

"I think you should go back to London when we get back," Lizzie told her with an empty expression, "If not London, then out of the Everfield."

"Fuck you, Lizzie Bennet," Tabatha shouted at her, "I came over here to be nice, to try and console you, I was gonna show you…" she stopped herself and put her phone back in her pocket.

"Show me what?" Lizzie asked as everyone looked back at them.

"It doesn't matter," Tabatha told her as she started to get up from her chair.

Max ran towards them and blocked her in, reaching into Tabatha's pocket to try and take her phone.

"Get your hands off me!" she screamed as Max took her phone out of her pocket.

"Passcode?" he demanded, pointing to the locked screen.

"I'm not telling you shit," she told him.

"I'm not gonna ask you again," Max warned her.

"Fitzy," she muttered, when she noticed Jane stood behind her brother.

"Pass her, her phone back," said Lizzy on hearing Fitzy's name.

"It looks like she has something to show us first," Jane said.

"My videos," Tabatha told them; the exhaustion she felt, meant she wouldn't be able to stand up to any type of confrontation and would crumble before they even got started.

"It's the last one, filmed at the Pemberly."

Max scrolled through her files, ignoring his temptation to look at the thumbnails showing an obvious nude video of Tabatha.

The shaky video started, and crackled sound began to fill the Jet; the Bennets all tried to get the best view of the screen as they could; Mrs. Bennet sat where she was and had no interest in moving from her seat.

Whack. Fitzy swung for Collin and hit him. Lizzie could just about make out what was being said and strained her ears as to not miss anything. Tabatha fell back into her seat and watched the Bennets staring at her phone.

When the video cut off after Fitzy's arrest, all three of them stared down at the docile Tabatha. She held out her hand for Max to return it to her.

"Collin owns the Everfield?" Lizzie whispered, not loud enough, as Mrs. Bennet shot out of her seat to join them.

"What's going on?" Mrs. Bennet demanded when she reached

them.

"I don't know," said Lizzie whose head was abuzz with information.

She couldn't help but feel sorry for Fitzy, who must be seated in a jail cell this very minute, defending her family, or so he thought he was. The small feeling she harboured for Fitzy, intensified the more and more she tried to rationalise what had happened.

Although, it would be impossible for her to help Fitzy get out of jail, or get his charges dropped (Fitzy's incarceration was really the least of her worries); Tabatha and Chrome had best hope they can get hold of their lawyer, this time.

Jane went back to her seat and tried taking her phone off aeroplane mode, she gave out a yelp of excitement as her reception restored itself to full bars .

A flurry of messages and missed calls inundated her phone, but nothing from the person she most wanted to speak with.

"I have cell reception!" Jane called back to her family as she began typing away ferociously.

'Meet me in the lobby at two,' she messaged James with a smile on her face, *'this is going to make the both of us rich.'*

On hearing about the newfound phone signal, Lizzie switched on her phone after Tabatha made her way back to where she originally sat. She was surprised by the amount of messages and missed calls she had, all from Fitzy; as she began to read through the messages, she heard a cork pop from the front of the plane.

Jane sent champagne bubbles flying everywhere, as she began to pour five glasses. Keeping one for herself, she handed one to her brother, who accepted it automatically and then her mother; who froze when she saw the glass coming in her direction.

It's a test, Mrs. Bennet thought, before slowly reaching for the glass and drinking it in front of everyone.

"How are you all drinking champagne at a time like this?" Lizzie asked them all after refusing her glass.

"A girl's gotta drink," Jane told her before offering a glass to Tabatha, who also refused, down to her being asleep. Jane drank what she was left with. "Lizzie, it's just a drink, you drink it at celebrations, I drink because it's eleven."

***

Charlotte was standing at the lobby, waiting for the Bennets to return. Mrs. Bennet flurried past her as soon as she set foot in the Everfield, prompting her children to follow.

"First things first," Mrs. Bennet told them as they waited for the elevator, "We save this hotel; that's what your father would have wanted."

The elevator doors opened and the Bennets entered, followed by Charlotte; Jane was the last to join them, looking around for James.

"Hurry up," Mrs. Bennet snapped with her finger hovering over the up button, waiting to take them upstairs.

"Mrs. Bennet," Charlotte said as she was shunned into the corner by all the Bennets.

"Not now," she replied, without looking at her.

"But…" said Charlotte.

"If you want to keep your job, well…working for the Everfield, I'm going to need you to keep it zipped."

The doors reopened and they all piled out; led by Mrs. Bennet who marched them down the hallway, past Jane's bedroom that had police tape covering her door.

"Well, we'll deal with that later," Mrs. Bennet called back to her daughter without stopping.

Jane took a moment outside her door, her stomach lunched to the ground as she examined the police tape, cordoning off her room.

"Jane," Mrs. Bennet called at her, forcing Jane to follow her down the corridor. Jane's first thought was to run, but that seemed impossible as long as her mother was staring at her.

"I'm not going to like what's behind your door, am I?" Mrs. Bennet said as Jane re-joined them. Jane stayed silent and waited for her mother to open her father's office.

Charlotte made her way to the front of them, "I need to speak with you," she tried to tell Mrs. Bennet as she opened the door.

Mrs. Bennet led them inside the office, ignoring Charlotte who walked with her, side by side.

She made her way to her husband's desk, opening up his draws and emptying their contents over the immaculately tidy desk. She began to flick through the paperwork she came across, with no idea what she was actually looking for.

When the desk gave her no resolution, she made her way to the large portrait of her that hung on the wall, swinging it off the wall, revealing the safe behind it. Charlotte ran around to join Mrs. Bennet when she realised what she was doing. The safe gave a beep after she entered the code.

"I need his key," she said to herself; defeated, she turned around and bumped into Charlotte, who was still standing at her side, "Out of my way, you stupid girl."

"Mrs. Bennet, I really must speak with you."

"How many times must I say? Not now."

They all stood in silence, looking at each other; the quiet room was broken when a flushing sound came from the bathroom. Everyone turned to face towards the door, holding their breaths as the door handle turned down.

"Mrs. Bennet…" Charlotte said, her voice trailed off as the door slowly swung open.

"Hello Annalise," Collin said as he stepped into the office, drying his hands and discarding the towel on the floor.

"What are you doing in my husband's office?" she demanded of him as she stepped towards him.

"It's not his office anymore," he told her, spitefully.

As soon as she was within kissing distance of him, she swung her arm around and planted a slap, firmly on his cheek.

"I can tell you're distressed and confused," he said, patting his cheek, feeling the heat coming from it, "My god, what is it with people hitting me recently," he joked.

"Out," Mrs. Bennet said from behind a dam of tears, ready to explode, "Get out," she shouted.

"I'll leave," he told her, "but first."

He pulled up his sleeve to show nothing was hiding there and began to wave his hands in mid-air. He clapped them together, as he slowly pulled his clasped hands apart; an envelope (folded in a Constantine), unravelled itself, turning uncreased as he pulled it to its full size.

"Maybe you were looking for this," he said, bowing down and holding out the envelope for her to take.

"What is it?" she asked.

"A little light reading," he told her as he strengthened himself out.

Lizzie raced to her mother's side and snatched the envelope from her hand and tore it open. As she began to scan through the pages, her breathing ceased as she tried to comprehend what her father had done.

'Call daddy's lawyer, now," Lizzie instructed her mother.

Mrs. Bennet stood there, staring at her daughter without moving.

"You have ten days," Collin told them as he put on his jacket, "ten days to pay up, or... all this is mine," he gestured around the room.

Mrs. Bennet began to cry, silent tears rolled down her face as the pressure of the last twenty four hours began to take its toll.

"Why?" Mrs. Bennet asked, "My husband has just died."

"He's not dead," Charlotte shouted from the back of the Bennet's. Everyone turned around to face her.

"What?" Mrs. Bennet said as she wiped away the tears that began to fall on her white blouse, causing little water marks to appear.

"He's alive.. He's not dead," she said in a relieved tone, finally managing to get it out.

"Then who died?" Collin asked; a look of dread appeared across his face.

Where the fuck are you?' Jane text James, *"so much shit is going down.'*

Chapter Twenty-Two

The Bennet family stood around Mr. Bennet's hospital bed as he lay there unconscious with tubes coming out his nose and IVs attached to each arm. The room was abuzz with sounds as machinery beeped and hummed to itself.

The evening light began to fill the room. No-one wanted to sit down, in case they missed him opening his eyes for the first time; all scared he'd wake up feeling all alone, even if it was just for a split second.

"What do we do when he wakes up?" Jane asked as they all looked up and turned their attention onto her.

"Ask him how he is feeling?" Max suggested.

"About the hotel," she corrected him, "How do we bring it up?"

"I don't want the first thing he hears," Mrs. Bennet told her, "being Collin is about to own the Everfield."

"Collin can have the Everfield," Mr. Bennet said with a croaky tone to his voice.

Mrs. Bennet jumped out of her skin and fell to her husband's side when she heard him speak.

"Shush, my darling," she told him while stroking his hair, "Not now."

All three of his children sat on the edge of the bed with a sense of relief.

"Daddy," Lizzie said, loud enough, to make sure he knew she was there.

"Give him the hotel," Mr. Bennet instructed his family, "I'm too tired."

"Too tired to give him a beat down?" Max asked.

"I could muster the strength to knock him into Tuesday, for sure," Mr. Bennet said with a smile across his face.

"You won't be the first," Jane said, taking out her phone, "You should see what Fitzy did to him."

Jane passed her father the phone after pressing play on the video Tabatha sent her. Everyone watched in silence as Mr. Bennet saw the altercation in the Pemberly.

"Wow," Mr. Bennet said after handing Jane back her phone, "I like that boy more and more, shame about his music," he told them, getting a sympathetic chuckle from the group.

Lizzie's phone started to ring ecstatically, breaking the silence of the room.

"Who is it?" Jane asked as they stared at Lizzie as she took her phone out of her pocket.

"No idea," she told them, looking down at the withheld number, "to be honest, I don't really care." She sent the call to voicemail and stood up to give her father a hug.

"Lizzie, It's me, Fitzy," he said from a jail payphone. A line of other men, all wearing the same orange jumpsuits as him, waited behind him for their turn to use the phone.

After recording his message, Lizzie received a notification.

"Well?" Jane asked as she noticed Lizzie's phone light up.

"It's not important," she told her after returning to her place on the bed.

"How often do you get calls?" Jane asked her.

"Often," she replied, trying to convince Jane of her popularity.

"Listen to the message," Jane instructed her.

"I'd rather not," she said looking at her father and smiling.

"Listen to it, darling," Mr. Bennet told her.

Unable to say no to her father, Lizzie picked up the phone and began listening to Fitzy's message.

"It's Fitzy," she told them after hearing his message.

"And?" Jane asked her.

"He's in jail, he's asking for my help."

"Lizzie, go to him," Mr. Bennet told her, his voice becoming stronger as he spoke with his daughter.

"Dad, I can't. Look at you…"

"Look at me, I'm fine," he told her, "If you don't go, I'm cutting you out of my will."

She joked as she reluctantly got off the bed, "Okay," she told them, knowing she wasn't going to win this one "I'm going."

"Take those disgusting fucking flowers with you," Mrs. Bennet pointed towards a huge bouquet of Lillys, "before I throw them out the window."

***

As Lizzie sat in the waiting area of the twenty second precinct, her mind immediately went back to the last time she visited a police station; again to bail out Fitzy.

"There's no way I can get these charges dropped, darlin'," a desk sergeant called over to Lizzie after a long and ominous looking phone discussion.

"The internet is on fire with your friend hitting Mr. Williams, I have to admit; I'm not his biggest fan and so many people from my neighbourhood get a real kick out of seeing that English guy give him a hitting. But, my hands are tied."

"So, he had been charged with assault?" Lizzie questioned him, getting out of the bench and moving across the cold concrete floor.

"Mr. Williams' lawyer is attempting to get him done for attempted murder,"

Lizzie's phone dropped as she heard what the officer was telling her.

"It's not gonna happen," he reassured her, "Just some spoiled rich kid, throwing his toys out of the pram. No offence."

"What do you mean?" Lizzie asked him.

"I know who your father is, Miss Bennet."

"You think I'm spoiled?" Annoyed by the stranger's character assassination of her.

"What?" he said, realising what he'd just said to her, "no, that's not what I meant. Most of these Wall street, silver spooned kids I see running around the city all think they're above the law."

"You think I fall into that category?"

"No," he said, unable to say anything else.

'When will he get released?" Lizzie asked through her teeth; daring him to bring up her wealth and upbringing again.

"Lizzie!" Fitzy said from a nearby doorway, "Your father! I'm so sorry."

"He's fine, in the hospital but recovering," she said as she made her way over to him as another officer removed his handcuffs.

"I really did fear for my life," Collin was saying on the local news that played on the television above the sergeant's desk.

"Speak of the devil," the desk sergeant told Lizzie as he increased the volume.

"He's nothing but an English thug," Collin told the reporter, the same reporter from the Everfield last night. Collin's bruised nose seemed to have intensified tenfold for his interview.

"If I had things my way, I wouldn't give this 'so called rapper' any attention, but my lawyers have told me I must make the public aware of what a danger he is."

"God, he's really milking this, isn't he," Fitzy told Lizzie as he hugged her, "Thank you for coming," he whispered in her ear before separating.

Music began to fill the reception area; everyone looked up at the TV.

"They've been playing clips of your videos all day!" the police sergeant told him in a supportive tone, "There's always an upside, when your album comes out, I'm buying it," he told him.

A smile was plastered across Fitzy's face as he danced along to his own song.

"Stop it," said Lizzie who thumped his arm, playfully.

"Silver lightning," he told her with a wink. "You saw she assaulted me, right?" Fitzy jokingly called back at the officers as they were leaving the building.

They re-joined the evening mist of the city, making their way towards the East river, following it up stream towards the Brooklyn Bridge.

"I suppose I need to thank you again," he told her as they walked slowly, side by side.

"I didn't do anything," not trying to be modest, "I just showed up."

"Yes you did," he said as slowly as their walking speed.

"I'm sorry," she told him, too shy to look him in the eye.

"For what? Kissing Collin?"

"Yeah, he told me you stole money from my father."

"You believed him? I know you're a smart girl Lizzie, but what you're saying sounds rather stupid to me."

"I found out my father was broke, and I just put two and two together."

"But you got six," he said with his cheeky grin, "what's going on with your father and the hotel?" he asked, turning the conversation down a completely different avenue.

"It's just a huge mess, Fitzy. I don't know what he's going to do; he owes money to Collin, from what I can tell, a lot of money and used the

Everfield as collateral."

"That's less than smart," he told her, "Maybe I could help," he suggested.

"How can you help?" she asked him, not knowing where he was coming from.

"Chrome and I have what's called a Unicorn," he told her, her face didn't give any indication of understanding what he was talking about.

"Our company has a valuation of over a billion dollars," he said, dead pan, looking at her dead in the eyes.

"A billion dollars? How?" Lizzie was completely shocked and stuttered as she tried to say more.

"We have a huge back catalogue of music and publish other artists' stuff, do everything in house ourselves and have mentored and signed so many singers and musicians who are either really on the up and coming or are huge already; just America is the market we've yet to crack."

"Who valued you at a billion dollars?"

"Collin's company," he told her, without realising what he was saying.

"Oh Fitzy, I really wouldn't believe a word that man says," she told him, happy for his intentions but not taking his offer of help seriously.

"It's not just him, he's arranged investors, that's why he brought us to New York, It's all above board, our lawyers are all over this."

"Lawyers who fail to bail you out, on two occasions?" she said with a half joking smile.

"They're corporate lawyers, not criminal. I'm going to sell off a stake off my company to raise money for your dad to save his hotel," he said admiringly to her.

"No Fitzy," she said to him, sternly shutting him down, "My father's debts are nothing for you to worry about, he'll deal with it."

"I want to help," he told her, as they walked across the bridge.

"I know you do," with a smile across her face, "But I'm confident he will find a way out of it."

"Look over there," he pointed in the distance towards the city.

"What are we looking at?" she asked, shifting her whole body, "I can't see anything."

"It's turned around" he said franticly.

As she spun around to face him, Fitzy leaned in and kissed her. He put his hand on her face as they embraced passionately.

"I should get home," Lizzie told him as they broke apart.

"Then I shall get you a car!" he skipped up the remainder of the bridge.

Within a matter of minutes, Fitzy found them a taxi and they were gliding up Manhattan towards the Everfield. The brightly lit hotel glowed brighter the closer they got to it. A small number of press was still camped outside, waiting for scraps of scandal to come their way.

"Let's go through the service entrance," Lizzie suggested as they were mere feet from pulling up.

"No," Fitzy said as he handed the driver a fifty, "Keep the change."

Fitzy opened the door and got out first, holding his hand out for Lizzie to accept. They walked hand in hand up the hotel steps. It wasn't until they almost reached the hotel steps that the paparazzi realised who they were.

They endured less than five seconds of flashes before arriving safe and sound in the Lobby, away from the vultures outside.

Lizzie made her way back to her floor and left Fitzy to meet Tabatha, who was seated at the Pemberly bar knocking back Porn Star Martinis.

Jane had been back at the Everfield for over an hour and spent her time seated at the Pemberly, sitting as far away from Tabatha as she possibly could, pretending she wasn't there. When she saw Lizzie arrive back and walking across the lobby, she drank the remainder of her drink and raced across the lobby to follow Lizzie, only reaching the elevator as the doors slid shut. Infuriated at being made to wait for it to come back down, she tapped her nude louboutins erratically as if the tapping sound would make the elevator come to her faster. She used the replacement keycard Michael provided her with and made her way to her floor; her vodka fuelled mind raced uncontrollably as she envisioned what was waiting for her between her cordoned off room.

When the doors slid open, she stepped out and saw a man standing outside her bedroom door; a member of NYPDs finest waiting for her return. She noticed Lizzie's door just about to close; she dove for it, before it shut completely, almost knocking a startled Lizzie on the ground.

"Jane!" Lizzie said as she regained her balance.

"Evening, Lizzie. I saw Fitzy got out, then, I saw Collin on the news, spewing some dribble about fighting for his life."

"He's more dramatic than you and mom combined," Lizzie joked as she searched her bureau for a pair of pyjamas.

Jane laughed along, "Hey," she said when she realised what Lizzie had just said.

"How's dad?" Lizzie asked concernedly as she stripped off and got herself ready for bed.

"Happy with his progress, apparently, he has a few tests tomorrow, and then should be home by the evening."

"God, that's fast," Lizzie said as she attempted to tie her hair up in a bun, instead settling on a messy ponytail.

"I'm gonna sleep here tonight," Jane told her as Lizzie made it obvious that she was ready for bed by switching off all the lights, apart from the lamp by the side of her bed.

"Why?" Lizzie asked.

Jane wasn't sure if she noticed the police officer stationed outside her door, or not.

"I'm worried about dad," she lied.

"Okay," Lizzie replied, thinking that the only person Jane ever worried about was herself.

Jane stripped down to her bra and panties, made sure the door was firmly locked and slid into the bed before Lizzie knew what was happening.

Lizzie turned around from putting her dirty laundry in the hamper to find Jane sprawled in her bed. "Sure, you can sleep in the bed," she said as she climbed in too.

Lizzie switched off her bedside light and moved onto her back, staring up at the ceiling.

Jane had made herself comfortable, her leg digging onto Lizzie's side; Lizzie could hear her breathing getting much deeper, on the brink of drifting off to sleep.

Lizzie couldn't help but think of her parents. Her father alone in hospital and her mum; pregnant at her age. Her family's financial situation also twirled around in her mind as she found the ability to nod off was impossible; a whole complex mess of family incidents plagued her ability to sleep.

Chapter Twenty-Three

Jane and Lizzie left for breakfast early the next morning and met Mrs. Bennet and Max in the ballroom, a table for four was pre-set in the centre of the cavernous room, with a mountain of food for them to devour.

They all sat in silence and mostly drank coffee, barely touching the food in front of them.

Mrs. Bennet had managed to cover the fading bruise on her face with makeup; a girl from the Channel came to the Everfield at the crack of dawn to touch her up.

"No one eating?" Max asked them, breaking their silence as he helped himself to a plateful of smoked salmon.

"I'm not hungry, dear," her mother said as she swirled the remaining of her cold black coffee around in her mouth; every tastebud latched onto the bitter Columbian beverage she was using to send away her desire to eat.

"I'm actually going to miss this," Jane said as she too drank her drink.

"Miss what?" Mrs. Bennet asked in a dismissive tone, "Are you going somewhere? Wanna move out?"

"You know, with daddy losing the hotel," Jane said slowly, knowing that each word she muttered, made her mother furious.

"We're not losing the Everfield," she said, slamming her coffee cup on the table, almost hard enough to shatter it in her hand.

"I hope we don't, but I don't see any way out of it," Jane told her.

"That's why, you don't and never will run your father's company," Mrs. Bennet spat bitterly at her.

"Lizzie, how was your date last night," Jane said to change the topic of conversation; Jane knew that talking about the future of her family company and her parents' succession plans always ended up in an argument; her parents usually threatening to disinherit them if they carried on winging about things.

"It wasn't a date," Lizzie told her as she thought about the kiss she and Fitzy shared last night, "I met him as he got out of jail."

"Sounds like a date to me," Mrs. Bennet told Lizzie as she poured herself another cup of coffee, "When me and your father were your age, I bailed him out countless times."

Lizzie chose to ignore what her mother just said and carried on speaking, "We went for a walk and kissed."

"Aww," said Max in a patronising, drawn out tone.

"And he offered to lend daddy money to pay off Collins debt," Lizzie said in a blasé way between sips of her tea.

"What?" said Mrs. Bennet, causing her to drop her cup and send its contents to spread over the table.

The three of them all stared at Lizzie with excitement in their eyes and grins across their faces.

"Excellent dear, you've done great. What a relief! Our prayers have been answered" she threw her hands into the air, muttering "thank you."
For a split second, she looked down at the carpet and gave the carpet a little wink; none of her children noticed her do this.

"Does he have the money?" Max asked.

"Apparently so, his and Chrome's company is larger than I thought," Lizzie told them.

Jane's ears peaked up when she heard Lizzie mention Chrome's name; she was just annoyed that things weren't going as well for them, as they were for Lizzie and Fitzy.

"When do we get the money?" Mrs. Bennet asked Lizzie, full of glee.

"We don't," she said, feeling bad to disappoint them.

"Bitch say what?" Jane shouted across the table.

"Excuse me?" said Lizzie trying to understand what Jane had just said.

"You heard your sister," Mrs. Bennet snapped at her, "Why are we not getting that money?" she too shouted, banging her wrist down on the table into the smashed cup, the broken shards of pottery had no feeling on her skin.

"Daddy can get us out of this, he'll find a way," Lizzie told them.

"Your father wants to give this place up," Mrs. Bennet reminded her, "He's weak, fallen over and doesn't have the balls to lift himself back up."

"That's our father you're speaking about," Lizzie reminded her.

"Yeah? And my fucking husband. My Darling husband, who's laying there like some snot nosed child in a hospital bed feeling sorry for himself, leaving us lot to deal with this fucked up situation."

"Oh, so now you want to help," Lizzie shouted at her mother.

"Meaning?" Mrs. Bennet snapped back, as Jane and Max watched them argue, turning their head from one to the other.

"You didn't seem that bothered to put the effort in when things were doing well, as long as your Visa balances was cleared, you were happy. I suppose the only time you got involved with the finances was to make sure that Saks would accept your store card."

"Now you listen very carefully, you spoiled bitch," drops of spit came out of Mrs. Bennet's mouth with every word she spoke, landing on Lizzie's cheek on a few occasions, "How dare you get in the way of the life your father and I," really emphasising her insolvent, "created for you kids. Sending you to the best schools, best rehab facilities," pointing over at Max who sunk in his chair at being singled out, "making sure you never went without. Your dumb daddy isn't thinking straight in that bloody hospital, he's tired and weak and looking at us," motioning her finger in a circular motion as she's speaking, "to help him out. Right now, from where I'm standing, you're looking like some ungrateful cunt who isn't willing to help out her family and wants to stop the legacy me and your father have being trying, for decades to create."

"You didn't create shit," Lizzie said after a long pause, "Daddy snapped you off a Milan runway when you were eighteen and brought you to America. You just so happened to win the lottery that night."

"I grew up in Hackney, you unsophisticated cow. You have absolutely no idea how hard I had to work to get to Milan, the hours I spent bleaching my skin and marching up and down London until my feet bled with my photographs in a folder under my arm; only getting jobs if I was willing to open my legs for these disgusting photographers, who only saw me for one thing. It took me nearly a decade, from the age of thirteen to get to the big runways, wearing the big labels. I didn't know hard work until I came here, married your father and got lumbered with you four."

"Four?" said Lizzie.

"Three…" Mrs. Bennet said correcting herself, "You three, clinging onto me, all under the age of five when your father was nowhere to be seen. The longest gap I had without seeing him was forty five days, a month and a half of just me and you winey fucking lot. I may not have been in the office every day with your father, but I made damn sure he was able to go; I gave up work when I moved here so your father could follow his dreams, I wanted to be in the movies but I stood by him so he could erect these fucking buildings. And I'll be damned If I've wasted my life just to let it all crumble now."

Without saying anything else, Mrs. Bennet leaped out of her seat, wiped the mall amount of blood and coffee that stained her wrist on the table cloth, picked up her purse and left her children to contemplate what she'd just said. They watched as she stomped her way across the ballroom, slamming the heavy door shut behind her.

Mrs. Bennet made way it across the lobby, past Tabatha who stood suspiciously close to the ballrooms entrance; she ignored her and pushed her way through a line of people waiting to use an elevator.

"You'll have to wait for the next one," she told them as she hurried the people inside to get out.

As she stepped in, Mrs. Bennet pressed the button for the fifteenth floor and waited to get out. She found herself on a deserted floor and proceeded to knock on the first door she came across.

After waiting almost two minutes, Fitzy opened up the door.

"Mrs. Bennet," he said when he saw her standing before him, "you wanna come in?"

He fully opened the door and made way for her to enter, shutting the door behind them.

***

Chrome was met by Tabatha as soon as he entered the Everfield, she had perched herself on her usual seat at the bar, able to command drinks at the snap of a finger and see all the comings and goings in the lobby. When she spotted her brother walk in through the main doors, she almost jumped over the wall of neatly trimmed shrubbery that separated them, way too excited to spread the bad news she had to tell him about .

"Chrome," she shouted as she jumped down off the stool, running to meet him with her drink still in her hand; sipping from the straw as she made her way to him. "You really shouldn't have gone to that Oprah gig," she told him as she threw her arms around him.

"I heard what's been going on," he told her as he put his small overnight bag down on the floor, "Is Jane okay?" he asked her.

"What? Yeah, she's fine. Don't believe everything you read, her father's still alive, she's not dressed in black like some wailing washer woman."

"He's fine?"

"I presume so," she told him, really not bothered.

Behind them, Max, Lizzie and Jane entered the lobby from the ballroom, waiting a few minutes after their mother left to absorb what she'd said; they sat in silence, waiting for one of them to make the first move to leave. Max had volunteered, saying: "I need a drink," and led them out.

"I'm going to the Pemberly," Max told Lizzie on seeing Chrome and Tabatha before his sisters, "Wanna join me?"

"I could do with one," Jane said without seeing who had recently returned to the hotel.

"Maybe just me and Lizzie," he said, nudging Lizzie hard in the ribs.

"Aww," she wined before looking across the busy lobby and seeing Chrome.

Chrome began to pick up his bag when he noticed Jane across from him; she had yet to spot him. He stood staring at her for a moment as she ran her hand through her long hair.

After an endless amount of personal grooming, Jane looked across and saw Chrome. Lizzie and Max had stepped back and left her in her own space.

They gazed at each other for a moment, their eye contact only breaking as Chrome began to run towards her.

"Chrome? Where are you going?" Tabatha asked before turning around and seeing who he was running towards, "fuck," she said under her breath when she saw Jane.

"Hi," Chrome said as he stopped suddenly in front of her.

"Hi."

An awkward moment of silence endured as they stared into each other's eyes, broken only by Chrome, without notice, leaning in and kissing her passionately, holding her with both hands by her side as they embraced.

Lizzie, Max and Tabatha all watched at their reunion; their kiss lasting a little too long for them to be still watching, but they did.

After they finally broke apart, Jane was the first to speak: "You left, without telling me."

"I know," was all he could say, "I was scared," he whispered.

"Of what?"

"Us," he said without hesitation, "About the speed things were going. I like you Jane and... I'm no good at commitment; sure I can follow an album through from conception to release but when it comes to my personal life... I chickened out... I ran and screened your calls and was scared for things going from like to..."

"Maybe we should just… go to the studio together, dinner now and then and see what, or if anything happens," she told him, knowing what he wanted to hear.

"I like the sound of that," he said with a smile across his face, "I've been working on this sick beat and I think you'd love it, wanna meet up tomorrow and hear it?"

"I'd love to," she told him as Tabatha joined them, carrying Chrome's bag.

"You left this," she told him, holding his bag for him to take; not impressed she had to carry it to him.

"Let's go upstairs," she told him, walking off towards to lift.

"Until tomorrow then," he said, kissing her on the cheek.

She re-joined her giggling siblings and watched Tabatha and Chrome wait for the elevator to open. When it did, they moved out of the way to let the passengers inside get out; two police officers stepped out.

On seeing the two officers enter the lobby, Jane turned her back to them and slinked behind Lizzie and Max.

Chrome and Tabatha entered the elevator and the doors almost immediately closed behind them.

Jane quickly looking over her shoulder, and saw Chrome and Tabatha were gone; she started moving slowly towards the Everfield's main doors, in an awkwardly sideways motion.

"What are you doing?" Lizzie asked as Jane continued to scuffle sideways.

"Jane Bennet?" one of the officers shouted over on noticing her unnatural mannerisms, and Lizzie and Max looking at her strange behaviour.

Jane began to move quicker as the two officers also began to walk faster, before running towards her.

"Stop, Miss Bennet," the other officer said as he grabbed her, with the other officer getting her by the other arm.

Handcuffs appeared out of nowhere and were attached to Jane's wrists.

"What's going on?" Lizzie asked the officer.

"You have the right to remain silent," an officer told her as she started to wriggle uncontrollably.

"If you do say something…"

"Jane? What have you done?" Lizzie asked, staring at her defeated face, "I'm gonna call Mom and get the lawyers down here."

"If you cannot afford a lawyer, one will…"

"Mr. Hilbert," Max shouted. Calling over the hotel's manager, who had just gotten out of an elevator.

"What's going on?" he shouted over at the police officers, as he came running over to them.

"Drugs," an officer told them, "Enough cocaine to feed every addict in a five block radius."

Jane was being led through the lobby, no longer putting up a fight. She noticed the large crowd starting to gather around her and the many cell phones pointed in her direction.

***

"I think I know why you're here," Fitzy said after shutting the door behind Mrs. Bennet.

He led her over to the seating area and invited her to take a seat.

"Can I get you anything?" he asked as he sat down next to her.

"How about a hundred mill?" she said without joking, as he read his trademark white T-shirt, that had: *'If girls were meant to be equal- they'd have dicks,'* written across his chest.

He laughed at her bluntness.

"She told you that I offered to help you guys out?"

"Yeah, she told me," she said as she thought back at the events in the ballroom.

"I'm more than happy to help you out…" he told her as a grin appeared across her face, "…With Lizzie's blessing," he finished off, making Mrs. Bennett's face drop as quickly as the smile had arrived.

"I'm sorry Mrs. B, without her say so, my hands are tied."

"Is there nothing I can do to persuade you to change her mind?" she asked, undoing a button of her blouse and putting her hand on his lap, moving it at a snail's pace, up his leg.

Fitzy burst into hysterics, "You're joking, right?" before slapping her hand away, "C'mon Mrs. B, I'm old enough to be your grandson."

"Son," she quacked back at him, and joining him with his laughter.

Knowing that the way to the money was through Lizzie, she got up from the sofa and started to hatch a plan. Her husband would need to be the one to get to her daughter.

"I admire you, Mr… Fitzy," she told him as she put her purse back on her shoulder.

"For what?" he asked.

"The way you handle yourself. My daughter likes you… and I can tell you like her too."

"I do like her, very much," they slowly began to make their way to the door.

"I'll give you a little bit of advice," Mrs. Bennet said, stopping dead to look him straight in the eye, "Not many people know this, but a man like yourself, with access to a wealth of resources, needs to make the right choices from day one, starting with the person you choose to share your life with. You started with nothing, just like my husband and I. You're just getting started on this little road we call life… The person you choose to walk side by side with you, for all I know, it may not be Lizzie, but she needs to be of equal measure to you, if not a better person than you can ever hope to be."

"Lizzie is incredibly smart."

"Where do you think she gets that from," she winked at him.

Fitzy smiled at her.

"Can I show you something?" he asked her.

"Go for it," she said.

He began to walk back on themselves and let her into a large dining room with a huge table. Sprawled across the table were blueprints, colour and stone swatches, documents and models of a skyscraper.

"What's it for?" she asked as she got closer to the blueprints.

"It was going to be our company's home," he told her, "You need to go big or go home," he joked at the size of the building. "I think the land Collin was securing for us is no longer going to be available. One day," he said with optimism in his voice.

Mrs. Bennet took a moment to examine the blueprints, before looking at him with a large smile across her face; the time she spent gleaming at him, unnerved him slightly.

"You know my husband, has a plot of land, not far from here, that he's doing absolutely nothing with and would fit this beautiful design, nicely."

"Really?" Fitzy said with amazement in his voice.

"Forget the loan you suggested," she said, "I think I may be able to help *you* out."

They stood staring at each other with smiles across their faces as Tabatha and Chrome joined them.

"What's going on?" Chrome asked, shocked to see Mrs. Bennet.

"I'll let you boys talk," she said and left.

Chapter Twenty-Four

"You ready?" Benjy asked Charlie, who was seated at the Pemberly bar, playing with the remains of the ice in her glass with her straw.

"All done?" she asked as she watched him take off his apron and throw it into Franky's face.

"Done," he said as he walked around to the front and kissed her, "how about a burger?" he suggested as he helped her with her jacket.

"Sounds great," she said as her lips tingled from their kiss.

"Have a good evening you guys," Franky said as he was making a round of drinks.

"Thanks," they both said as they took one another's hands and began to leave.

"No hand holding," a formidable voice said from behind them, "ten inches between yourselves," Charlie's mother said as she hurried up to them, putting on her coat as she jogged, "Wait for me, where we going?"

"For a burger, mom," Charlie called back without looking back, instead smiling at Benjy as they separated their hands.

They smiled and waved at Kitty who was busy with a customer at her flower stall; she waved back as the doorman opened the door for them, and let them leave.

As they left, Collin walked in, almost pushing Charlie's mother out of the way, "watch it," he told her as he made his way over to the Bennets, who all stood in the centre of the lobby, waiting for him.

Mr. Bennet was standing on the end, holding onto a stick and Jane was missing from the line.

He walked over to them and stopped a few feet away.

No one moved; they all stared straight ahead.

Lizzie broke the silence as her footsteps echoed around them, as she made her way towards Collin.

"This is for you," she told him, reaching into her pocket and handing him a folded piece of paper.

He took it from her and unfolded it.

"Is this going to bounce?" he asked as he looked down at the cheque.

She shook her head and pointed to a pile of boxes in the corner of the lobby, the things he'd left in the suite he'd forced her father to let him use.

She looked down at her watch, "If it's not gone in twenty nine minutes, they'll find your possessions incinerated."

"Ohh, you naive girl, you can incinerate it all, I'll just buy more shit," he said, flicking the cheque near her face.

Behind his shoulder, she could see Fitzy enter the lobby, coming up to her, brushing past Collin to kiss her.

"I'll be seeing you, Lizzie," Collin said as he left the hotel.

"Does this mean… we're dating?" Fitzy asked Lizzie after their kiss ended.

"I don't know," Lizzie shrugged.

"Do you want to be my girlfriend?" he asked her, looking back at her whole family, who were looking at them, with beaming smiles across their faces.

"Yes," she said as he reached in for another kiss.

Acknowledgment

I'd like to begin by thanking Davie Toothill, who's encouragement got me through this writing process. I'd also like to thank Jonjo Holcroft, my first true friend and his family.

This book would not have been possible without all the amazing tutors I've had through my life; Sandra Cain, Dr. Devon Campbell-Hall, Dr. Sara Bailey, Dr. Tom Masters, Mike Lynch and Seamus Finnegan.

And finally, my family; My dad for all his love and support, my mother and my siblings, Emma and Daniel for always being there for me.

And Kelvy, words cannot describe what you've done for me and how you make me feel.